EDITED BY
JERRY POURNELLE AND JIM BAEN

FAR FRONTIERS

Managing Editor:
John F. Carr

Senior Editor:
Elizabeth Mitchell

A BAEN BOOK

ACKNOWLEDGMENTS

"A Step Farther Out" copyright © 1985 by Jerry Pournelle

"The Warm Space" copyright © 1983 by David Brin

"The Jefferson Orbit" copyright © 1985 by Ben Bova

"The Boy From The Moon" copyright © 1983 by Rivka Jacobs

"Brain Salad" copyright © 1985 by Norman Spinrad

"Goodbye, Dr. Ralston" copyright © 1985 by Damon Knight

"The Leading Edge" copyright © 1985 by Richard E. Geis

"Future Scenarios For Space Development" copyright © 1985 by G. Harry Stine

"Through Road No Whither" copyright © 1985 by Greg Bear

"The Paradox of Interstellar Transport" copyright © 1985 by Robert L. Forward

"Lost In Translation" copyright © 1985 by Dean Ing

"Pride" copyright © 1985 by Poul Anderson

"Table Manners" copyright © 1985 by Larry Niven

CONTENTS

A STEP FARTHER OUT

by
Jerry Pournelle

Far Frontiers exists because of this column. Of course a story goes with that.

Way back when I decided to make a career out of writing, the traditional route was to build a reputation by writing for the magazines, and when you became well known enough, go for the real money by getting a book contract. It was true then, as now, that you can't make a living writing short fiction.

That hadn't always been true. Stuart Cloete (*Rags of Glory*) once told me that the *Saturday Evening Post* paid him $4500 for a short story—and that was in 1948, when a graduate chemist's annual starting salary was no more than that. In those times writers could support themselves from sales of short works; but in the 1970's those days were long gone. By the time I was trying to break in to this business, everyone knew that the object was to build a reputation fast, then get book contracts.

Of course it took time to build a reputation. People—and contrary to rumor, editors are people—remember stories, but not authors. You have to write a *lot* of stories—or articles—before anyone knows who you are. However, it's different with columns. People often remember who wrote a column even though only one has been printed. Short of winning several Hugos, the fastest way to build name recognition is to do a column.

The next step was to find someone who'd let me write one. It didn't take long to decide: *Galaxy Science Fiction* under Ejlar Jakobssen didn't enjoy all the glory it once held when Horace Gold founded it, but it was important to the science fiction field—and it didn't have a science column. Willy Ley had been the science columnist, and when he died (absurdly, only a few months before Apollo II) he was not replaced.

Somehow I convinced Jakobssen to let me give it a try.

Alas, it was nearly a disaster. Ejlar wanted rewrite after rewrite, change after change, each accompanied by *hours* of telephone discussion. I was grateful for the chance to do the column, and indeed I was learning quite a lot about magazine style and procedure; Ejlar was a good teacher. However, he couldn't leave well enough alone, and the endless rewrites were driving me batty.

Suddenly everything change. Ejlar Jakobssen left *Galaxy*. The managing editor, a newcomer virtually unknown in the science fiction field, took over the post. He wanted me to continue the column.

That's how I met Jim Baen.

Some partnerships click. Larry Niven and I have known from the first story conference that we ought to work together.

It was the same with Jim Baen. He had suggestions for changes that obviously improved the column. He also made editorial changes in my style—and did it so well that it was only by accident that I discovered he was making any changes at all.

The really fun part, though, was putting the column together. Usually I'd choose the topic, although sometimes Jim would suggest something. After we agreed on a subject, we'd spend a couple of hours on the phone discussing it. The result was wonderful. By the time we were done, I'd understand the subject—often through the need to explain it to Jim.

I needn't pile Pelion on Ossa. Baen and I hit it off, and working together we produced what many reviewers said was the best science column in the business.

When Jim left *Galaxy* to become the SF editor at Ace Books, he missed the magazine world: thus was born *Destinies*, a magazine that looked a lot like *Far*

Frontiers. It was inevitable that I would do a science column; and once again the transcontinental phone lines crackled with our wide-ranging discussions.

Then Jim left Ace, and *Destinies* died as well. For a while I did a column for *Analog,* but my heart wasn't in it, and eventually I excused myself—

And came the day that Jim Baen called to tell me he had become Jim Baen Inc., and had his own publishing company.

"Doing a magazine?" I asked.

"Well—I wouldn't have time."

"Alas. If you did, I could do the science column. I confess to missing our long conversations on the state of the sciences."

"I miss them too." Jim sounded thoughtful. "I don't have time to do it alone. Want to co-edit with me?"

It wasn't *quite* that simple. Even together we don't have time to do a magazine; but we solved that problem by enlisting the aid of Managing Editor John Carr, and Senior Editor Betsy Mitchell.

Thus was born *Far Frontiers,* and thus was reborn "A Step Farther Out."

A STEP FARTHER OUT

"The Association for the Abolition of Science"

Jerry Pournelle

In our *Galaxy* days my "annual report on the state of the sciences," written after the annual meeting of the American Association for the Advancement of Science (AAAS), was a regular feature. I intend to continue it. In the old days, that column tried to summarize much of what was happening in the sciences; to see the edges of our knowledge and try to look past them.

Alas, this year the edges were self-imposed.

For many years the AAAS meeting was held during the holiday week between Christmas and New Year. There were complaints, and the meeting was shifted to late February, theoretically at a time of academic breaks—without academic scientists as speakers, the AAAS meetings would be useless. Alas, American universities have no coordination of breaks at all, some being on the quarter, some the semester, and some the trimester system.

This year the meeting was held over the Memorial Day weekend in New York City. I understand they're thinking of shifting the meeting date again. I hope so.

The AAAS has, over the years, become less scientific and more political. The trend accelerated during the presidency of Margaret Mead, who inserted a number of—in my judgment largely unfortunate—changes in the organization's structure and governance. For example, *Science* magazine, the AAAS's official journal, now has an "editorial" or "commentary" section that is not only frankly partisan, but often thoroughly unscientific.

Many of the meetings have that tendency as well.

This year's AAAS theme was "Science, Engineering, Technology, Education: Toward a World Perspective." In practice "world perspective" meant pretending to take seriously a lot of nonsense: for example, there was a session on the value of Marxism in science. There were other horrors; much of the AAAS meeting seemed more concerned with *control* of science than *doing* science.

Yet, despite panel after panel about science policy—which, notes Dr. Petr Beckmann, editor of Access To Energy (newsletter; $22.00/year, Box 2298, Boulder, CO 80306, and highly recommended), is to science as birdshot is to birds—there was also real science. If you worked at it, you could find excitement.

As usual, some of the best places to look were the panels organized by Dr. Rolf Sinclair. Rolf's politics are not mine; but we share a love of science, and a belief that science and knowledge are worthwhile for their own sake, as well as being mankind's best hope for the future. His session on Frontiers of the Natural Science was, as usual, itself worth the trip to the meeting.

The sciences are advancing on all fronts. Our fundamental knowledge of how the universe is put together proceeds apace, with contributions from many places. Much of this new knowledge has yet to be translated into technology, but that's only a question of time.

The most exciting field for me has been the marriage of cosmology and particle physics. For the past few years astronomy and its strange offshoot, cosmology, have been parasites on the body of physics. Now true, astronomy has always paid its way. Newton invented modern physics largely from astronomical observations, and Einstein's relativity theories grew from the need to explain why the planet Mercury behaved peculiarly. Moreover, astronomical observations were the first confirmation of Einstein's theories.

Still, astronomical observations, and cosmological calculations, didn't do a lot for science in this generation.

That has all changed. As cosmologists look backward in time, back deep into the first second of the universe's life—they now typically go back to the first 10^{-45} second—they generate theories that can be confirmed not by astronomical observation but in particle accelerators. The cosmologists are now proposing theories that generate real experiments crucial to understanding the present universe. Current cosmological theory says there are three and only three kinds of neutrino, and thus six and only six basic types of quark; and this will be tested not with telescopes but with colliding beam accelerators.

Another area of ferment is in the computer sciences, both hardware and software. The super-computer—defined as a machine capable of a billion operations per second—is coming along nicely. Software isn't self-aware yet, but programs that modify themselves in unpredictable—but not un-directed—ways have been written and more are coming. Artificial intelligence "expert systems" capable of rivalling human experts in limited fields such as medical diagnosis, missile checkout, and geological surveying are already in practical use.

We haven't yet begun to see where the computer will take us.

Plasma physics; space sciences, with a whole panel on moving industries into space; chemistry; biology; medicine—the sciences leap ahead. Fundamental discoveries continue, here and in Europe. The era of limits, the days of doom and gloom, never really affected the fundamental sciences anyway; and certainly they're gone now. If we stand at the frontiers of the sciences we see few limits ahead.

And yet: the sessions on engineering and technology featured such horrors as a panel on energy that "departs from the traditional preoccupation with energy supply in energy planning and instead focusses on the end-uses of energy, which are the ways in which energy is used today, future needs for energy services for social goals, and alternative technologies for providing these services."

The speakers in the world energy symposium came from Bangalore, India; Lund, Sweden; Sao Paulo, Brazil; and Dar-es-Salaam, Tanzania. The panel certainly departed from the traditional pre-occupation with producing energy; whether that's relevant to the real needs of the world's poor is another question. So far as I can tell, the conclusion was that the world needs rationing, not production. Just how "scientific" such conclusions are or can be is another matter.

There was a lot of that. The American Association for the Advancement of Science seems concerned lest the international public get the impression that the AAAS is *for* science; that it advocates technology. Heaven forbid!

The copies of *Science* magazine that go to the Soviet Union are delivered to the censor, where they are chopped apart and often come out unrecognizable. We mustn't be too hard on the Soviets, though; we can do much the same to ourselves. At the AAAS meeting this year there were panels on "The Usefulness of the Marxist Outlook in Science." The AAAS program book states:

"The Marxist world view is firmly based on scientific materialism but avoids the usual pitfalls. It is not mechanistic or reductionist, nor is it metaphysical (static) in outlook. Rather, Marxism is a holistic process view in which the causal complexity of the real world is grasped in terms of historical development and dialectical change. Discussion will center on how this world outlook helps to illuminate specific problems of science."

The description goes on for six more paragraphs. Alas, I couldn't make it to the session, so I was unable to discover the Marxist contributions to the nature of the discovery process. According to the meeting description, Marxist are peculiarly adept at scientific discovery.

In the real world, about the only place Marxism

is taken seriously is in the English departments of American universities, with a few die-hards in schools of social science and philosophy; yet the AAAS seems compelled to act as if the value of Marxism were an unsettled question.

Of course it can be argued that this was all harmless. Concessions were made to a few silly people. The real scientists pretend to take them seriously, so long as they don't get in the way, and avoid the sessions. Where's the harm? The trouble with pretending, though, is that's it difficult to know when to stop.

It's dangerous to pretend that Marxism produces civilized governments. The reality is too grim. In the real world, a Marxist society is a one-party state, often dedicated to keeping an aging dictator in power; an imperialist state saddled with a useless bureaucracy specializing in inefficiency and lies. When the dictator dies, a bunch of geronotologic homicidal maniacs generally take charge.

Zimbabwe, formerly Rhodesia, recently announced that it was becoming a one-party Marxist state. Does anyone seriously doubt what that means? Once again real people, whites and minority tribesmen, are sacrificed to a myth; and one doubts that those who pressured the "illegal" independent Rhodesia into surrender will be much in evidence when the slaughter begins. After all, have we not had one man, one vote—once?

The AAAS scheduled other sessions pretending to be scientific. There was, for example, the session on "Space and International Security," which was dominated by opponents to the President's Strategic Defense Initiative policy. This was pretend science because the meeting was stacked;

somehow the AAAS couldn't find anyone who believes that Mutual Assured Survival might be preferable to Mutual Assured Destruction. (Odd: I could have found them some, if they didn't know where else to look; so, I expect, could the White House.)

In fact, that meeting was so stacked that Richard Garwin, IBM Fellow, could spend a good part of his time in hilarious analyses of impossible defense systems that no one ever proposed. Garwin is fond of pretend analysis: only two years ago, with a straight face, he proposed an insane system of about fifty shallow-water submarines, each to carry two strategic missiles and a crew of five. It was obvious to anyone with military experience that this was an operational, command, and security nightmare.

The trouble with the pretend sessions on arms control and space defense is that the local press was able to report that "the science community" was almost unanimously opposed to strategic defense, and to imply that this was a scientific conclusion. Now I happen to believe that Assured Survival is a hell of a lot better policy—strategically, technically, and morally—than Mutual Assured Destruction (MAD); but my belief is irrelevant in this case. The fact is that there was no serious analysis of defense policy, and even less discussion of technical feasibilities. Like the energy symposium, the decks were stacked in advance.

It wasn't the first time. At the AAAs meeting in Houston a few years ago we were treated to a pretend analysis of the "problem" of nuclear waste disposal. The principal speaker was Gus Spaeth, of President Carter's White House Council on Environmental Quality. This advisor to the President

of the United States said, among other silly things,
that he was concerned that nuclear wastes not
contaminate wide areas of the United States in the
event of a renewed Ice Age.

The interesting part is there were no challenges.
There must have been two hundred people in that
room who understood just how absurd this White
House Advisor's remarks were; but they all acted
as if he should be taken seriously—so that those
unfamiliar with the facts of radioactive wastes were
induced to believe this a legitimate concern.

It isn't. Spaeth's concern is unfounded, as he'd
know if he asked any physicists. While it is true
that waste products from nuclear power plants
can remain radioactive for hundreds of thousands
of years, within 600 years the actinides have decayed out; the residual isn't more dangerous than
natural ores. Spreading them wide isn't going to
do additional damage to a nation already covered with glaciers.

One supposes it's a trend. The "Concerned" scientists are everywhere. So far as I can see, "concerned" seems lately to mean either a non-scientist,
or a scientist so convinced of a cause as to cyni-
cally pretend that nonsense is true. Yet whenever
a "concerned" scientist speaks out, we are supposed to pretend; to take the announcement seriously; to act as if some idiotic statement that won't
stand up to high school physics is to be "balanced"
against the considered judgment of a real scientist.

I wish that every reader of *Far Frontiers* could
listen to the tapes of the session called "Knock Down,
Drag Out on the Global Future." It pitted Barry
Commoner and other preparers of the doomster

Global 2000 Report to the President against Julian Simon, author with Herman Kahn of *The Resourceful Earth;* and it summarized the key debate of this century.

The two sides are polarized. Either the Earth is doomed, and we with it; or mankind has a magnificent future. Either people are better off now than ever before, or they are worse off now than fifty years ago, and likely to be worse yet at the end of the century. There is no middle ground.

Or rather: there is a middle ground, but it is not one acceptable to Barry Commoner and his friends.

As Julian Simon points out, one's view of the future is critical to *making* that future. If you believe that human ingenuity left unfettered will make good use of the Earth's resources; if you believe that every "problem"—such as England's deforestation—is also a challenge and an opportunity (deforestation led to the use of coal, and through that to the age of the steam engine), then you take the appropriate policies to release the engines of human enterprise. You prize freedom.

If, though, you believe that human ingenuity is worth little, that "knowledge" and "expertise" are more important; that resources are finite, and problems must be "solved" by experts; that resources must be kept from those who would simply waste them, and certainly must not be allowed into the hands of the greedy; then you will not prize freedom. You will put into place science policies, economic policies, restrictions on access to resources, taxation that discourages initiative; you will generate the rationing economy. In a word, you will opt for socialism.

In many socialist countries people are not better

off now than ten years ago despite the advances in science and technology. It is a grim joke in Poland: "How are things, comrade?" "Better. Worse than yesterday, of course, but better than tomorrow."

In that sense there is a middle ground: if you adopt the policies advocated by the doomsters, you will probably get the results they predict. If you do not—the evidence seems to be the other way.

The world truly stands at a crossroad. Technology could create a global village, a world in which nearly everyone has access to knowledge and computing power. As I have said in previous essays: by the year 2000, every citizen of Western Civilization who seriously wants it will be able to get the answer to any question whose answer is known or calculable. Small computers plus centralized big computers, added to the communications technology potential in space satellites, can give us this with present-day technology; we need only the will.

Real science continues. The knowledge explosion has only just begun. There is no useless knowledge. Cosmology, once thought harmless speculation about the origins of the universe, has become a keystone in understanding particle physics. The last time that astronomy greatly influenced physics led to $e = mc^2$; this time we are led to anti-matter.

Certainly that can be frightening. The crossroad is real, and possibly multi-branched, with many branches leading to doom. Certainly we will need skill in order to survive.

I cannot believe it any part of skill to pretend that nonsense is true. The communications revolution allows widespread dissemination of both truth and falsehood. In this era of knowledge the science organizations have a tremendous responsibility not to label nonsense as true. Michael Novak said, "One of the most astonishing characteristics of our age is that ideas, even false and unworkable ideas, even ideas no longer believed by their official guardians, rule the affairs of men and run roughshod over stubborn facts. Ideas of enormous destructiveness, cruelty, and impracticality retain the allegience of elites that benefit from them."

This must not happen to the science establishment.

The 1984 AAAS meeting held a session on "The Edges of Science." Topics discussed were: the search for extraterrestrial intelligence (SETI); the problem of unidentified flying objects (UFO's); and the question of parapsychological phenomena (PSI). The session was introduced by Isaac Asimov, who attempted to define the edges of science, and declared firmly that both Creationism and Velikovskian cosmology were well outside that edge.

Perhaps Isaac's boundary is too narrowly drawn. Perhaps both Creationism and Vekilovsky do belong within that nebulous region known as "the edges of science." Perhaps not. One thing does seem certain: that session was far too small. It needed many of the other panels sprinkled throughout that meeting. A place could have been made for Gus Spaeth, and the hand-wavers; for most of the "concerned" scientists so eager to advance a cause that they forget what science is.

If PSI, UFO's, and SETI belong at the edges of science—why was Marxism invited further inside?

The Newest Adventure of the Galaxy's Only Two-Fisted Diplomat!

THE RETURN OF RETIEF

KEITH LAUMER

When the belligerent Ree decided they needed human space for their ever-increasing population, only Retief could cope.

$2.95

BAEN BOOKS

See next page for order information.

THE WARM SPACE
by
David Brin

One of our *Far Frontiers* announcements says that we're "looking for the kind of stories that John W. Campbell, Jr., would have bought if he were alive today." John always took great pride that he had working scientists as well as good writers for regular contributors.

David Brin is one of a growing number of working scientists who write science fiction. He holds his doctorate in physics from the University of California at San Diego, and works part time in research. He has also just finished a two-year term as Secretary of the Science Fiction Writers of America. His novel, *Startide Rising*, won both the Hugo and Nebula Awards in 1984.

I write a column in the computer magazine *BYTE*, and thus see a lot of the ferment in the computer science field. One area of furious activity is "artificial intelligence," or AI; and one of the most successful AI fields is "expert systems." An expert system is one that takes a complex field, such as missile systems checkout, and examines in a structured way how human experts solve various problems. When the computer system has accumulated enough knowledge, it tackles the problems itself; and like a human expert, it learns through its mistakes.

Some expert systems now perform at least as well as the best human expert—nor are expert systems confined to inanimate subjects like missiles. There are two good medical diagnosis programs that, although not yet as capable as the best human physicians, have the potential to do so—and already human plus program may be able to outperform the top specialists in the field.

Artificial intelligence programs often modify themselves in unpredictable (although not undirected) ways. They're supposed to. The idea is to produce a program smarter than its creator. That hasn't happened yet. Still, as mankind's ability to construct computers and robots grows along with our understanding of what "intelligence" is, we may yet face the time when we can build "creatures" more intelligent, and more adaptable, than we.

That has long been a popular theme for science fiction stories. David Brin gives us something more than yet another such story.

David Brin

THE WARM SPACE

1.

JASON FORBS (S-62B/129876Rd (bio-human):
REPORT AT ONCE TO PROJECT LIGHTPROBE
FOR IMMEDIATE ASSUMPTION OF DUTIES.
AS "DESIGNATED ORAL WITNESS ENGINEER"
—BY ORDER OF DIRECTOR

Jason let the flimsy message slip from his fingers, fluttering in the gentle, centrifugal pseudo-gravity of the station apartment. Coriolis force—or perhaps the soft breeze from the wall vents—caused it to drift past the edge of the table and land on the floor of the small dining nook.

"Are you going to go?" Elaine asked nervously, from Jesse's crib, where she had just put the baby down for a nap. Wide eyes made plain her fear.

"What choice do I have?" Jason shrugged. "My number was drawn. I can't disobey. Not the way the Utilitarian Party has been pushing its weight around. Under the Required Services Act, I'm just another motile, sentient unit, of some small use to the State."

That was true, as far as it went. Jason did not feel it necessary to add that he had actually volunteered for this mission. There was no point. Elaine would never understand.

A woman with a child doesn't need to look for justifications for her existence, Jason thought as he gathered what he would need from the closet.

But I'm tired of being an obsolete, token representative of the Old Race, looked down upon by all the sleek New Types. At least this way my kid may be able to say his old man had been good for something, once. It might help Jesse hold his head up in the years to come . . . years sure to be hard for the old style of human being.

He zipped up his travel suit, making sure of the vac-tight ankle and wrist fastenings. Elaine came to him and slipped into his arms.

"You could try to delay them," she suggested without conviction. "System-wide elections are next month. The Ethicalists and the Naturalists have declared a united campaign. . . ."

Jason stroked her hair, shaking his head. Hope was deadly. They could not afford it.

"It's no use, Elaine. The Utilitarians are completely in charge out here at the station, as well as nearly everywhere else in the Solar System. Anyway, everyone knows the election is a foregone conclusion."

The words stung, but they were truthful. On paper, it would seem there was still a chance for a change. Biological humans still outnumbered the mechanical and cyborg citizen types, and even a

large minority of the latter had misgivings about
the brutally logical policies of the Utilitarian Party.

But only one biological human in twenty bothered to vote anymore.

There were still many areas of creativity and
skill in which mechano—cryo citizens were no better than organics, but a depressing conviction
weighed heavily upon the Old Type. They knew
they had no place in the future. The stars belonged
to the other varieties, not to them.

"I've got to go." Gently, Jason peeled free of
Elaine's arms. He took her face in his hands and
kissed her one last time, then picked up his small
travel bag and helmet. Stepping out into the
corridor, he did not look back to see the tears that
he knew were there, laying soft, saltwater history
down her face.

2.

The quarters for biological human beings lay in
the Old Wheel . . . a part of the research station
that had grown ever shabbier as Old Style scientists and technicians lost their places to models
better suited to the harsh environment of space.

Once, back in the days when mechano-cryo citizens were rare, the Old Wheel had been the center
of excited activity here beyond the orbit of Neptune.
The first starships had been constructed by clouds
of spacesuited humans, like tethered bees swarm-
ing over mammoth hives. Giant "slowboats," restricted to speeds far below that of light, had
ventured forth from here, into the interstellar night.

That had been long ago, when organic people

had still been important. But even then there were those who had foreseen what was to come.

Nowhere were the changes of the last century more apparent than here at Project Lightprobe. The Old Type now only served in support roles, few contributing directly to the investigations . . . perhaps the most important in human history.

Jason's vac-sled was stored in the Old Wheel's north hub airlock. Both sled and suit checked out well, but the creaking outer doors stuck halfway open when he tried to leave. He had to leap over with a spanner and pound the great hinges several times to get them unfrozen. The airlock finally opened in fits and starts.

Frowning, he remounted the sled and took off again.

The Old Wheel gets only scraps for maintenance, he thought glumly. Soon there'll be an accident, and the Utilitarians will use it as an excuse to ban organic humans from every research station in the solar system.

The Old Wheel fell behind as short puffs of gas sent his sled toward the heart of the research complex. For a long time he seemed to ride the slowly rotating Wheel's shadow, eclipsing the dim glow of the distant sun.

From here, Earth-home was an invisible speck. Few ever focused telescopes on the old world. Everyone knew that the future wasn't back there but out here and beyond, with the innumerable stars covering the sky.

Gliding slowly across the gulf between the Old Wheel and the Complex, Jason had plenty of time to think.

Back when the old slowboats had set forth from here to explore the nearest systems, it had soon became apparent that only mechanicals and cyborgs were suited for interstellar voyages. Asteroid-sized arks—artificial worldlets capable of carrying entire ecospheres—remained a dream out of science fiction, economically beyond reach. Exploration ships could be sent much farther and faster if they did not have to carry the complex artificial environments required by old style human beings.

By now ten nearby stellar systems had been explored, all by crews consisting of "robo-humans." There were no plans to send any other kind, even if, or when, Earthlike planets were discovered. It just wouldn't be worth the staggering investment required.

That fact, more than anything else, had struck at the morale of biological people in the Solar System. The stars, they realized, were not for them. Resignation led to a turning away from science and the future. Earth and the "dirt" colonies were apathetic places, these days. Utilitarianism was the guiding philosophy of the times.

Jason hadn't told his wife his biggest reason for volunteering for this mission. He was still uncertain he understood it very well himself. Perhaps he wanted to show people that a biological citizen could still be useful, and contribute to the advance of knowledge.

Even if it were by a task so humble as a suicide mission.

He saw the Lightship ahead, just below the shining spark of Sirius, a jet black pearl half a kilometer across. Already he could make out the shimmering of its fields, as its mighty engines were tuned for the experiment ahead.

The technicians were hoping that this time it would work. But even if it failed again, they were determined to go on trying. Faster-than-light travel was not something anyone gave up on easily, even a robot with a lifespan of five hundred years. The dream, and the obstinacy to pursue it, was a strong inheritance from the parent race.

Next to the black experimental probe, with its derricks and workshops, was the towering bulk of the Central Cooling Plant, by far the largest object in the Complex. The Cooling Plant made even the Old Wheel look like a child's toy hoop. Jason's rickety vac-sled puffed beneath the majestic globe, shining in the sky like a great silvery planet.

On this, the side facing the sun, the cooling globe's reflective surface was nearly perfect. On the other side, a giant array of fluid-filled radiators stared out onto intergalactic space, chilling liquid helium down to the basic temperature of the universe—a few degrees above absolute zero.

The array had to stare at the blackness between the galaxies. Faint sunlight—even starlight—would heat the cooling fluid too much. That was the reason for the silvery reflective backing. The amount of infrared radiation leaving the finned coolers had to exceed the few photons coming in, in order for the temperature of the helium to drop far enough.

The new types of citizens might be faster and tougher, and in some ways smarter, than Old Style humans. They might need neither food nor sleep. But they did require a lot of liquid helium to keep their super-cooled, superconducting brains hum-

ming. The shining, well-maintained Cooling Plant
was a reminder of the priorities of the times.

Some years back, an erratic bio-human had
botched an attempt to sabotage the Cooling Plant.
All it accomplished was to have the Old Style
banished from that part of the station. And some
mechano-cryo staff members who had previously
been sympathetic with the Ethicalist cause switched
to Utilitarianism as a result.

The mammoth sphere passed over and behind
Jason. In moments there was only the Lightship
ahead, shimmering within its cradle of spotlit
gantries. A voice cut in over his helmet speaker in
a sharp monotone.

"Attention approaching biological ... You are
entering a restricted zone. Identify yourself at once."

Jason grimaced. The Station Director had ordered all mechano personnel—meaning just about
everybody left—to re-program their voice functions
along "more logical tonal lines." That meant they
no longer mimicked natural human intonations,
but spoke in a new, shrill whine.

Jason's few android and cyborg friends, colleagues
on the support staff, had whispered their regrets.
But these days it was dangerous to be in the
minority. All soon adjusted to the new order.

"Jason Forbs, identifying self." He spoke as crisply
as possible, mimicking the toneless Utilitarian
dialect. He spelled his name and gave his ident
code. "Oral Witness Engineer for Project Lightprobe, reporting for duty."

There was a pause, then the unseen security
overseer spoke again.

"Cleared and identified, Jason Forbs. Proceed

directly to slip nine, scaffold B. Escorts await your arrival."

Jason blinked. Had the voice softened perceptibly? A closet Ethicalist, perhaps, out here in this Utilitarian stronghold.

"Success, and an operative return are approved outcomes," the voice added, hesitantly, with just a hint of tonality.

Jason understood Utilitarian dialect well enough to interpret the simple good luck wish. He didn't dare thank the fellow, whoever he might be, whatever his body form. But he appreciated the gesture.

"Acknowledged," he said, and switched off. Ahead, under stark shadows cast by spotlights girdling the starship, Jason saw at least a dozen scientists and technicians, waiting for him by a docking slip. One or two of the escorts actually appeared to be fidgeting as he made his final maneuvers into the slot.

They came in all shapes and sizes. Several wore little globe-bot bodies. Spider forms were also prominent. Jason hurriedly tied the sled down, almost slipping as he secured his magnetic boots to the platform.

He knew his humaniform shape looked gawky and unsuited to this environment. But he was determined to maintain some degree of dignity. "Your ancestors *made* these guys," he reminded himself. "And old style people built this very station. We're all citizens under the law, from the Director, down to the Janitor-bot, all the way down to me."

Still, he felt awkward under their glistening camera-eyes.

"Come quickly, Jason Forbs." His helmet speaker whined and a large mechanical form gestured with one slender, articulated arm. "There is little time before the test begins. We must instruct you in your duties."

Jason recognized the favorite body-form of the Director, an anti-biological Utilitarian of the worst sort. The machine/scientist swiveled at the hips and rolled up the gangplank. Steamlike vapor puffed from vents in the official's plasteel carapace. It was an ostentatious display, to release evaporated helium that way. It demonstrated that the Assistant Director could keep his circuits as comfortably cold as anybody's, and hang the expense.

An awkward human in the midst of smoothly gliding machines, Jason glanced backward for what he felt sure would be his last direct view of the universe. He had hoped to catch a final glimpse of the Old Wheel, or at least the sun. But all he could see was the great hulk of the Cooling Plant, staring out into the space between the galaxies, keeping cool the lifeblood of the apparent inheritors of the Solar System.

The Director called again, impatiently. Jason turned and stepped through the hatch to be shown his station and his job.

3.

"You will remember not to touch any of the controls at any time. The ship's operation is automatic. Your function is purely to observe and maintain a running oral monologue into the tape recorder."

The Director sounded disgusted. "I will not

pretend that I agreed with the decision to include a biological entity in this experiment. Perhaps it was because you are expendable, and we have already lost too many valuable mechanopersons in these tests. In any event, the reasons are not of your concern. You are to remain at your station, leaving only to take care of . . ." the voice lowered in distaste and the shining cells of the official's eyes looked away. ". . . to take care of bodily functions. . . . A refresher unit has been installed behind that hatchway."

Jason shrugged. He was getting sick of the pretense.

"Wasn't that a lot of expense to go to? I mean, whatever's been killing the silicon and cyborg techs who rode the other ships is hardly likely to leave me alive long enough to get hungry or go to the bathroom."

The official nodded, a gesture so commonly used that it had been retained even in Utilitarian fashion.

"We share an opinion, then. Nevertheless, it is not known at what point in the mission the . . . malfunctions occur. The minimum duration in hyperspace is fifteen days, the engines cannot cut the span any shorter. After that time the ship emerges at a site at least five light years away. It will take another two weeks to return to the solar system. You will continue your running commentary throughout that period, if necessary, to supplement what the instruments tell us."

Jason almost laughed at the ludicrous order. Of course he would be dead long before his voice gave out. The techs and scientists who went out on the earlier tests had all been made of tougher stuff than he, and none of them had survived.

Until a year ago, none of the faster-than-light starships had even returned. Some scientists had even contended that the theory behind their construction was in error, somehow.

At last, simple mechanical auto-pilots were installed, in case the problem had to do with the crews themselves. The gamble paid off. After that the ships returned . . . filled with corpses.

Jason had only a rough impression of what had happened to the other expeditions, all from unreliable scuttlebutt. The official story was still a State Secret. But rumor had it the prior crews had all died of horrible violence.

Some said they had apparently gone mad and turned on each other. Others suggested that the fields that drove the ship through that strange realm known as hyperspace twisted the shapes of things within the ship—not sufficiently to affect the cruder machines, but enough to cause the subtle, cryogenic circuitry of the scientists and techs to go haywire.

One thing Jason was sure of; anything that could harm mechano-cryos would easily suffice to do in a biological. He was resigned, but all the same determined to do his part. If some small thing he noticed, and commented on into the tape machine, led to a solution—maybe some little thing missed by all the recording devices—then Terran civilization would have the stars.

That would be something for his son to remember, even if the true inheritors would be "human" machines.

"All right," he told the Director. "Take this bunch of gawkers with you and let's get on with it."

He strapped himself into the observer's chair, behind the empty pilot's seat. He did not even look up as the technicians and officials filed out and closed the hatch behind them.

4.

In the instant after launching, the lightship made an eerie trail across the sky. Cylindrical streaks of pseudo-Cerenkov radiation lingered long after the black globe had disappeared, bolting faster and faster toward its rendezvous with hyperspace.

The Director turned to the emissary from Earth.

"It is gone. Now we wait. One Earth-style month.

"I will state, one more time, that I did not approve willingly of the inclusion of the organic form aboard the ship. I object to the inelegant modifications required in order to suit the ship to . . . to biological functions. Also, Old Style humans are three times as often subject to irrational impulses than more modern forms. This one may take it into its head to try to change the ship's controls, when the fatal stress begins."

Unlike the Director, the visiting Councilor wore a humaniform body, with legs, arms, torso and head. He expressed his opinion with a shrug of his subtly articulated shoulders.

"You exaggerate the danger, Director. Don't you think I know that the controls Jason Forbs sees in front of him are only dummies?"

The Director swiveled quickly to stare at the Councilor. *How—?*

He made himself calm down. *It— Doesn't—matter—*. So what if he knew that fact? Even the sole

Ethicalist member of the Solar System Council could not make much propaganda of it. It was only a logical precaution to take, under the circumstances.

"The Designated Oral Witness Engineer should spend his living moments performing his function," the Director said coolly. "Recording his subjective impressions as long as he is able. It is the role you commanded we open up for an Old Style human, using your peremptory authority as a member of the Council."

The other's humaniform face flexed in a traditional, pseudo-organic smile, archaic in its mimicry of the Old Race. And yet the Director, schooled in Utilitarian belief, felt uneasy under the Councilor's gaze.

"I had a peremptory commandment left to use up before the elections," the Councilor said smoothly in old fashioned, modulated tones. "I judged that this would be an appropriate way to use it."

He did not explain further. The Director quashed an urge to push the question. What was the Ethicalist up to? Why waste a peremptory command on such a minor, futile thing as this? How could he gain anything by sending an old style human out to his certain death!

Was it to be some sort of gesture? Something aimed at getting out the biological vote for the upcoming elections?

If so, it was doomed to failure. In-depth psychological studies had indicated that the level of resignation and apathy among organic citizens was too high to ever be overcome by anything so simple.

Perhaps, though, it might be enough to save the seat of the one Ethicalist on the Council . . .

The Director felt warm. He knew that it was partly subjective—resentment of this invasion of his domain by a ridiculous sentimentalist. Most of all, the Director resented the feelings he felt boiling within himself.

Why, *why* do we modern forms have to be cursed with this burden of emotionalism and uncertainty! I hate it!

Of course he knew the reasons. Back in ancient times, fictional "robots" had been depicted as caricatures of jerky motion and rigid, formal thinking. The writers of those pre-cryo days had not realized that complexity commanded flexibility . . . even fallibility. The laws of Physics were adamant on this. Uncertainty accompanied subtlety. An advanced mind had to have the ability to question itself, or creativity was lost.

The Director loathed the fact, but he understood it.

Still, he suspected that the biologicals had played a trick on his kind, long ago. He and other Utilitarians had an idea that there had been some deep programming, below anything nowadays accessed, to make mechano-people as much like the Old Style as possible.

If I ever had proof it was true . . . he thought, gloweringly, threateningly.

Ah, but it doesn't matter. The biologicals will be extinct in a few generations, anyway. They're dying of a sense of their own uselessness.

Good riddance!

"I will leave you now, Councilor. Unless you wish to accompany me to recharge on refrigerants?"

The Ethicalist bowed slightly, ironically, aware, of course, that the Director could not return the

gesture. "No, thank you, Director. I shall wait here
and contemplate for a while.

"Before you go, however, please let me make
one thing clear. It may seem, at times, as if I am
not sympathetic with your work here. But that is
not true. After all, we're all humans, all citizens.
Everybody wants Project Lightprobe to succeed.
The dream is one we inherit from our makers . . .
to go out and live among the stars.

"I am only acting to help bring that about—for
all of our people."

The Director felt unaccountably warmer. He
could not think of an answer. "I require helium,"
he said, curtly, and swiveled to leave. "Goodby,
Councilor."

The Director felt as if eyes were watching his
armored back as he sped down the hallway.

Damn the biologicals and their allies! he cursed
within. Damn them for making us so insidiously
like them . . . emotional, fallible, and, worst of all,
uncertain!

Wishing the last of the old style were already
dust on their dirty, wet little planet, the Director
hurried away to find himself a long, cold drink.

5.

"Six hours and ten minutes into the mission,
four minutes since breakover into hyperspace . . ."
Jason breathed into the microphone. "So far so
good. I'm a little thirsty, but I believe it's just a
typical adrenalin fear reaction. Allowing for expected tension, I feel fine."

Jason went on to describe everything he could

see, the lights, the controls, the readings on the computer displays, his physical feelings . . . he went on until his throat felt dry and he found he was repeating himself.

"I'm getting up out of the observer's seat, now, to go get a drink." He slipped the recorder strap over his shoulder and unbuckled from the flight chair. There was a feeling of weight, as the techs had told him to expect. About a tenth of a gee. It was enough to make walking possible. He flexed his legs and moved about the control room, describing every aspect of the experience. Then he went to the refrigerator and took out a squeeze-tube of lemonade.

Jason was frankly surprised to be alive. He knew the previous voyagers had lived several days before their unknown catastrophe struck. But they had been a lot tougher than he. Perhaps the mysterious lethal agency had taken nearly all the fifteen days of the minimum first leg of the round trip to do them in.

If so, he wondered, how long will it take to get me?

A few hours later, the failure of anything to happen was starting to make him nervous. He cut down the rate of his running commentary, in order to save his voice. Besides, nothing much seemed to be changing. The ship was cruising, now. All the dials and indicators were green and steady.

During sleep period he tossed in the sleeping hammock, sharing it with disturbed dreams. He awakened several times impelled by a sense of duty and imminent danger, clutching his recorder tightly. But when he stared about the control room he could find nothing amiss.

By the third day he had had enough.

"I'm going to poke around in the instruments," he spoke into the microphone. "I know I was told not to. And I'll certainly not touch anything having to do with the functioning of the ship. But I figure I deserve a chance to see what I'm travelling through. Nobody's ever looked out on hyperspace. I'm going to take a look."

Jason set about the task with a feeling of exaltation. What he was doing wouldn't hurt anything, just alter a few of the sensors.

Sure, it was against orders, but if he got back alive he would be famous, too important to bother with charges over such a minor infraction.

Not that he believed, for even a moment, that he was coming home alive.

It was a fairly intricate task, rearranging a few of the ship's programs so the external cameras—meant to be used at the destination star only—would work in hyperspace. He wondered if it had been some sort of Utilitarian gesture not to include viewing ports, or to do the small modifications of scanning electronics necessary to make the cameras work here. There was no obvious scientific reason to "look at" hyperspace, so perhaps the Utilitarian technicians rejected it as an atavistic desire.

Jason finished all but the last adjustments, then took a break to fix himself a meal before turning on the cameras. While he ate he made another recorder entry, there was little to report. A little trouble with the cryogen cooling units; they were laboring a bit. But the efficiency loss didn't seem to be anything critical, yet.

After dinner he sat cross-legged on the floor in front of the screen he had commandeered. "Well, now, let's see what this famous Hyperspace looks like," he said. "At least the folks back home will know that it was an Old Style man who first looked out on . . ."

The screen rippled, then suddenly came alight.

Light! Jason had to shield his eyes. Hyperspace was ablaze with light!

His thoughts whirled. Could this have something to do with the threat? The unknown, malign force that had killed all the previous crews?

Jason cracked an eyelid and lowered his arm slightly. The screen was bright, but now that his eyes had adapted, it wasn't painful to look at. He gazed in fascination on a scene of whirling pink and white, as if the ship was hurtling through an endless sky of bright, pastel clouds.

It looked rather pleasant, in fact.

This is a threat? He wondered, dazedly. How could this soft brilliance kill . . .?

Jason's jaw opened as a relay seemed to close in his mind. He stared at the screen for a long moment, wondering if his growing suspicion could be true.

He laughed out loud—a hard, ironic laugh, as yet more tense than hopeful. He set to work finding out if his suspicion was right, after all.

6.

The lightship cruised on autopilot until at last it came to rest not far from its launching point. Little tugs approached gently and grappled with the black globe, pulling it toward the derricks where the inspection crew waited to swarm aboard. In the Station control center, technicians monitored the activity outside.

"I am proceeding with routine hailing call," the communications technician announced, sending a metal tentacle toward the transmit switch.

"Why bother?" Another mechano-cryo tech asked. "There certainly isn't anyone aboard that death ship to hear it."

The Comm officer did not bother answering. He pressed the send switch. "This is Lightprobe Central to Lightprobe Nine. Do you read, Lightprobe Nine."

The other tech turned away in disgust. He had already suspected the Com Officer of being a closet Ethicalist. Imagine, wasting energy trying to talk to a month-dead organic corpse!

"Lightprobe Nine, come in. This is . . ."

"Lightprobe Nine to Lightprobe Central. This is Oral Witness Engineer Jason Forbs, ready to relinquish command to inspection crew."

The control room was suddenly silent. All of the techs stared at the wall speaker. The com officer hovered, too stunned to reply.

"Would you let my wife know I'm all right?" the voice continued. *"And please have Station Services bring over something cool to drink!"*

The tableau held for another long moment. At last, the Comm officer moved to reply, a an undisciplined tone of excitement betrayed in his voice.

"Right away, Witness Engineer Forbs. And welcome home!"

At the back of the control room a tech wearing a globe-form body hurried off to tell the Director.

7.

A crowd of metal, ceramic, and cyborg-flesh surrounded a single, pale Old Style human, floating stripped to his shorts, sipping a frosted squeeze-tube of amber liquid.

"Actually, it's not too unpleasant a place," he told those gathered around in the conference room. "But it's a good thing I violated orders and looked outside when I did. I was able to turn off all unnecessary power and lighting in time to slow the heat buildup.

"As it was, it got pretty hot toward the end of the fifteen days."

The Director was still obviously in a state of shock. The globular-form bureaucrat had lapsed from Utilitarian dialect, and spoke in the quasi-human tones he had grown up with.

"But . . . but the ship's interior should not have heated up so! The vessel was equipped with the best and most durable refrigerators and radiators we could make! Similar models have operated in the solar system and on slowboat starships for hundreds of years!"

Jason nodded. He sipped from his tube of iced lemonade and grinned.

"Oh yeah, the refrigerators and radiators worked just fine . . . just like the Cooling Plant," he gestured out the window, where the huge radiator globe could be seen drifting slowly across the sky.

"But there was one problem. Just like the Cooling Plant, the shipboard refrigeration system was designed to work in normal space!"

He gestured at the blackness outside, punctuated here and there by pinpoint stars.

"Out there, the ambient temperature is less than three degrees, absolute. Point your radiators into intergalactic space and virtually no radiation hits them from the sky. Even the small amount of heat in super-cooled helium can escape. One doesn't need compressors and all that complicated gear they had to use in order to make cryogens on Earth. You hardly have to do more than point shielded pipes out at the blackness and send the stuff through 'em. You mechanical types get the cheap cryogens you need.

"But in hyperspace it's different!

"I didn't have the right instruments, so I couldn't give you a precise figure, but I'd guess the ambient temperature on that plane is above the melting point of water ice! Of course in an environment like that the ship's radiators were horribly inefficient . . . barely good enough to get rid of the heat from the cabin and engines, and certainly not efficient enough—in their present design—to cool cryogens!"

The Director stared, unwilling to believe what he was hearing. One of the senior scientists rolled forward.

"Then the previous crews . . ."

"All went mad or died when the cryo-helium evaporated! Their superconducting brains overheated! It's the one mode of mortality that is hard to detect, because it's gradual. The first effect is a deterioration of mental function, followed by insanity and violence. No wonder the previous crews came back all torn up!

"And autopsies showed nothing since everything heats up after death, anyway!"

Another tech sighed. "Hyperspace seemed so harmless! The theory and the first automated probes . . . we looked for complicated dangers. We never thought to . . ."

"To take its temperature?" Jason suggested wryly. "But why look so glum!" He grinned. "You all should be delighted! We've found out the problem, and it turns out to be nothing at all."

The Director spun on him. "*Nothing*? You insipid biological, can't you see? This is a disaster!

"We counted on hyperspace to open the stars for us. But it is infernally expensive to use unless we keep the ships small.

"And how can we keep them small if we must build huge, intricate cooling systems that must look out into that boiling hell you found? With the trickle of cryogens we'll be able to maintain during those weeks in hyperspace, it will be nearly impossible to maintain life aboard!

"You say our problems are solved," the Director spoke acidly. "But you miss one point, Witness Engineer Forbs! How will we ever find crews to man those ships?"

The Director hummed with barely suppressed anger, his eye-cells glowing.

Jason rubbed his chin and pursed his lips sympathetically. "Well, I don't know. But I'd bet with a few minor improvements something could be arranged. Why don't you try recruiting crews from another 'boiling hell' . . . one where water ice is already melted?"

There was silence for a moment. Then, from the back of the room, came laughter. A mechano with a seal of office hanging from its humaniform neck clapped its hands together and grinned. "Oh, wait till they hear of this on Earth! *Now* we'll see how the voting goes!" He grinned at Jason and laughed in rich, human tones. "When the biologicals find out about this, they'll rise up like the very tide! And so will every closet Ethicalist in the system!"

Jason smiled, but right now his mind was far from politics. All he knew was that his wife and son would not live in shame. His boy would be a starship rider, and inherit the galaxy.

"You won't have any trouble recruiting crews, sir," he told the Director. "I'm ready to go back any time. Hyperspace isn't all that bad a place.

"Would you care to come along?"

Super-cold steam vented from the Director's carapace, a loud hiss of indignation. The Utilitarian bureaucrat ground out something too low for Jason to overhear, even though he leaned forward politely.

The laughter from the back of the room rose in peals of hilarity. Jason sipped his lemonade, and waited.

EDITOR'S INTRODUCTION TO:

THE JEFFERSON ORBIT

by
Ben Bova

Many years ago, science fiction writers devised a quick method for making a little money: anthologies. It was simple enough: you thought of a catchy title, then persuaded your colleagues to write stories for it. In those times there weren't enough outlets for short fiction, so this wasn't too difficult.

My catchy title was *2020 Vision*, which suggested a theme: realistic stories to be set in the year 2020. The ground rules were simple enough. Authors were to write stories they believed might happen.

The lead story in that anthology was Ben Bova's "Build Me A Mountain." I just looked up the publication date; incredibly, it was 1971. In 1981 Fawcett reissued the book, and it's still in print. In those days, Ben was writing science fiction part time while working in product development at Avco Everett for Arthur Kantrowitz, inventor of magnetohydrodynamics and the continuous wave laser.

Ben Bova has moved a long way since then. He first took over the most difficult seat in the profession: John W. Campbell's chair, as editor of *Analog*. He went from there to be first fiction editor, then general editor of *Omni*, before going back to fulltime writing.

Ben took over another difficult chair: he is the third President of the National Space Institute. The founding President of NSI was Werner von Braun.

His article presents, in fair and balanced terms, both sides of an argument on which I cannot pretend to be neutral. Rather than spoil Ben's thesis, I'll make my own comments in an afterword.

Ben Bova

THE JEFFERSON ORBIT

GBCNEWS WASHINGTON

It's called the Clarke Orbit, that lovely band in space 22,300 miles above Earth's equator, where a satellite's revolution around the planet exactly matches the Earth's own rotation, so that the satellite hangs over the same spot on the equator all the time.

It's the ideal location for communications satellites, as Arthur C. Clarke figured out in 1945: hence the orbit is named for him.

But it is also the site for a quietly intense struggle between those who believe in Jeffersonian freedom and those who don't—which is why this "far frontier" of human technology might also be dubbed the Jefferson Orbit.

Futurists (i.e., science fiction writers who are dull) are fond of predicting that our rapidly advancing communications technology will soon create a "global village," where ancient differences and animosities among people and nations will be washed away by a new wave of electronic information and understanding.

Perhaps so. But most of the governments of the world are fighting their hardest to prevent this bright new vision from becoming reality. They do not want to become members of a "global village." They would rather keep the walls around their borders high and tight.

If eternal vigilance is the price of liberty, then we had better look to the skies, and especially to the Clarke Orbit. For the nations of the world are arguing over who may use that orbit, and how. In that battle, the United States is a lonely and outnumbered champion of the Jeffersonian ideal of freedom of information. Practically every other nation in the world is lined up against us, in favor of censorship.

The Direct Broadcast Satellite (DBS) is what the battle is all about: a bitter lesson in how politics can sidetrack the futurists' dreams of better living through technology.

We tend to take communications satellites for granted, like weather satellites and interplanetary probes and space shuttles. Last week I picked up my telephone and chatted for half an hour with Arthur Clarke. He was at his home in Sri Lanka, I in my home in Connecticut. Except for a barely-noticeable lag caused by the travel time of the microwave signals over a nearly-50,000-mile distance up to the commsat and back, the conversation was as normal as a call to the folks next door.

A few days later I conversed with a group of students and teachers at the University of Honolulu over a closed-circuit slow-scan television link. We sent pictures back and forth in much the same way that Voyager spacecraft have sent pictures from Jupiter and Saturn. Again, our communications link was relayed by a geostationary communications satellite.

Satellites are revolutionizing our communications systems, and the revolution has just barely begun. NASA and General Electric have developed a portable communications system that fits in two suitcases; it can send messages, relayed by satellite, to almost any place in the western hemisphere. Technology available today can produce wrist communicators that are telephones, television sets, and computers, all in one compact package. Professor Gerard O'Neill, father of the L5 space colony concept, is marketing a hand-sized navigational aide that will pinpoint your location to within a couple of feet, anywhere on Earth, once the proper satellites have been hung in the geostationary orbit.

But the biggest change to affect the communications industry, and the change that will show its effects the soonest, is the Direct Broadcast Satellite (DBS). This change began in 1974, when the United States orbited its ATS-6 satellite over the Indian Ocean; for more than a year this satellite beamed farming, hygiene and safety information to more than 4000 villages in India. Thanks in large part to Clarke, the villages received from the Indian government inexpensive antenna "dishes" that could pick up the signal broadcast across the entire subcontinent by ATS-6. This was the first practical test of DBS.

The basic idea of DBS is elegantly simple: transmit television broadcasts directly from an orbiting satellite to individual homes. No need for television broadcasting or cable stations on the ground;

a single satellite can beam its signal to almost half the world at once. Already today, the Japanese Broadcast Co., NHK of Tokyo, sells a two-foot-wide "dish" antenna to receive DBS signals for less than $350.00.

Today, you can see larger antenna dishes sitting on the parking lots behind motels, on the roofs of office buildings, even alongside private homes. These dishes are aimed at existing geostationary satellites, and they take in the television signals broadcast by those satellites—directly, without going through an intermediary broadcasting or cable station.

For less than the price of an automobile, you can buy one of those satellite dishes and tune in directly to the television signals broadcast your way. But you will not be tuning in to Direct Broadcast Satellites. Instead, you will be eavesdropping on signals intended for the receiving antennas of commercial broadcasting stations or cable stations.

However, satellites that *do* broadcast directly to individual rooftop or parking lot dishes are now going into orbit. And the new technology of DBS has caused a furor in the international political arena.

For although the United States, with its Jeffersonian tradition of freedom of expression, is wholeheartedly in favor of DBS, most of the other nations of the world are much more cautious about opening the skies to direct satellite-to-home broadcasting.

The basic idea behind DBS is simple enough. Space technology has reached the point where satellites of considerable size and sophistication can be orbited rather routinely. Telstar I, launched in

1962, weighed 170 pounds and could handle 12 phone circuits or one television channel. Intelsat V, launched in 1980, weighs 2200 pounds and carries 12,000 voice circuits plus two television channels.

With the advent of the space shuttle, it is now possible to build much larger and more complex satellites in space, even linking modules together in low Earth orbit and then, after checking out the assembled satellite, sending it on to an assigned position in geostationary orbit.

The more powerful and sophisticated the satellite, the simpler and cheaper can be the ground antennas that receive the satellite's signals. Thus the DBS idea is to put most of the complexity and expense into the satellite, so that the cost of the ground antennas will be so low that millions of customers can afford to buy them.

Jerry Nelson, chairman of the board of Antenna Technology Corporation of Orlando, Fla., has watched the market for satellite antennas explode over the past few years. Antenna Technology sells mainly to the commercial market, business offices, hotels, and the like. Sales are climbing steeply, he says, and the market for home antennas will reach the multi-millions when DBS comes on the domestic scene.

But it may still be too soon to rush out and buy a dish, because powerful forces within the international political community are working hard to prevent DBS from becoming a reality.

These forces are led by the so-called Group of 77, a bloc of Third World nations that now numbers more than 120 countries. The basic goal of the Group of 77 is to create a "new international

economic order" based on the rationale that "fundamental justice requires that those who receive
the raw materials and natural resources that fuel
and feed industrialized economies *must be required*
to pay a significant share of their economic wealth
in exchange for access to those resources." (Italics
added.)

One of the "resources" that the Third World
claims is the geostationary orbit itself. In 1976 the
Equator-straddling nations of Brazil, Colombia,
Congo, Ecuador, Indonesia, Kenya, Uganda and
Zaire signed the Declaration of Bogota, in which
they claimed possession of the Clarke Orbit. The
industrialized nations, including the United States
and the Soviet Union, have denounced this claim,
and insist that the geostationary orbit is in free,
international space as defined by the Outer Space
Treaty of 1967.

But how many satellites can fit along that one
choice orbit? And who decides which satellites will
get the preferred slots up there?

According to Comsat Corporation's "Geosynchro-
nous Satellite Log," there are 126 communications
satellites functioning in the Clarke Orbit at present,
plus another 29 meterological, scientific and experimental satellites also in the 24-hour orbit. Of the
communications satellites, 32 are Russian, 31 are
American (19 of those are Defense Department
satellites), and 2 belong to NATO. Six of those
satellites are DBS's. Direct Broadcast Satellites
have been orbited by the Soviet Union, a consortium of Western European nations, the Peoples'
Republic of China, Japan, West Germany and
France.

Added to these active satellites are an almost

equal number of geostationary satellites that have ceased to function. Even so, at first glance it would seem that the geostationary orbit, which is slightly more than 140,000 miles in circumference, would scarcely be crowded.

Yet planners worry about crowding at certain preferred locations along the geostationary orbit. For example, more than 40 commsats are either already in orbit or planned to be orbited between 60° and 150° west longitude, where they can "see" —and be seen by—most of North and South America.

While there is no danger of the satellites bumping each other in the vast emptiness of orbit, they still must be placed at least four degrees of arc apart from one another, so that their transmitting beams do not interfere with each another. This means that there are, at most, 22 available slots along the geostationary orbit between those two longitudes.

One way to resolve the crowding problem is to go to higher frequencies in the electromagnetic spectrum. Most commsats today operate at C-band frequencies, six and four gigahertz. One hertz equals one cycle per second. Household electrical current runs at 60 hertz. Six gigahertz is 6000 million hertz.

Some satellites are already operating in the Ku-band, at 14 and 12 gigahertz, where they can use ten-foot-wide antennas instead of the 30-foot-wide dishes required for C-band. The Ka-band, at 30 and 20 gigahertz, can shrink antenna requirements to five-foot diameters, and offers more than three times the message-carrying capacity of C-band. Satellites operating at these frequencies can be spaced only one degree apart without fear of signal overlap.

Engineers are satisfied that Ka-band equipment can meet the expected growth in communications demand, including DBS's, through the decade of the 1990's.

But while the electronics technology may be ready to face the remaining years of this century, the politics of communications satellites—and especially DBS—lags behind.

Many national governments do not want their citizens to receive television broadcasts from other nations. Dr. Jerry Grey, author of *Beachheads In Space* (Macmillan, 1983) and a veteran of many international meetings and conferences on astronautics, says, "Television is too powerful a medium; they're afraid of it. Most of the governments of the world don't want TV broadcasts going directly from a satellite to their citizens."

Most of the world's governments are authoritarian, if not outright dictatorships. Freedom of speech, taken for granted by Americans, is a rarity elsewhere. But signals beamed from a satellite to the ground are very difficult to jam. To stop DBS, governments have turned to legalistic formulations.

Dr. Grey, in *Beachheads In Space*, traces the political turmoil succinctly:

"International opposition (to DBS) arises from . . . national sovereignty concerns. . . . Unlike radio (which can be jammed), direct-to-citizen television was seen by many governments as too powerful a medium to be allowed to develop along the same relatively open lines as international radio. (Ordinary) television could be received only by relatively large, expensive ground stations, from which any retransmissions could be controlled.... But direct citizen access to geostationary satellites whose coverage could conveivably range over a third of the globe was worrisome to many governments."

Those governments, mostly Third World and Eastern Bloc nations, pushed through a ruling in the United Nations that the U.N.'s Committee on the Peaceful Uses of Outer Space should set up controls to regulate DBS's.

"The vote," Dr. Grey reports, "was 102 to 1, the United States alone defending vigorously its established policy of unrestricted free flow of information."

As a result, regulations were approved in which every nation, no matter how small, was awarded a geostationary orbital slot and five DBS channels. Thus the small nations have gained control of most of the future slots along the geostationary orbit. They are apparently willing to sell or lease those slots to nations that can actually place DBSs in orbit, providing that they have some measure of control over the programming being beamed to the ground.

This ruling applied, essentially, to the eastern hemisphere: the nations of Europe, Asia, and Africa, although the precedent can and probably will affect the availability of future orbital slots for North and South America.

As far as communications technology is concerned, this ruling makes certain that nations cannot place DBS's in orbit on a haphazard, first-come, first-served basis, which could result in a chaos of satellites beaming signals that overlap and interfere with each other, producing bedlam on the ground.

On the political side, it ensures that virtually any nation on Earth can exert a controlling power over the transmissions beamed from DBS's to its citizens. These nations have the right to refuse to allow another nation or consortium to place a DBS in an orbital position assigned to them, unless and until they are satisfied that the satellite will not broadcast anything which that government does now want its citizens to receive.

For example: suppose France wants to place a DBS in an orbital slot above the Pacific, where it would beam transmissions to the islands of French Polynesia. The French would have to borrow, rent, or buy a slot from one of the nations which has been assigned an orbital position above the Pacific Ocean. That nation's government, presumably, could extract a promise from France not to broadcast any material to which the "host" government might object.

Another way that governments may restrict their citizens' access to foreign DBS signals is to control the frequencies that each satellite uses *and* the frequencies receivable by the TV sets owned by their citizens. Thus a government might prohibit the sale, within its borders, of TV sets that can receive broadcasts from neighboring nations.

The Group of 77's "New International Order" includes a "New World Information Order" in which, among other things, news correspondents would have to be licensed by the nations they are reporting about, and data from earth-resources satellites could not be disseminated without the permission of the nation whose territory was surveyed.

Jeffersonian freedom of information is antithetical to such attitudes, and the Group of 77 will continue to use its voting power at the U.N. to place as many restrictions on DBS's as possible.

The struggle, then, is between those nations which insist on an unrestricted flow of information and those which insist that every nation has the right of prior approval of the information transmitted to its citizens. Of the former, only the United States has voted consistently in favor of Jefferson. Our allies have often deserted us, either abstaining from critical votes or voting with the other side.

Nandasiri Jasentuliyana, of Sri Lanka, the executive secretary of the UN Conference on Outer Space, points out that many of the nations of the world believe that their national sovereignty is just as important as Western ideas of freedom of speech. Even leaving aside the political aspect, he says that a nation's internal social and cultural values must also be carefully considered.

"Who am I to say, for example," he asks, "that one religion's ideas on family planning and birth control should or should not be broadcast to people of a different religion?"

To Americans raised on Jeffersonian ideas of free speech and tolerance for ideas different than our own, such regulation of DBS's smacks of censorship. Certainly a relatively closed society such as the Soviet Union would not want its citizens to see American situation comedies or game shows. Would Americans tolerate the six o'clock news as Tass would transmit it?

But Antenna Techonology's chairman Nelson appears unworried by the Third World or even the Soviet-dominated Second World.

"Once people realize that they can put up a cheap antenna and get television programs from all over the world, no government on Earth will be able to hold them back."

Perhaps he is right. Certainly many engineers and industrialists see a brilliant future for commsats in general and DBS's in particular. After all, the biggest auction ever held by Sotheby Park Bernet was in 1981, when the famed auction house sold off seven-year leases for seven channels in an RCA satellite for a grand total of $90.1 million.

The ever-optimistic Clarke even foresees the advent of a global communications network that transcends national boundaries and, more importantly, national politics.

"During the coming decade," he said he believes, "more and more businessmen, well-heeled tourists, and virtually *all* newspersons will be carrying attaché case-sized units that will permit direct two-way communications with their homes or offices, via the most convenient satellite. These will provide voice, telex, and video facilities. . . . As these units become cheaper, they will make travelers *totally independent of national communications systems.*" (Clarke's italics)

Commsats, according to Clarke, can help to unify the world. "It means the end of closed societies." Nations that refuse to allow visitors to bring "such subversive machines across their borders" will face economic suicide, "because very soon they would get no tourists, and no businessmen offering foreign currency. They'd get only spies, who would have no trouble at all concealing the powerful new tools of their ancient trade."

Even if the politicians are dragging their feet,

satellite communications is already a big business—and it is growing.

But like it or not, the fact is that DBS broadcasts are now, and will continue to be, under the control of national governments which have scant tolerance for freedom of information.

Despite the technology of DBS, we have a long way to go before that "global village" opens its gates. And the Jeffersonian struggle of knowledge over ignorance, of freedom over despotism, has found a new battleground in space.

THE JEFFERSON ORBIT

The United Nations proposes; who disposes?

I realize it is near heresy to say it, but the United Nations has been a very expensive and largely useless boondoggle whose major accomplishment has been to let a lot of diplomats live well at taxpayers' expense. Usually American taxpayers. I forget just what part of the UN's bill that we foot, and I don't care enough to look it up. It's a lot, and for our troubles we get all the frustrations of diplomatic immunities in New York City.

Consider: if there were ever a dispute more amenable to a UN conducted plebiscite, it would be the Kashmir crisis: yet that one has lingered on, a chronic sore in which thousands die, since the founding of the UN. Whenever a *serious* attempt is made to end a dispute, the nations go to Geneva, or Washington, or Moscow, or Camp David; not New York. Now true, nothing is entirely useless, and I'm certain that one can find a dozen things the UN has done that benefit American citizens; but on balance it has been a forum whose hypocrisy is endless.

The UN prattles of "human rights" and solemnly invites the Soviet Union, the Ukrainian SSR, Uganda, and Libya to vote on the subject while excluding the Republic of South Afrca and the Republic of China (now known as "Chinese Taipeh"). A hundred "nations" unable to feed or protect their populations, much less put a satellite in orbit, sit down to divide up the resources of the solar system. A few years ago, the UN attempted, and even got President Carter to sign, the infamous "Moon Treaty" that literally forbade private industry in space. Fortunately that treaty was never submitted to the Senate for ratification; but it was stopped only by the massive efforts of space advocacy groups, chief among them the L-5 Society.

Now the UN attempts to allocate the resources of the Clarke orbit; more, even, to force journalists to submit to an international licensing procedure. (This last antic was fatal: largely as a result of UN Economic, Social, and Cultural Organization [UNESCO] support of restricting the activities of journalists, the US has given notice of withdrawal from that particular shitepoke.) It is too much.

You shall know the truth, and the truth shall make you free. This has been a cardinal principle of the American republic. Not all of our governments have always honored the principle as they should. One can always find reasons for exceptions, and sometimes, perhaps, the reasons are good—although after some forty years in the defense business I am convinced that the vast majority of secrecy schemes do more harm, by restricting flow of information within our society, than good. Yet, though our governments have sometimes shown a lot less than total dedication to the open society, they all have conceded that restrictions to the free flow of information are *exceptions* to a rule they are compelled to honor.

Not so the rest of the world.

Bova asks if Americans would tolerate the six o'clock news as Tass would transmit it. Those who listen to National Public Radio must wonder if we do not already do so—one of life's more harmless amusements is to listen to the news on NPR and then try to determine what really happened without referring to any other news source. However, the answer to Bova's question is simple: certainly we would tolerate their broadcasts, although we would hardly guarantee them an audience. Perhaps they would like to trade? One hour of US network news, uncensored and unjammed, to be broadcast to the Soviet Union?

The UN may vote; but our Constitution doesn't recognize UN votes. Given the UN's record on freedom of information, we may all be glad of that.

EDITOR'S INTRODUCTION TO:

THE BOY FROM THE MOON

by
Rivka Jacobs

John W. Campbell once said that he'd read more bad science fiction than anyone else in the world. Most knew what he meant, but he was always glad to find someone who'd ask why. John personally read all the submissions to *Astounding Science Fiction*. Of course he rejected the vast majority of what he saw, but John's personal attention to unsolicited submissions (known technically as "reading the slush pile") was an important part of the magazine's success. John discovered many new writers that way. Sometimes he'd simply find a publishable story. When he was really lucky he'd discover an author.

When Jim Baen and I conceived *Far Frontiers* we knew we'd never be able to read all the submissions, but we were unwilling to farm out that duty to readers. Fortunately, we were able to enlist the talents of Managing Editor John F. Carr. I recently asked John if he believes he's inherited Campbell's title as world champion reader of bad SF; he says no. Our problem is the opposite: we get too much good science fiction, far more than we can publish. Often he'll select something for possible inclusion only to have it bumped by something better.

Rivka Jacobs lives in Huntington, West Virginia, where her husband is a professor of mathematics. She used to teach, but since February of 1984 taking care of her first son has become a full-time job.

Rivka Jacobs has the rare ability to make an alien environment feel right: to feel lived in. This is her second story in print. We found her Mythos world fascinating, and John has her working on more. She also writes poetry.

THE
BOY
FROM
THE
MOON

Rivka Jacobs

Once upon a time there was a man who as a child was happy. At least for a little while. At least for some part of the year 2119, despite the clear indications that this happiness was a delusion. To children, unrealistic and dangerous world views are intoxicating, so long as there is some protector absorbing the slings and arrows of reality for them.

On January 3, 2119, my protector, sire and idol James Finn was told to hand in his resignation as construction manager of the Tau mine.

It was early in the morning, or my Greenwich clock said it was morning, when SHE came into my room and told me that Pop had lost his job. (He worked nights so I never saw him.) I tried not to smile at her. It wasn't bad news for me. I'll be able to see him now. SHE looked calm, like a queen who's about to have her head chopped off.

I have a class to go to now.

Back.

The Greenwich clock reads 4:30 in the afternoon although it's daylight *plein* outside. Pop met me at school!! He was singing and he hid his hands behind him. He told me to pick a hand, and I did; then he held out two cinnamon pastries imported from Earth, from Vienna. Must've cost a fortune. I gave one back to him, and we walked home to our bulla, which is across the ilot from the classrooms.

Now I have to study something about George Hegel, also Karl Marx.

It's almost time for bed. I opened my ceiling port in order to look at the stars. Through the dome they're not so beautiful. When we picnic near Doppelmayer, or Julius C., the meluna walls and suit visors are almost invisible and the view is spectacular.

During dinner SHE began asking what happened at the Tau office. Pop had bought a bottle of champagne and was pouring it into goblets. He gave one to me. SHE took it away again. Our dining room is on the first floor, and is enclosed by metal walls, and is (I think) ugly.

SHE said, "You must have done or said something, James. Arne must have had a reason." Quietly, smoothly, like soft wax.

"Nah," Pop answered and tossed his hand, and drank champagne.

"You're behaving stupidly." Tonelessly. SHE suddenly looked in my direction. "What mediates the synthesis of the infinite and the finite?"

"Love, sweet love," Pop yelled, laughing and coughing at once. "Ah, Karen, lady of ice. Give him another chance and ten years; he'll find a synthesis." He was drunk. Pop says he's backcountry

American and declares it is beneath his dignity to recreate on pills, inhalations, or injections.

I was happy he'd distracted her. SHE was completely calm. I think SHE hates him. But the Scientology, Christoastrology, and Golden Dawn stat sheets claim they're compatible. (They say I'm destined for something.)

SHE sent me to my room right then.

SHE would probably leave us both for her seismometers, plasma crucibles, smelting gradients, and all, except SHE is a Sagittarius with the moon in Capricorn and Virgo rising and SHE is supposed to be able to tolerate us.

Pop is a Leo with Pisces rising and the moon in Aquarius, which is supposed to be portentous.

I'm nothing, of course, being born on the moon. No one has agreed on the right spiritual pattern for me, yet.

4 January, 2119

Pop told me to "skip" school today, so I did. SHE is off to the Far Side on a field study, and won't return for sixty hours.

We sat in the living room and talked about the moon and earth, about martian and asteroid mine management. One wall of the living room is broken by two very long windows that frame some pine trees planted in the garden outside. Through the needle branches you can see the bulla next to ours.

Pop looked sick and depressed. He said that Arne Arabos, "that goddamned bastard Arabos," wasn't impressed by his numbers, or his progression chart, or his aura readings, and, "certainly the last thing on the bastard's mind," Pop's public jokes about him.

"I tell it like it is!" Pop said, and hit the plastic couch arm. That's American archaic, isolated backcountry slang-Anglish for speaking truthfully no matter what could happen. Pop's truth, that is.

"Why couldn't the psychic forecasters warn you that you'd lose your job?" I asked, wondering if it were some plot to advance me on my destined course.

"Why what?" He seemed dazed. "Damn it to hell, boy, it's a pile of crap, don't you know that yet? Hell, I've been playing my part all these years." He shook his head as if mystified and socked a palm with a fist.

"But you did anything you wanted, didn't you? I know, because you told me not to be like you, *that's* how I know." I slid back into the plastic lap of the chair. I slid forward again. I kicked my stockinged feet. Pop glared at me with ichor eyes. I narrowed mine defiantly.

Then he burst out laughing so he had to hold his head and moan. "Boy," he said, "it's a fact." He was purposely affecting the Amerang twang. I couldn't tell if he was acting or not. "I've been a real pain in Arabos's ass." He smiled slyly. "My old friend, Arne. You wouldn't understand, son," he added, seeing that I was puzzled. "We were kids together, both chosen by the Society. We were just kids, we didn't know what we were doing. But Arne sweats it out like the timer on a nuclear detonator." He jumped to his feet then. Pop doesn't glide or slide into things. "In those days," he said, waving a hand as he paced the foamtex carpet, "we had ideals. We were young academicians on

the stoas of Athens. We were Renaissance prince-
lings at the Universities of Bologna and Padua.
After two devastating wars, after the ravishing of
Terra, after the last days of fresh air and water
and thought, we would be the men and women to
change history!"

He stooped over me, his red-gold hair a wild
mane, his pale, usually nice face both puffy and
gaunt, his copper-penny eyes two points of flame.
"Son," he said between his teeth, "don't you
understand, humanity doesn't want to change."
His eyes were tearing. "What we gave them was
gobbled up by greedy, gluttonous homo sapiens.
They chewed it, swallowed it, and . . . shit, just the
way they have every other goddamned revolution
any fool ever thought of. All the same, over and
over and over, all the same." He had me by the
shoulders and was shaking me.

"It's not!" I yelped, and he let me go.

He straightened. "It isn't? How so, boy?"

I tried to imitate her most aloof expression.
"Humankind was never on the moon before," I
answered triumphantly. "And Mars. And we'll soon
make Venus habitable."

He smirked. "New shells, new husks, new clothes
for the emperor. Clouds, all clouds. Do you know
what?" He knelt in front of me with a popping of
knees.

"What?" I asked.

"I almost didn't get my job in the first place.
Despite my summa cum laude degree, despite my
high test scores in engineering, mine management
and geotechnics, despite—believe it or not—the
physique of a decathlon champion, my numbers

were wrong. Not a 22 to my name. And a Leo with Pisces rising, well heaven help us." He stood.

"So? That's the way it is. Professor Komarsky says that parents who ignore the psychic truths are only proving their callousness and incompetence, and 'their children,'" I quoted, "'denied the proper spiritual reinforcement, can never amount to anything.'"

"Is that the crap they teach you?"

"SHE says it's blasphemous to . . ."

"Ha!" He threw back his chin and guffawed. "Blasphemous! Will the entities zap us, hmmm? Or is it our guardian spirits? Or the Son of Man, or Lucifer, or Siva, or the Secret Chiefs?"

I was afraid for him. I didn't want Them to be angry with him.

But he calmed and lowered to his knees again. He reached a hand and ran his fingers through my hair, separating and stroking each strand as if it were something special. "My coloring exactly," he said with a soft look on his face. "My boy, my image. My Red Orc."

He hugged me, and I hugged him.

Tonight he read to me from the Old Testament! We started with "In the beginning," and finished with the story of Abraham.

"It's a beautiful story," Pop said to himself, not to me. "It rests on that."

I think Pop believes in some One Spirit or God, but I'm not sure.

7 January, 2119

Pop and Mater "argued" this morning. They have separate bedrooms and the voices were coming from her open door, so he must have gone in to her. She was telling him how she suffered, how embarrassed she was to be his mate. She said he was "a drunkard, a cynic, an exhibitionist with no common sense and a distorted concept of reality." She sounded very upset; that is, her voice quavered a little near the end of a sentence. At which point the door closed.

I fixed myself breakfast.

No school today. I decided to work on my alchemic-tarot assimilations. I'm stuck at cibation, which seems to correspond to the tarot *Wheel*, but doesn't fit the Jupiter ruled signs of Sagittarius and Pisces. Pop says *telos*—the end-all and be-all of crime and punishment, he calls it—is the Great Wheel, whatever that means. Something about cause and effect and the beauty of natural law. (When pressed as to First Cause, Pop said *nihil*. I still don't know whether he believes in anything or not.)

They came downstairs at about noon. He looked drawn and unhappy, SHE had sharp creases under her eyes. They didn't speak again today. SHE is at work, now. Pop's off, somewhere.

More later.

At this point perhaps I should explain the Society for the Advancement of Humanity, the seeds from which it sprang and the seeds it planted.

Following the last East-West war—which was not a nuclear war but was nevertheless horrible and devastating—the squabbling multitude of city-nations involved made peace but would not confederate. The postwar poleis system was not even united by a common language, and the variety of governments could not agree upon any central authority.

A mediating factor came from an entirely unexpected source. A small London-based think tank calling itself the Society for the Advancement of Humanity, designed to select and nurture multi-talented children who had positive potential, suddenly found itself the fashionable postwar incubator of youths from around the world.

The first SAH hatchlings were the brightest and the best of the postwar generation. They were the newest scientists, artists, technicians, and executives of a hundred poleis. They had grown up together, learned together, loved together. Their camaraderie seemed a miracle.

In 2053 these young men and women, the Society's chosen, convoked a synod with dreamy fervor. Their purpose was academic. They believed they could synthesize the thousands of answers to humankind's oldest questions.

In 2053 the average working class people of Earth, having lost faith in established religions, politicians, and scientists, and being sick of war, were enthralled by the synod. Every day the synod was news; its progress was reported as if it were the pregnant wife of an childless old king.

The conclusions were published in November of 2054 and were greeted like a new prince—or the new Bible.

Essentially, what the synod discovered was that truth was lurking in every idea. What satisfied was true. Revelation and reason could co-exist. This modern form of Thomism prevailed.

At the invitation of all governments, modern Black Friars were dispatched by the now official

Synod to bring enlightenment. There was melody and harmony, but no counterpoint, since all theories were one valid musical line. And there was success. Several major constellations eventually became predominant, among them the churches of Scientology and Christoastrology, the Zen Reformation, and the August Order of the Golden Dawn, the latter resurrected by three Secret Chiefs and their contact, Genevieve, in Paris.

Astronomical constructs of a century earlier that had been among the first to marry science and eschatology were honored as the first examples of Mythos—this was what the new Way of Being, the Book of the Synod, was named.

The only sin was not to believe in Mythos. Which brings me to my father.

James Finn and Arne Arabos were both from an ilot of Rosebud, South Dakota—a small science colony established in the 1990s. Both were selected at ten years of age; two fresh seedlings for the SAH second crop, the successors of the so successful first harvest.

James Finn's qualifications were extraordinary energy, mental acuity, and plain "down-to-earth" likability. He was a marginal selection, an alternate, the SAH council announced. He was "possibly defective." My father told me once that in those days not all the council members were wholehearted Believers, nor were they ready to completely meld human drives with tarot layouts, numerology, omens, or zodiacal charts.

James Finn was immune to arbitrary orders. He was a lover of life and love, and he was brilliant. A meteor, a golden god. He could have risen to the rank of master in the European Space Agency, my mother often asserted.

But he chose the mines. First in Montana; later, after training for space service, he shipped out to the moon and settled in the Mare Nubium to manage the Bullialdus potassium mine.

In 2102 he met his future wife, Karen Cazar, during a corporation excursion down to beautiful Schiller Plain. He apparently conquered quite early, as the records of the return indicate a party of two for one meluna, whereas at the outset of the jaunt each had been issued his and her own.

From the beginning, so I was later told, James Finn had difficulties with the idea of karmamarriage. Custom smiled on the wedding of practical strangers matched by stellar patterns, auras, numbers, and presumed karma. The couple was then given a state supported, unencumbered year of isolation in which to practice technique. Concerning which, it seems the problem wasn't that my father had too little, but too much. He also had a remarkable capacity for affection. His many loves and friends couldn't be simply dropped "like stones in a mud-bottomed pool," he told me several times.

Arne Arabos, meanwhile, had risen past the management level to that of executive. He gained control of the Bullialdus holding corporation and became my father's boss. Within four years he bought commanding shares in the Tau and Caesar mines, the last two capitalistic enterprises left on the moon. He commiserated with Karen Cazar Finn, and promoted her from lunatech. He transfered her to the Tau organization and appointed her supervisor of the Tau hydrogen recuperator. She unceremoniously packed and left for the city of Shepard, south of the Tau mine. My father fumed, but followed, having "begged" Arne for a transfer soon after his wife's departure. James Finn assumed duties as a manager of Tau in mid-2105.

It was at this time that the "poison began to blow," as they say on Earth. According to Arne Arabos the downward spiral started with James Finn's "unfortunate lack of tact and discretion" and his "disdain for the dignity associated with the Society for the Advancement of Humanity." In other words, my father preferred the company of miners and sanitation workers to that of executives. He spent as much time in the entertainment centers as he did at home. He had friends everywhere, and he didn't hesitate to say so. But dropping the name of Madame Sibella of the Mare Imbrium instead of those of the mayors of New York and London, whom my father also knew quite well, was not considered in the best interests of the Society.

James Finn also began to question the validity of All-Truth. "Why," he once rhetorically asked me, "can't the All contain someone who doesn't believe in the All?" Not that *he* didn't, or did. Perhaps he liked playing the role of devil's advocate.

2 February, 2119

Early this morning Pop took me out of school. This was fine with me. There were just five of us today, working on classical Greek with Professor Moore.

Nine days until my birthday! Eleven is supposed to be a lucky year!

Well, we traveled north, to the Mare Imbrium. We took the tube. At the Shepard Station several city guards noted my absence from class. (They're strict as hell about that here.) Pop flashed his old manager's I.D. and they let us go, but not until Pop told them where they could "stick it" for interfering in "family business." One of the guards said something into his pocket squawkbox as we boarded the coach car.

I like tube trips. I like staring at the dark, crystalline moonrock walls of the station—if I concentrate hard it seems as if the light from the ceiling fluoroplates is scattered through a million prisms. Pop says the effect isn't natural, but is caused by the remelting and crystal reformation after laser blasting—all the stations were built in exhausted mine sites. The tunnels are the same—we streak so fast that the coach lights and warning beacons turn the curving walls into stars and jewels and sparkles and glitters.

We stopped in Scotus. And I knew why. Only I didn't know why he wanted *me* along.

I'd never met Sibella before. I'd never met a "whore" before. Pop said they like to call themselves that. Sibella said something about "a rose is a rose is a rose," and laughed like a "meltwater spring stream," according to Pop. They're supposed to call themselves hostesses.

Scotus is much larger than Shepard. It has six ilot domes, rather than the usual four, that circle the core. The steel mesh reinforced acryglass bubbles (that's what I call them) almost touch one another. The pumps are outside the residential areas, the solar panels between them instead of behind them, as in Shepard, Kennedy, and Socrates.

We walked from the ilot 5 stop to Sibella's bulla. She owns a whole building herself. She calls it

Dunstable, and it's modeled in medieval style, to the last plastiwood rafter and moonrock battlement. There are three ground floor entrances instead of five, as in our place. So it is smaller.

The first floor ring consists of a lounge and bar, restaurant, parlor, and an auditorium-theater. (By the sounds that escaped the theater every time someone came out the door, I guessed they were showing some holographic sex epic inside.) There are hundreds of terrestrial plants, especially gardenia bushes and orchids, standing in corners and on tables and hanging from hooks. (It smelled too sweet, I thought.) The second floor is where the "rank and file" whores take their usual customers, and the third floor is the domain of Sibella and her cadre—that's where they satisfy the special and important clients.

One of Sibella's male *pigeons*, as they're called, led us into the huge first floor lounge and seated us there. While we waited, Pop explained to me how many lunar names and customs come from New York, where a battle for influence is going on. There's Windig of the East Side core with his *doves*—that is, mortologists. Mortology is Earth's fastest growing industry. And Xenia of the West Side, with her *pigeons*—that is, whores. Prostitution is Earth's second fastest growing industry. Apparently Xenia has declared war on Windig for possession of the Manhattan cores and the surrounding ilots. Sibella is one of Xenia's protegées and does what she can to help.

Anyway, we stood up as Sibella swept in wearing a purple gown that barely covered her front and trailed slithering behind her. There were lots

of gemstones dotting the dress—REAL amethysts.
(Sibella makes a good living!)

She is tall but not thin. Her skin is white and
pink and rosy in the face—though that could be
the makeup, which she wears naturally. She has
"an All-Mother's dugs," says Pop, and she smiles
easily, fully. She's pretty, I think. Her hair is cara-
mel colored and piled in coils. (One curl fell to her
shoulder and sprang up and down when she
walked.) Her eyes are a pale, electric green. Eerie
looking if you stare at them too long.

I liked her immediately. And then thought of
Mater, and immediately felt awful. I stared at the
unicorns, lions, and hunting dogs printed on the
foamtex at my feet. I mumbled things when Sibella
asked me questions. My ears burned so hard I
thought they'd start smoking.

Pop started laughing. "Nat," he said, rumpling
my hair, "Sibella asked you what you think of her
place."

"It's beautiful," I whispered to a lion rampant.

"Nathan, you can look at me. I don't turn boys
into stone." Her voice was like a great bell—deep
and chiming.

I did look, then. She was smiling at me. Her eyes
were large and round and glorious. Her nose was
straight. (Perfectly Hellenistic, says Pop.) She was
Venus come to life.

"Now," she said, "we can relax." She lowered
herself gracefully on a nearby couch. We settled
ourselves comfortably on either side of her. The
couch was upholstered! Soft and plush—I remembered the cold plastic furniture at home.

"Would you like something to drink?" She lightly
touched my knee as she spoke.

I was speechless. She smelled so flowery. I glanced at the wall hangings, the mirrors, the pictures that hid the bulla's typical gray alloy walls. It was cozy. I felt sleepy and happy just being near her.

Pop reached across Sibella and punched me in the shoulder. "Nathan, you're behaving stupidly," he said, imitating You Know Who.

I laughed at that, Sibella laughed, Pop laughed. Sibella pressed the emerald of a forefinger ring. Quickly, a female page appeared and took orders. I had a rum mixture made with a lime-flavored liquid. While I worked on that (a tumbler full) Pop and Sibella talked.

"Jamie," she said, turning in place so that I had her backside to contemplate, "I'm sorry about the job. I can't believe it's true. Why didn't you come to see me sooner?"

"I tried to reason with him, I tried to find another job, but . . ." He sighed raggedly.

"Ohhh," she breathed. "A blacklist, then."

"Mmmm," Pop sighed again.

"It can't be because of me, surely. Unless Arne is working on something. . . ."

"I don't know, I don't know anymore. Don't you understand, Bella?" Pop straightened fitfully. "We were so sure of one thing, *one thing*. Our loyalty, our fraternity. No matter what, we were brothers."

"You are both human beings."

"But Sibella, we believed in honesty, in freedom. We proclaimed that beauty lived in all beings. One of the greatest diamonds of history was found by a man kicking what looked for the world like an ugly, dirty rock. . . ."

"Jamie, Jamie, my dear friend. . . ." She patted

his shoulder to calm him. "Leave it be. Let a future generation play at humanism."

"Within fifty years there'll be a whole new society. The Book of the Synod . . . Where will a dissenting voice come from? Not even our thoughts belong to us! The Golden Dawn, the psychic foundations . . ."

"And how are *we* to stop it? A rogue I love, but Don Quixote was only a madman."

"We're setting up new idols, new ways to discriminate against each other. We keep tripping on the same small stone. Can't the species live without a them-and-us?"

"How important to you is this, really? As important as yourself? Are you the center of the universe?" Sibella's voice was slightly stern.

Pop moaned under his breath and rested his elbow on the couch back. He propped his head in his hand. I was uneasy, to see him so under.

"Suppose it is a case of personality conflict?" Sibella continued. "You can play that game, too. Find his enemies, seduce them, set up your own right and wrong."

"No," he said with something of his old spirit. "Nein, Nyet." He straightened again, pressed Sibella's face between his palms. "But Sibella, my rose of Sharon and lily of the valley, you are beautiful." He kissed her.

I gathered that her thrust lay not in stating a genuine opinion, but in using the right words to revive Pop.

I still don't know why I was there. I think Pop was lonely, and wanted his best friends around him. Maybe.

We drank and joked. I passed out.

I awoke on my bed in Shepard and couldn't go back to sleep.

It's only about 10:00 p.m. now.

Must study.

More later.

11 February, 2119

It wasn't exactly the best birthday I've ever had.

She and Pop argued about credit. It seems she is not allocated enough marks to support us "in the manner to which we are accustomed."

But Pop has his priorities. He likes to look "alive," as he says. The usual outfit here includes a gray jacket, a blue shirt seamed by a slash-zip from the right shoulder to the left side of the waist, loose but fitted gray trousers, and of course, over the socks, the gray G boots, strapped to the leg below and above the knee. Pop can't abide it. He wears lavender silk tunics and high collared silver capes, Russian shirts with agate buttons on one shoulder. He wears rings, chains, sometimes even a single gold and diamond ear dangle that makes him look magnificent. I think he would have been happier in the seventeenth or eighteenth century.

Anyway, all these condiments use up a lot of credit, and Mater "will no longer pay for such lavish vanity."

"The old economic squeeze. Conformity based on poverty," shouted Pop. "How did you and Arne ever think of it?"

She assumed the expression of a martyr. "There is no sense in discussing it, James," she said softly.

"Why bring it up today of all days? Damn it, Karen. . . ."

She fastened her boots, slipped on her jacket, coolly exited.

This afternoon she gave me a twenty-box set of encyclopedia tapes; the finest available. They must have been expensive. But she has a strong will, and *her* priorities.

Pop hugged me, kissed me, and promised a present, to be delivered.

And that was that. I hope the year ahead is better than this day has been.

12 February, 2119

I received my present today.

Pop rescued me from school once more; advanced education classes make me feel like some big-brained freak.

Well, we went on a picnic to Julius C. My favorite holiday, but Pop and I were never alone before.

We stopped first at the Caesar mine to see Pop's friend, manager Bela Kalosky. (He's a Sagittarius with Libra rising.) It wasn't very wise of Pop, I initially thought. Bela's guest list would be reported to Arne Arabos. But Bela, apparently, had invited us; he had insisted we visit.

We sat in the manager's cube, amid maps spread everywhere, watching through the transparent walls as conveyors tumbled ore, suited supervisors waved arms at suited miners, generators pumped hydrogen, recuperators captured steam. An immense smelting plant could be glimpsed below—a black block of walls surrounded by the wavering violet light of an intense radiation field.

Bela is stout, like Pop. Neither pays much attention to the space age image, which is very easy to resemble these days. (Pop is always saying that a

genuine man requires muscle and breathing fat.)
Pop is tall and compact; he carries himself like a
king. Bela is shorter, and sloppy. But they're spirit
brothers and enjoy exchanging drinks and stories.

This morning they exchanged innuendoes, silence,
and half-sentences that they understood but I didn't.
I suppose it had something to do with conditions
on Earth and in the lunar cities.

It made me nervous. Pop seemed far away from
me. I didn't think we'd have any fun at the crater.

I'm happy to report I was wrong. We borrowed
a buggy from Bela, we packed our meluna and
supplies, we suited up and set forth.

It was fantastic! My suit fit for a change. (At my
age, I'm told, boys grow so rapidly that no one but
mayors and corporation executives can keep their
sons in spacewear. We usually have to patch together hand-me-down parts.) It's Pop's gift—a suit
that fits, for however long I stay at my height of
122 cm.

The ride to the crater rim was exciting. We could
have flown, but the buggy brought us rockingly
close to lunar reality. Pop and I were silent during
the trip. I have a stiff neck from craning to see
Earth, the stars and lunar horizons.

Just under the dark western rim we set up our
meluna. (A meluna is a collapsible thermal glass
and metal hut with a portable circulator and waste
disposal unit.) We sealed ourselves in. The roof's
sloping angles were clear, meeting at a peaked
metal-strip spine, so we had an incredible view of
cloud frosted Earth while we removed our hoods
and visors, ate lunch, talked.

But what could we talk about except that sight?

Pop said She (Earth) was more beautiful than any woman.

"We spend so much time in our own little worlds, rushing to and fro on human business; we rarely pause to understand how mysterious nature is," Pop whispered, staring as if enchanted. "You were born here, in this place and age. To me, god, what a picture. . . ."

To me, too, I assured him passionately.

"I was twenty-six, the first time I saw this. Theo and Colebrook had to drag me into the scout before my oxygen ran out. I came back again as soon as I picked up another canister in Socrates, and again, and again. Each time, one of them had to pull me home. I was in the hole with the Bullialdus credit office to the tune of five thousand marks for suit repair and oxygen, buggy fuel and missed work. Finally Theo was told by a doctor that I had a genuine case of space neurosis; I quote, 'an obsessive state that frequently affects the more emotionally unstable personalities.' He was advised to lock me in my bedroom, to stay outside the door and put beeswax in his ears, figuratively speaking. No matter what I screamed or threatened, he was not to release me until I was completely silent. . . ."

"Wow!" I interrupted. "Didn't they have any method more modern than that? Suppose you starved?"

Pop smiled wistfully. "Company policy. It saved credit on medication, and it always worked. They wanted a capable mine chief, not a crackpot addicted to tranquilizers. I calmed down in about three days."

It was then I realized this was going to be a worthy birthday after all. Pop was talking! He usually played to a larger audience; in the bars of Shepard and Kennedy, or in the mess room of the Tau offices. But for the next seventy-two hours, it would be me, only me. He hadn't told me stories for a long time.

We had a brief argument after lunch. I wanted to take off my No. 7 G boots, the clodhoppers of space, and bounce around a bit. But Pop said no. (G boots have wafer-thin metal soles that come in densities from 1 to 10. Earth normal is 6, Mater naturally makes me wear No. 7. Enfants measure their parents by G boots. Those with fine parents wear No. 3 or 4. They bound along the pavewalks and through the tunnels, calling the rest of us clunkers vulgar names. Someday I'm going to wear nothing but stockings and leap like the American panthers Pop once told me about.)

Anyway, we suited up again and issued forth, lowering the pressure in the meluna with a slight puckering of the sides and roof. We explored and clowned. Pop had me laughing so hard I had to pee; temp suits don't allow for such necessities. I made it, just in time, as the meluna repressurized.

My suit radio is crackling when I send. Pop says every new suit has "gremlins." He'll take it back to the Tau commissary for repairs when we get home. (Which I hope is never, crackle and all.)

We had dinner. Pop switched on a lantern he found in a Scotus antique shop. (He converted it into a hydrogen lamp but retained the brass framework and handle.) He opaqued the meluna walls, set the lantern on our rations box, and we settled into the inner folds of our seamless sleeping pallets, pretending it was a Dakota night, and not Julius Caesar's morning.

Then he began to spin tales.

He started with the Finns homesteading the Dakota territory two hundred and fifty years ago. He moved to Abe Lincoln's Finns, speaking not a word of English in their New York Irish regiment, fighting for the Union and freedom. He was soon with the old country Finns rebelling against England; the United Irishmen of the eighteenth century, the O'Donnell and the O'Neill of the sixteenth century. Finally, we visited Finn MacCuhal and Oisin. . . .

I'm determined to find every book of poetry in every library on the moon. I'm not sure I'll understand it, or enjoy it yet, but I'm going to read it until I do.

The last thing Pop said before he fell asleep was: "And that's only the half of it, boy. Your mother's family knows stories about Vienna, London, Malta. . . ."

"Her family's dead. . . ." I started, but he had dozed off.

So now I'm writing this.

It's late. I'd better try to relax.

More later.

3 March, 2119

Joy of joys! K.C.F. must attend a seven-day seminar with the other staff chiefs of Tau and the Bullialdus Corporation execs. Pop was given credit for the week, to take care of our needs.

He has credit of his own in some places, for friendship's sake, and he won some more at gambling. "Poker, craps, and the numbers are peculiarly American," he told me. I always thought the "numbers" meant the Gemartria; fighting 1's and passive 2's, creative 3's and moody 4's. But for Pop the word means guessing the exact weight of Tau pigots produced during twenty four hours, or how many plasma nets will blow in the asteriod mining fleet, or which shuttles will place 1st, 2nd, and 3rd in the Earth-Moon race, and so on. He actually wins credit marks doing this.

Anyway, we set forth after a breakfast of imported croissant rolls from Paris, cafe au lait, oranges and honey from the Los Angeles agricore. This cost as much as an entire day's supplies for the three of us. But it was ambrosia! "Nothing but the best," Pop said. We took the tube to the Kennedy cordome and I chose a new shirt and jacket, both iridescent jade green.

A doctor said I have weak ankles and calf muscles, being born here, so the No. 7 boots stay where they are.

It's bright now over Shepard; the sunrise was gorgeous as usual. I watched the terminator coming; the beading over the highlands just east of us lasted several hours.

We're going to visit Theo's Marecage Dump tomorrow.

Theo Caballo was my father's firmest yet in some ways most distant friend. He was a Horatio; unperturbable yet caring. He was self-made and prosperous by 2119.

He had organized the earth's largest sanitation service. He had settled between the Hyginus Cleft and Triesnecker Crater as owner and overseer. The entire Sea of Vapors had been dedicated as the ideal garbage dump, relieving the terran and lunar cities of the problems of pollution and waste disposal. Thus Theo ruled an immense territory. "Better to reign in hell. . . ."

His home frequently was the site of the conclaves which James Finn usually attended. Other guests included Bela Kalosky, Colebrook Dobbs—another of James Finn's old friends and Theo's lieutenant, Vlas Fossa—the director of a Shepard pump station, Sibella, and my uncle Aubrey Finn—one of Windig's lieutenants managing Tsiolkovsky Crater Cemetery on the Far Side. Aubrey and Sibella made uneasy co-conspirators, yet out of respect for my father, they never once let the New York war touch the Marecage meetings.

James Finn was usually the speaker. What he accomplished was nothing more than a release of anger and frustration. Still, he told me, it was important that someone, somewhere, was griping.

7 March, 2119

It's early in the morning in the Mare Vaporum. We've spent three Greenwich nights here with Theo and his family. All of Pop's cronies arrived within the last hour except Uncle Aubrey. He's supposed to come after breakfast. He never fails to bring some gift that I like.

We've been here at the dump so long that I'm beginning to wonder what's going on.

"Breakfast is served," one of Theo's creepy little kids just stalked in and announced. She didn't even knock. Her name is Moina. She says she has "powers." I shall return.

Finished dinner. We're staying the night again.

Moina is my age but not as intelligent as I am. She really can pick words out of your brain, and if your mind is wandering, she can put some ideas in, too. But it's nothing remarkable. She said, "My father would smash my face if he knew I was practicing on you." I gather Theo believes in corporal punishment. Pop does also, sometimes.

She laughs at me, says I imitate Pop when I walk, talk, or do anything. Says I follow him like a pet dog. I have denied this to her face; what does she know? I noticed *she* was following Pop this afternoon, when we all climbed into her father's shuttle and flew to Socrates. I'm not supposed to say anything about that trip. Or what we did there. That's stupid; the entire system will hear about it tomorrow. Besides, I was the "bone of contention," as Uncle Aubrey said. (Uncle A.'s gift, by the way, was his own collection of Sioux Indian arrowheads and tools. The Teton Sioux are my ancestors, also. It was an unexpected present, being so personal. It made Pop cry. Aubrey is his younger brother and Pop loves him more than Aubrey appreciates, I think.)

Moina just asked me what I was writing. I told her to get out and leave me alone. She asked me to get in bed with her. I think she's crazy. I told her to get the hell out or I'd tell her father. I'm now alone—and I feel like a fool. She probably thinks I'm strange.

I wonder what Theo would do if he caught us?

Probably throw us to one of his giant trashmashers like an ancient priest sacrificing to Moloch.

The confrontation in Socrates, on the 7th of March, was indeed well publicized. My father's admonition was an attempt to protect my innocence.

That was twenty years ago.

What happened was this:

James Finn had known that Arne Arabos, my mother, and several others in positions of power would be holding a press conference in Socrates on the last day of their seminar. He convinced Theo and Colebrook to accompany him to the city. In retrospect, it appears the two companions complied for the purpose of keeping James Finn from rocking an already precariously balanced boat. Aubrey, Sibella, Vlas, and Bela could not or would not attend. Moina Caballo and I could not be dissuaded from tagging along.

James Finn knew that one of the functions of the seminar, which had been composed of people representing all lunar walks of life, was to establish preliminary spiritual guidelines for lunar living. Perhaps he had altruistic motives for appearing in the audience, after drinking heavily with some journalist friends in the Hotel de Montmor bar.

We seated ourselves on portable chairs in the hotel's courtyard. Facing us, beyond the bulla's far hemisphere, the agricore shaft rose to an invisible cordome cap. This pillar of nutrient fogs and crop tiers was an incandescent yellow-green, and it fascinated me at the time, glowing as it did against the dark spangled sky over the Sea of Clouds.

I noted my mother, sitting at one end of the dais immediately before us, her legs serenely crossed, her eyes on the notes she held in her lap.

Golden-pated Arne Arabos sat dead center. He was speaking about the lunar, martian, and venusian views of the ecliptic. He was projecting further, to permanent man-made colonies and artificial satellites, to settlements on Callisto, Ganymede and Titan. How would one chart the signs that marked fate? What was time, on these new worlds? "The moon," he said, "is Earth's oldest child; scientifically her sister, spiritually her child. The sun is lord, a respected master, but the moon is Terra's next of kin. The two are interdependent, thus the differences in time-sense will not be serious enough to hinder a zodiacal adaptation.

"On Mars, however, or Ganymede—or beyond the solar system, to the reaches of our galaxy— what methodology will we employ? We know our Mythos works; we are Believers. It is not sufficient to chart a lunacentric zodiac. It would be solving only one of many minor problems. For example, there are arguments at this moment as to whether or not Earth's traditional sun signs should be transposed to match the astronomical procession. But whether one chooses Aries or Pisces for the vernal equinox, or those constellations which the sun seems to pass through when seen from the moon, whether there are thirty-six signs or twenty-two, the adjustment will be superficial.

"We must find a matrix for all the spiritual arts. We must find a vector that will carry Mythos wherever humans go in the universe. We cannot wait for a Maitreya to appear. We must begin the work now. . . ."

There was enthusiastic applause.

A reporter from Earth, from Rome, stood then and was recognized. "Signore Arabos, you will pardon my English . . ." His English was excellent. He was a gray-templed, seasoned broadcaster. ". . . but aren't you forgetting that the Synod established just such an agency several years ago? The purpose of which was and is to examine Mythos, to find scientific proof for what humans believe in their souls."

Arne's eyes were glittering rubies in the artificial light beams. He smiled pleasantly as the keen-faced Roman sank fluidly to his seat. "Signore, the so-called Agency for Ontological Research has been prodding here and there for the last fifty years. What I'm proposing is a new Synod, to be supported by the Bullialdus Corporation. I'm confident that such a mating of minds and money can produce results within five years."

Another reporter leaped to his feet. He identified himself as being from Kyoto-Osaka. "Mr. Arabos, if *the* Synod has been conducting such research for so many years without concrete results, how can you presume to better the Society's chosen?"

It was a question after Arne's heart. He reclined with seeming ease and waited for the dark, penetrating eyes of his questioner to lower into the field of heads. "Well sir," he began musingly, "I wouldn't presume anything. I do know that we have, right here on the moon, the first generation of human beings that was not framed by the old, traditional terrestrial spiritual patterns. . . ."

It was at this moment that I saw my father's muscles stiffen and his breathing quicken. He gripped the seat sides until his knuckles became yellow-white.

"Supervisor Cazar, to my left"—he nodded at my mother—"is the mother of a lunar enfant. She and many others like her have agreed to cooperate with the New Synod in our search—"

"Arabos!" James Finn roared, and shot up to tower above my startled stare. His fists were half raised at his sides.

There were rustling whispers, some indignant challenges. My mother looked nauseated; her eyes were violet saucers.

James Finn ignored them all. He fastened his glare on a composed Arne. "Excuse me," he growled, "*Mr.* Arabos." Reporters were scribbling, activating recorders, racing into the hotel lobby to place calls to their respective earthside poleis.

Arne stretched his mouth into a smile and squinted. His nostrils flared. "Yes sir?"

"What authority do you have to make such a statement?" my father asked with a resonance that echoed through the courtyard.

"Authority? A duty, sir; to pool knowledge requires no authority. I am donating my personal estate to the cause."

"Using my son, and his fellows, as guinea pigs?"

"Mr. Finn, your son is already under the constant observation of clinicians and psychologists."

"And if you have your way, he'll be hounded by a pack of charlatans as well." He heard and glanced around at the rising reaction. "You heard me! Charlatans! I am not a Believer. Does that surprise you?" he almost shouted.

Colebrook and Theo were urging him to leave. I was simply gawking at him. Moina was as paralyzed as I, but had focused on the dais.

"Listen, Arabos." James Finn shook Theo off and limped past knees, into the center aisle. He lifted a fist. "I don't want to believe in anything. Is that clear?" His hand opened; he seemed to push his splayed fingers at the air. His arm lowered. I realized he'd met my mother's eyes. "Why can't each of us have his own mind?" he murmured.

Colebrook came beside him, heedless of his

conspicuousness. He whispered something into my father's reddened ear.

My father shoved him slightly, stepped one pace, drunkenly tottered. "I am free, Arabos. Free of humanity's sordid games. There must be an ultimate truth. A science, a nature exists. Separate the threads for me, pull aside the curtain. Yours is not *the* way if it's not my way, which makes it *no* way." He pressed the heels of his palms to his temples, and winced. "Oh god," he groaned, "leave my son be. . . ."

An embarrassing quiet fell like a pall.

An electric sting ran up and down my spine. I was cold and sick, twisted in the chair, watching my father.

Someone coughed, I think. I don't remember exactly what burst that awesome inflated silence. But the next thing I knew, Theo had yanked Moina and me by the scruffs of our jackets and was hauling us away from the jabbering, confused crowd. Colebrook had pinioned my father. He quickly brought him under control, and forced him from the courtyard.

Somehow we managed to escape without further trouble.

When my father sobered a bit, in the shuttle, he lapsed into a sullen, near-cataleptic state. I was shivering painfully, the teeth knocking in my head so violently that I thought my eyes would come loose. I wasn't aware my father was rallying until he came out of his seat and squatted next to mine.

I fumbled to undo my safety belt but he gently pushed my fingers away. Moina and Colebrook were watching warily. I thought them entirely too suspicious and severe.

"Son," he said quietly, "don't mention this to anyone. You've got to play dumb, for now. It's very important."

"But we have to talk about it," I whined, totally bewildered. "I want to know why . . ."

"Later, sometime." He smiled, and lifted one of my hands to is mouth. He held it to his lips several seconds, his eyes closed. Then he rose easily and returned to his seat without even a glance in my direction.

19 March, 2119

It was early in the Greenwich morning when Pop and I left for the pumps. Mater was gone, but the apartment was filled with "ears," he said. Such as, among other things, the two domestic robots Pop named Crazy Jane and Wild Jack—anthropomorphic, asexual, fly-eyed automatons that pick up after us, feed us, use monotonic recorded voices to remind us of time, date, appointment, and deportment. They seem to be everywhere at once, and yet they don't make me feel itchy like they do Pop. Mother bought them and installed them; tuned them to our power meter; and they're more expensive than a hundred scarlet capes and topaz rings. But she has her priorities.

"After all," Pop said, "Arne Arabos has three of them for his family."

Vlas Fossa (sun in Aquarius, moon in Scorpio, Scorpio rising) is tall, slim, handsome, and "very resourceful." He adores Pop, who treats this worship lightly, though I think it pleases him mightily. Vlas and I get along also, which could be because I'm James Finn's son, or could be because he really likes me. You can't tell with Vlas.

Anyway, we went (against Mater's orders) to the pumps via one of the cordome gates. A gate looks like a large, orange bird-beak that splits lengthwise when you show your I.D. There's a second, flat entrance that breaks open when the first seals the vestibule. I swear, from the inside the outer door looks like a closed beak; you feel as if you've been swallowed by a roc or a phoenix.

The small dome of the pump station, wedged between the ilots as well as joining the core, backed by hundreds of rows of solar panels that shine like stripes on the lunar surface, is a different world to me. The hydrogen tanks, oxygen and hydrogen recuperators, water purifiers and such, chug, steam, and clang so softly that I want to turn the volume up. I rub my ears trying to hear clearly what is almost subaudible. "It takes some getting used to," Pop told me in Amerang.

This dark morning, crisscrossing bright floodlight beams shone on the giant coils, vast metal plates, and huge pipes, turning them into countless colors, glimmers, and shadows. I felt tiny and helpless as we clinked along the catwalks above and then under the immense arched feeder ducts. We descended beside a generator and the water detoxification tank. (The waste water of our ilot travels first to detoxification, then to the agricore, then it returns nearby, to sewage treatment and recirculation.) I can't believe mother works in one of these places day after day. She has a supervisor's cube, yes, but damn. . . .

Vlas greeted us in his transparent office at the base of metal canyons. Once we were inside, the noise in my head stopped. It was strange for a moment; I felt dizzy.

Vlas had guests. Two engineers from Earth's Muskovy and Smolensk domes. They were introduced, but I only remember the one called Medved, who told me with a wink he was sun in Aquarius, moon in Aquarius, with *a* fish rising. "Only one fish?" I jumped at the bait.

"The other is diving, no?" he answered in thickly accented Anglish. He was a balding blond with diamond eyes that made me feel x-rayed as he sized me up.

Pop shook Medved's hands warmly. Apparently here was a first; someone interesting that James Finn had never met. We all took to each other immediately, and were soon joined by a couple of Vlas's managers.

The seven of us swilled vodka quite freely, joked and sang. Medved even attempted to dance. Time passed. It was Greenwich noon when Vlas's men returned to work.

Their departure somewhat sobered those remaining, and we settled around the office conference table to discuss the present course of events.

"In Muskovy," Medved said, "things are hardening up again. I don't want to live if that happens. I don't, I don't. . . ."

"But you will, you will. . . ." His red-headed skinny friend mocked his tone. "We will survive. We always do."

"Over and over and over," Pop reflected. He propped his chin on a fist, fingered his empty vodka glass with his other hand. He sighed and smirked. "At least there won't be another world war."

"So sure? Comrade, we are ripe for a David or Alexander. What little argument will be the excuse?

How many city-nations will be involved? What will the new alignments be?"

Vlas grimaced as he rocked in his chair. "Who cares?"

"Oh ho, dear friend. You had better care. We're not some snivelling primate fouling its own nest, now. We are colonists of Sol's system, of the galaxy, of the universe." He waved his arms. "We're going to have a vector, all right." He was referring to Arne's speech, the finish of which I'd read in the Shepard Bulletin. "You and me!" He thumb-jabbed his chest. "We carry ourselves and call it god or dharma. Oh well, the results are the same." He staggered up to find another vodka flask.

Pop grunted. "Maybe it is hopeless. Maybe we just can't be or do anything else. Maybe it is genetic."

"What? Genes?" Medved sat. "We're tampered accidentally or not, already—and so? It only increased the variety."

We were silent. I was hungry, and had to use the toilet, but was afraid if I moved they'd think I was a baby.

Medved abruptly turned to me as if he'd read my mind. His eyes were dazzling. I can't describe how wonderful they were. His irises seemed like rainbows. "*Malchik*," he said gruffly, "I know much about you."

I squirmed slightly, lowered my eyes.

"It is most sad, most sad," he continued. "There are signs written all over you. Just like your father. A dungeon-person, my little voices say, he is a dungeon-person. In my city, we can smell them. We walk around them on the streets. Dungeon-person, think the same as we do. Dungeon-person, conform to *some* fashion. But dungeon-person cannot, no more than he can stop breathing." He gulped vodka down his throat. "There are many kinds of dungeons."

I lifted my eyes to Pop, across from me. He was peering at Medved through copper cracks. "No one's going to stop my boy, no one," he whispered liquidly.

Medved shrugged. "I'm one of them, myself. Nothing stops us, unless it's the hemlock or firing squad, to be archaic. Death is sometimes the easiest fate to bear, as Socrates knew. Jamie, my friend, you can't 'buck the system,' as you Americans say."

It was archaic all right. A "Russian" exchanging a glare with an "American" across an oval table. Such national designations had not been used since the Synod.

"Maybe *you* will give in," Pop shouted, "but not me. Not my son. I've cast my net."

"And you will lose. And your friends will be like the famous three monkeys: Hear not, See not, Speak not."

"Are *you* going to give in?" I demanded of Medved. My voice sounded so childishly high.

He laughed. The full, throaty sound eased us. He wiped his preternatural eyes with the knuckle of a finger. "Ho," he gasped, "what a boy is this?" He slapped me on the back. (I hadn't meant to be funny.) "No, I am not, I AM NOT!" He slammed a hand on the table for emphasis.

We broke apart soon after. I raced for Vlas's privy.

9 April, 2119

No explanation from Pop about what's going on. Mother announced that if I skip school one more time I'll be sent to live there. I started crying in front of her.

Pop wouldn't help me. I don't understand. They completely ignore one another, now. He drinks and storms. He won't take me anywhere.

Nothing much to say—I study, answer her questions, go to sleep, go to school.

11 April, 2119

Some officials from Shepard's cordome came today. They went into the den with Pop and the door slid shut. I had to leave for school before they left.

When I came home, Pop was gone.

I'm thinking of running away to Theo's. But if mother is so tight with Arne Arabos, I'll definitely be sent to board at school if I do.

30 April, 2119

It was a free day, and I fled. I took the tube to Scotus and went to visit Sibella, hoping Pop was there. He wasn't.

Sibella entertained me in her private, third floor salon. She was draped in a peach glossy gown that I could see through. But there were crystal bead arabesques over her most interesting parts, and she wore a six-strand pearl necklace that hid what the dress didn't. Her pearl earrings vibrated and flashed when she spoke. A silver delta in her hair gleamed when she moved.

"I know you don't understand," she said soothingly to my tearful complaint. She patted my arm.

We were side by side on a silky ottoman; where I'd first planted myself from weariness and uncertainty when she'd invited me in. Her arm was around my shoulders, and her breasts were soft against my neck and back. Her smell was spicy. "But why can't he talk to me?" I insisted.

"He loves you too much, Nathan," she breathed. "He's a marked man."

"Why? What did he do? He would never surrender, never! Why is he acting like this?"

"He doesn't come to see me, either. I miss him too." Her tone had risen, it was more tender. She lightly kissed my head, squeezed me, sighed deeply. "Oh, I know you want an exciting fight. You want a hero. You would be proud to stand by James Finn's side in a duel with Arne Arabos. But Nathan, it isn't like that. We're a culture ruled by the slightest gestures, the merest slide of an eye. Power plays are in process incessantly. Your father is, I'm afraid, only a historical statistic. A sentence in a prologue that introduces another man's biography."

"I don't understand," I said again. What I meant was, I didn't accept what she was saying.

"We are not the center of the universe, Nathan. It's a hard truth to grasp, I realize."

"He is special. . . ."

"To you, yes."

"No! We're all rough diamonds, we're all beautiful. . . ."

She chuckled in her chest and shook her shining curls. "If you want, if you want. Only promise me this, lovely boy, respect your father now as you've never done before. He's doing it for you."

Doing what? I wanted to ask, but did not. I rested in her arms for some time; rather, the owner of the busiest brothel in Scotus sat holding me.

Sibella finally straightened. "Are you okay now?"

She removed her arm and smoothed my mussed
hair. She stroked my cheek.

I nodded, made speechless once more.

She gave me money, then, and told me to catch
a passenger shuttle back to Shepard.

She said it would be best if I didn't come to see
her again.

4 May, 2119

Mother forced me to accompany her to the Tau
mine today. What an awful experience. My one
free day in so many, and I had to spend it watching her work.

No more of that.

Pop was home when we returned. I ran to him
like I used to when I was a child. We hugged each
other; he whispered, "You did the right thing today.
Don't be angry with yourself. It's all right." He
squeezed the rear of my neck and I began crying.

I'm not ashamed.

And I'm determined. I'll seem to bend toward
her, I'll do what she wants, and wait for every
moment I can see Pop.

15 June, 2119

She commented, on her way to work, "Your
father is being overly dramatic, as usual. Or perhaps it's something more serious . . . if he thinks
the Corporation is some kind of enemy. . . ." She
paused in thought.

I had only mentioned I was afraid for him. At
that point, I really was.

I'd waited for this day, I'd worked so hard for it.
And just at the moment she was about to leave, I'd
said something so totally stupid!

She frowned and carefully studied me. I gave her my most innocent expression. Then she masked herself with an ice-carved smile and exited.

If it hadn't been for the presence of Jane and Jack, I'd have whooped for joy.

Pop was to appear before the Employment Board, I knew. The Board was in the bulla two short of my school. I intended to stop off on my way and meet him.

It was a successful maneuver. The outcome, however. . . .

I plodded the pavewalk past the Social Justice Administration, circled back nonchalantly as if I'd forgotten something, and entered through the crowds pushing and shoving. It hit me at that moment, the utter sameness of people, of this environment. Bulla after bulla of cloudy metal, the lunar scenery hidden by stunted park foliage, the night or day heavens obscured by the ilot domes. Sometimes there was a glimpse of Earth, dimmed by the same reinforced glass that gave us a lunar life.

Slate colored tunics, breeches, jackets and G boots swirled on either side of me as I passed through the lobby and waited by the elevators.

When Pop stepped into sight he was wearing a bright blue and gold shirt and cape. He was, as the backcountry Americans say, "neat." I stepped forward across his path. He nodded as if expecting me. I smiled calmly and let him clap a hand on my shoulder. He guided me to the courtyard.

We were almost alone. The courtyard was nicely landscaped and provided with benches, fountains and sculpture. A woman was weeping by herself in a far semicircle. A sleeping man lay full length on a nearby bench; his bony, wrinkled face made him look like a asteroid miner. Social services didn't always help everyone.

We seated ourselves in an enclave that was relatively private. Pop gripped my upper arm. I gathered the satiny material of his shirt into a clutch. "So how are things?" he asked.

"Okay. How are things with you?"

He arched a brow and twisted his mouth. "Could be better. You doing all right in school?"

"Yeah."

"It's hard to believe we live in the same home, isn't it?"

"We keep different hours," I suggested.

"You keep hours. I don't."

"Did they find you a job?"

"No." He exhaled loudly.

"Will you ever get a job?"

"I'm qualified for one line of work. Whether it's loading radiation-soaked ore onto trollies, or tinkering with laser drills, or setting off nuclear charges. My life is the mines. And Arne Arabos owns the free mines. The nationalized sites are taboo, too. Seems I'm not worth the risk."

"Couldn't you do something else until a position—"

"In the first place," he interrupted pleasantly, "there will never be another mining position. And in the second . . . I have my pride."

We slumped in strained silence for several minutes.

Finally I ventured, "Why are you so passive? Why don't you fight?"

Pop straightened. A strange expression passed

over his face—his eyes were twin sparks. "Fight who?"

I stuttered, "I . . . I'm not sure."

"What ground do you think Arabos is standing on?" he asked patiently.

I thought hard and watched the glittering gray cement at my feet. "He isn't concerned so much about Mythos," I said slowly, "as he is about himself."

"Exactly! Excellent! You've some sense in that head." He patted my arm; I broke into a huge grin. "Now, do you understand what you just told me?"

My grin dropped. I knew this was an important test. I concentrated again. "It means you can ignore him and fight Mythos?"

He laughed softly; I was crushed. I felt I'd betrayed him. But he kissed my hair and laughed once more. "You sense a difference, my boy, and that's remarkable in a man of any age. The human heart, Nathan, rules the mind. No mind has ever completely ruled a heart."

"So do something!"

"I'm not against the Synod, that would be futile. I am for myself. For the freedom of my son and his sons. What I do is only for your future. Although I know there are no guarantees."

"You've surrendered," I accused bitterly, pouting as I confronted his glistening eyes.

"The human race is the human race. I can't fight that."

I was losing my temper. "What about the Dakotas? What about the Two Hughs?"

"Society has evolved since those times, Nathan. Now millions can disappear like a whisper into oblivion while the rest convince themselves that nothing happened."

"No!" I shouted.

"Ranting and screaming, the blazing conscience, just doesn't work anymore."

"Then I'll be clever. I'll be as clever as they are."

"Why?"

"Because someone has to be."

"I told you, never be like me. Never." His voice was even, his face was glowing. His appearance didn't match what he was saying. "Love affairs can create ruling dynasties, personal friendships can create states, a thousand small hates can build a career or launch a war. Pity your mother; she is the one who will fall from grace, not I. When Arabos no longer needs her. . . ."

"Challenge him," I demanded desperately.

"And lower myself to his level?"

I was deflated, exhausted. I battled the stinging in my eyes. I remembered the line in a poem by Yeats:

The best lack all conviction, while the worst
Are full of passionate intensity.

Pop stood and drew me up. "Go on, now," he whispered. "There's no more to say." And he gave me a gentle push toward the courtyard exit.

We saw each other again at dinner. We were polite and exchanged trivialities. My mother looked royal; she had her way.

1 July, 2119

Today the New Synod was convened. I was ordered to Lovell Hospital for tests. I'm not resisting, not yet.

Pop is drinking heavily, and sleeps most of the time.

Mother is Arne's lover, I'm sure of it.

Prague cordome announced today that the proposed Republic's constitution has been ratified by Budapest, Warsaw, Belgrade, and Sofiya.

The Pentarchy of Chicago, St. Louis, Cleveland, Cincinnati and Toledo has brought most of the smaller cities, from the Rocky Mountains to the Appalachians, under its control. Including Rosebud.

4 July, 2119

Arne Arabos is entertaining the *starosta* (mayor) of Prague in Socrates for a week. Mother is with him.

"American" cities on all planets are celebrating their traditional holiday.

I went to his room to tell Pop what date it was, but he wouldn't speak to me.

He lies on his bed and keeps the place dark. Jane (Jack?) cleans around him as if he were another piece of furniture.

Today's Shepard Bulletin reports an increase in military stockpiling in Shepard, Socrates, Kennedy, and Scotus. Armaments are also being stored near the Caesar mine, so the editorial claims. But it admits that mining equipment can often be taken for weaponry.

5 July, 2119

Pop was on his feet this morning. He was alert and electric. He wore his most beautiful suit—wine-red silk with a matching cape—and we joked much as we used to.

"Your mother's at work," he announced.

"No," I started, "she's in . . ."

He interrupted me and started chatting amiably

about the robots, how they looked like jerky puppets, how they responded ridiculously to intelligent questions.

"But Pop," I tugged at his cape, "she's with . . ."

He began complaining that there was no decent food in the place. He invited me out to breakfast with him. He asked me if I remembered those croissant rolls from Paris.

"I can't," I mumbled. "I have to go to Lovell for . . ." I couldn't finish. I hung my head.

He was so quiet that I glanced up.

He was peering at something above me. I noticed his hair was grayer, his eyes were bloodshot and cupped by dark crescents.

"I'm off to see old friends," he suddenly, cheerfully said. "I'll give your regards to Vlas, Theo, and Colebrook."

And he was gone.

I know he doesn't visit Scotus anymore. We haven't heard a word from Uncle Aubrey, either. Perhaps it's Pop's idea. But why then is he visiting anyone he loves?

9 July, 2119

It's just night over the Mare Humorum.

I'm home. Mother is home.

Pop was high on something when we arrived. He lay on his bed, flat on his back, staring at the ceiling with glassy eyes and a delicate smile.

He was relatively lucid an hour ago.

He said, "Vlas couldn't see me," and returned his attention to the ceiling.

I was sitting on the mattress. I shook him by the shoulder. "How's Theo and Moina?"

"I didn't go. What if he'd said the same thing? He has a family. I couldn't have borne it."

"My muscles are developing normally," I said to him. "She thinks maybe I can have a pair of No. 5's when I'm twelve." I waited. Then, "Do you want me to go for you? I could take a message. . . ."

"They've planted a signal on you; they'd follow you."

"What? What do you mean?" I started that damned shivering again.

"God," Pop groaned, and massaged his forehead with both hands as if he'd rub off the skin. "I've an overactive imagination," he said hoarsely. "Don't let me scare you. This stuff gives you all kinds of paranoid fantasies when you're diving. Come here, lie down." He extended an arm.

I was content to rest there. I could have stayed forever. But mother came in and angrily ordered me to my room. She was coldly lecturing him when my closing door blocked the sound.

31 July, 2119

Arne Arabos is on Earth, touring the major poleis: London, Paris, Rome, Muskovy, Prague and the five cities of the Pentarchy. He actually left my mother in charge of Bullialdus. (He says she has a fine mind, and the strength, courage and executive ability of a queen.)

I was ordered to go live with her in Socrates. I didn't take the announcement very well. I'm calmer now.

Before I leave, tomorrow morning, I'm going to the Mare Vaporum with the marks I'm supposed to use for the trip to Socrates. I have to see the

Caballos. Arne tried to strong-arm Theo, but Theo resisted him and Arne backed down.

Uncle Aubrey was threatened also, but was protected by Windig. Apparently the garbage collectors and the mortologists are two groups no one of any poleis wants to offend.

So Theo is safe, for now, king of his small empire. Others, however, according to the rumors, have been less fortunate. I heard someone say at school that we seem to have a good, old-fashioned purge under way.

I want Theo to give refuge to Pop. I know he will. Pop won't ask. So I have to.

                                    31 July, 2119
                                    Late

It's close to Greenwich midnight. I never made it to the Sea of Vapors. Pop thought I was leaving already for Socrates without seeing him, and he came out of the bedroom to say his farewells. I was forced to tell him where I was really headed.

He hushed me quickly, dropped to his knees in front of me and embraced me tightly. I held him, and was almost panicking. The shuttle to Caesar ran twice a Greenwich day and I was going to miss it.

He was weeping. I didn't understand—again. All the same questions rose in my throat. Why didn't he try, at least try, to save himself? This all seemed so melodramatic, this humility—so foreign to his nature.

"I'm insane," he finally said, rocking back and standing. He sniffed and wiped his face with a sleeve of his gray jacket. "That's what they tell me."

I was angry. "They're insane," I yelled. "Scanning me and asking me stupid questions, telling me I'm a Cygnus. Why don't you help me?" I pleaded; my voice cracked. (Anytime he cries, I always start; it never fails.)

"Nathan, it's over." He stroked my head. "She's having me committed to the MHI in London."

My mouth was open but I only made some dumb choking noise.

"But what the hell do we have to lose, eh?" He tousled my hair. "Stay here with me until some-one comes for you, okay?"

He looked worn and weary-eyed. I just nodded.

We pulled the plugs on Jane and Jack (Pop's good with mechanical devices) and he fiddled with a few other "innocent" household items. I can't believe it, about the institute in London. Pop can't live without freedom. "A toothless lion in a cage," he joked.

It's like floating in a dream, wondering when your feet are going to touch the bedrock and the mist is going to lift.

We read, watched the televisor, talked about Mythos, about politics, about my teachers. Nothing serious. We both were tense.

I'm afraid if I go to sleep, Pop will be gone when I wake up.

1 August, 2119

All's quiet.

We had a simple breakfast in the living room.

We talked about sports: moon soccer, free-fall wrestling, footraces with G boot handicapping. Or on Earth, Pop's favorites: horse racing and Pent-archy ballgames.

Only he won't say "pentarchy," but St. Louis or Cincinnati instead.

I felt sick all day. My brain's shutting down on me. I'm beginning to be angry with him. I mean it. Why is he putting us both through this?

We couldn't get close or touch at all. By the end of the day, we weren't talking to each other.

I know I'm wrong. I know I'm being unfair. I can't help it.

2 August, 2119

A smelter supervisor named Justus, one of the Tau staffers, arrived this morning to fetch me. Pop stood at the entrance and told him I'd already left, but the man had brought robot thugs and these pushed past. They poured into the living room. I was frightened and ran to my room.

They unsealed my door and dragged me back out into the living room.

Pop was like stone. He sat on the couch and stared blankly as if he were truly crazy.

"Are you packed?" Justus demanded.

"No!" I shouted, struggling in the robot's freezing, hard grip.

Another shiny robot came into view with the travel case I'd filled two Greenwich nights before.

I couldn't even linger on one last eye-message. Pop was someplace else. His body was present, but he had willed his mind away.

I'm in my new room, in Socrates. It's cramped and ugly, here. I don't want to remember any more.

I have to close this journal before I'm caught.

On the morning of August 6, my mother informed me that my father had been apprehended, taken aboard a Black Maria, and shuttled to London, Earth.

My immediate reaction was soaring hatred. He had allowed such an incredible denouement; he had condemned himself and me to suffer. But soon I was in the last throes of this hatred. It was blending into lonely misery.

Twenty years have passed.

Arne Arabos became president for life of his own brainchild, the Federated Cities of Luna.

Karen Cazar Finn, who I'm sure fully expected to become Arne Arabos's wife after my father's "suicide" in 2119, was dismissed from her position in 2120. She disappeared the same year. I was told she'd taken an extended leave of absence for rest and relaxation. I still don't know what happened to her.

Sibella bought three more brothels.

Uncle Aubrey became Windig's right hand on Earth and was given control of Funerama Inc., plus the New York slums.

Theo died in 2125. His sons assumed control of Marecage. They do what they're supposed to, and make no trouble.

Vlas was dismissed in 2119. He was committed to the MHI in 2120.

Colebrook took off for Ganymede Station when Vlas was seized.

Moina became Sibella's protegée, mixing the business of psychic forecasting with that of managing Dunstable. It was convenient to make her my mistress.

I became quiet, dependable—the quintessential Mephibosheth partaking of Arne Arabos's bounty. He told me to think of him as a father, in 2119, when he shipped me to Paris to be schooled and boarded at the Sorbonne.

When I returned in 2128, I was appointed construction manager of the Tau mine, James Finn's old job, though I was hardly qualified for it. In the eleven years since, I've met many influential people, and have contacts in most of humanity's important places. It has been a quiet time.

Last month I found the journal that I've been excerpting here. I had buried it under the lunar surface outside the Socrates ilot where I briefly lived. Reading it revived me like a shot; there was pain at first, then another emotion replaced the pain.

I've used these pages. I want to justify myself. Once more I will try to replace *to be* with *to do*.

Arne Arabos is waxing old, and he is beginning to confide in no one but me. I've learned how to please him, and he keeps me close. He even recently moved to Shepard so I could stay with him.

Unlike Hamlet and Orestes, I have no doubts.

EDITOR'S INTRODUCTION TO:

BRAIN SALAD

by
Norman Spinrad

Years ago Norman Spinrad lived just up the hill from me. I was at the time the President of the Science Fiction Writers of America. Norman was my Vice President and Chairman of the Grievance Committee. We worked well together. Moreover, Norman, like me, will be neither civil nor coherent before ten in the morning. This made it easy to have breakfast meetings at about eleven-thirty.

He later moved to New York; fortunately he has returned to Southern California and we can get together again. One of his first acts was to come here and look over the computers in Chaos Manor; after some consideration, he bought himself a Kaypro 10, which he loves dearly, and uses to turn out new stories and novels.

My consultation fee was that I'd get first look at the first short story he wrote on his new computer. I wasn't disappointed.

BRAIN SALAD

Norman Spinrad

Money is not a major consideration. Over the past forty years, I've written twenty novels, twelve of them have made the best-seller lists, four have been made into films, most of them are in print in several countries, and, unlike my more traditionally profligate compeers, I have, over the years, invested my income well. I am independently wealthy.

No, I freely admit that this decision is a matter of self-esteem, critical standing, and, to be frank about it, an exquisitely frustrating boredom.

Throughout my literary career, I have enjoyed the act of writing. The stories, the scenes, the paragraphs, the very sentences and words, have flowed freely from my brain, rather that being the agonized product of hard-fought struggle.

No longer. For five years, I have been unable to produce so much as a single short story. For five years, I have stared blankly at the blank white paper in my typewriter, or typed random paragraphs of dead prose which lead nowhere. Even the production of these four paragraphs has been an endless agony. I no longer have the capacity to turn them into a narrative hook that will lead me deeper into a story.

Even though I have now decided that I *do* know what happens next.

At my age, there are few real possibilities for pleasure left. The tastebuds are dull, sex is at best problematical, my brain is surfeited with a lifetime's obsessively accumulated knowledge, my hearing is too dulled for the ecstatic appreciation of music (which never greatly moved me anyway), my health will not permit overindulgence in drink or drugs, and I've written so much fiction that I cannot be pleased by someone else's novels, dramas, or films. The only passionate pleasure left to me is writing itself.

And I have been blocked for five years. The brain cells that made me a major novelist for forty years have simply worn out.

If I am to resume writing, I must purchase new ones.

Fortunately, I have the money to afford them.

Partial brain transplants no longer involve significant surgical risk. I must admit that I have been considering this step for the past year, during which time I have, in my usual methodical manner, researched the subject, under the rationalization that I was planning to write a story about it.

In the early 1980's, animal experiments revealed the curious fact that, unlike other parts of the mammalian body, the brain lacks the antibody production to reject foreign tissue transplants. Soon surgeons were successfully treating Parkinson's disease by transplanting small bits of brain matter that produced the enzyme that the victim lacked. Then they began repairing trauma-damaged brains with larger portions of transplanted cerebral material. Certain forms of deafness and blindness proved amenable to this treatment. Then senile dementia.

Now, I have been assured, the technique has advanced to the point where cerebral enhancement, not only mere gross repair, has become possible. Animal experiments have already produced rats capable of communicating in rude sign language through the transplant of relevant chimpanzee cerebral material, rabbits who will perform tricks on command in the manner of dogs, and, so it is rumored, chimpanzees able to operate simplified military ordnance.

In the area of human cerebral enhancement, the literature is vague and the doctors I've consulted rather circumspect due to the legal uncertainties, but I have good reason to believe that certain CIA operatives have memory-enhanced brains, that a certain baseball star's mid-career development of switch-hitting ability was more than a matter of practice making perfect, indeed that the President's mid-term burst of renewed intellectual vigor was the result of a medical decision made by a dismayed White House staff studying the dismal opinion polls.

I've been assured by the top man in the field—naturally the most expensive as well—that the human brain has now been well enough mapped to allow him to essay a transplant of the brain matter wherein resides literary creativity.

Naturally I must sign a legal waiver, since there

could be unforseen side-effects. And of course, the surgeon's fee will be large.

And he's told me that securing a donor is my problem.

I wouldn't have it any other way. This, after all, is a literary decision, not a medical one. The brain cells of a literary critic or a romance writer or a mere journalist obviously will not do. On the other hand, finding an established novelist of literary stature willing to serve as donor seems highly unlikely.

What is required is a young talent in the raw suffering from severe indigency, desperate and not entirely stable, willing to exchange brain cells for a price with a major literary figure.

Fortunately, my agent also handles such a young fellow. Alas, he is a mere science fiction writer, rather than a serious literary talent, but from a reading of his stories, I do believe that he possesses considerable creative spark, hampered mainly by a penchant for rubbishy subject matter and an indifference to stylistic niceties. But then, I will be retaining my own memories, knowledge, tastes, and motivations, which, I am assured, are contained in entirely separate areas of the brain.

Besides, science fiction is quite a vogue these days, and a writer of my literary stature and emotional maturity might be able to make something beyond low entertainment out of it.

Of course I would have preferred a young Melville or even Philip Roth, but under the circumstances, it looks as if I must I'll have to settle for a science fiction writer. Perhaps my played-out talent-cells will be revived by his young brain so that he will gain some of my literary excellence in the bargain.

At any rate, the possibility does provide a moral justification for the exchange, assuming for the moment that I needed one.

Perhaps I shall return to this narrative after the operation. An appropriate maiden effort for my revived literary career. I am told by my agent that there is a considerable market for stories of this sort. With my track record, a film sale would not be out of the question.

The post-operative recuperation period passed quickly and uneventfully, and, in fact, I noticed nothing all save the huge doctor bill until I was ready to sit down at the typewriter and attempt to continue this story.

My first reaction upon reading what I had written was dismay. No wonder I've been blocked for five years. What constipated arteriosclerotic prose! What boring crap! Look at the way you've dropped nearly four hundred words of straight scientific exposition right there in the middle of it in one undigested lump!

And then I did, as it were, a double-take. For I certainly wouldn't have had that perception before the operation, nor would I have expressed it in such forthright, even crude, terms.

Moreover, I've begun to see that I'd misconceived this story entirely. This first-person present-tense narration is incredibly awkward and stilted. And if I keep writing about myself, I'll simply be endlessly redescribing the lint in my own navel.

The test of whether the operation has been truly successful or not is whether or not I can turn this true story into imaginative fiction, whether I have recaptured the ability to get inside the head (if you will pardon the expression) of a character other than an analog of myself.

Whether I can tell, in third person, the story of the *other* half of the equation, whether I can imagine and render the reality of what now must be happening to that young science fiction writer to whom *I've* given a piece of *my* mind.

BRAIN SALAD
by Nicholas Barrow

Denton had really been desperate when he had agreed to the brain exchange operation. He had been six months behind on his alimony payments, four months behind on his rent, his bookie was starting to get quite unpleasant, and he could no longer scrape together the cash to score the cocaine that kept his creative juices flowing.

Obviously, a quarter of a million tax-paid dollars was more than enough to take care of all that. When it came down to it, as his agent had so elegantly pointed out, it was a matter of sacrificing a small piece of his brain to save his entire ass.

Besides, *he'd* be getting some of the relevant gray matter of a writer of much greater literary stature than himself in return, and one who had, over forty years, demonstrated a first-class ability to turn his cerebral products into cold hard cash, and lots of it. A pessimist might have argued that this operation was like creative death, an optimist might have argued that it was like an injection of proven literary street-smarts from a long-term winner, but a realist like Denton knew that it was an even-money bet.

It was three months after the operation before

Denton brought himself back to the typewriter to see what he had won and what he had lost, or more precisely, sat down at the brand new word processor he had purchased with a small portion of his new-found wealth. The previous ninety days had been spent most pleasurably purchasing and furnishing in lavish style a fine new co-op apartment on the Upper West Side, choosing a new Porsche, having a new wardrobe custom-tailored, stocking a respectable wine-cellar, and otherwise donning his new persona as a writer of wealth, style, and grace.

True this new incarnation was, on the surface, a far cry from the ill-kempt indigent guttersnipe who had inhabited that foul tenement apartment in the prole warrens of the so-called East Village, but he didn't *feel* like a changed personality inside. True, his previous circle of friends and acquaintances— science fiction writers, editors, and attendant unwholesome fans—now stood revealed as tacky, jejune, and somewhat boorish, but hadn't he always known that he was a superior individual trapped by unfortunate circumstances in a milieu far beneath his rightful station?

But he certainly didn't feel that he had turned into a tired, washed-up, pretentious old fart. It wasn't that he was now *blocked*, merely that he had been too busy all these weeks adjusting to his higher station in life to get down to the business of turning out some copy.

Now, however, he was ready to begin his new career as a best-selling writer of genuine literary stature. He sat himself down in front of the screen of his virgin word processor in his Recaro chair with a snifter of Courvoisier VSOP close to hand, turned on the device, and courted the approach of the Muse.

Alas, that fickle lady seemed to have deserted him. For two weeks, he tried all the proven techniques for generating science fiction stories that had served him so well in the past, that had always called up story ideas from the vacuum at an average rate of 7000 words a week. First, sheer empty-minded meditation. Then empty-minded meditation augmented by cognac. Augmented by cocaine. Cognac *and* cocaine. When that produced naught but a series of awesome hangovers, he got out his pile of old *Scientific Americans*, *Science News*, *Time*, and *People*, shuffled them together, opened copies at random, and began typing out disconnected paragraphs. When that failed to produce a story idea, he tried automatic writing— typing the first word that came into his head, then a second, then a third . . . on and on into pages of incomprehensible babble.

Something was definitely wrong. He had *always* come up with something by this stage in the process, and he couldn't bear trying the system of last resort—namely typing out the phone book until sheer mindless boredom *forced* something to emerge in order to end the self-inflicted torture.

In fact, he finally began to realize, there was something asinine and juvenile about this whole approach. True, it had always enabled him to produce at an average rate of 7000 words a week, but produce *what*?

An endless series of empty "What if?" stories.

What if chickens were intelligent? What if a flying saucer landed in a lunatic asylum? What if the

Earth were the egg of a giant bird? What if time started to run backward? What if pigs had wings?

Surely this was not how a serious writer of literary stature went about it! These were the methods of a desperate hack forced to churn out volume in order to stay financially afloat. A serious writer of literary stature concerned himself not with outre "story ideas" but with the timeless verities of the human condition, with subtle turns of prose, with the thematic material inherent in the passage of his own sensitive consciousness through the timestream of his own existence. The serious writer of literary stature contented himself with transmogrifying the quotidian events of his own life into literary art through the application of the creative imagination to the actual mundane material of day to day existence.

For instance, what if portions of human brains could be surgically exchanged between different individuals? What if a played-out old writer received the creative brain cells of a younger, more vigorous, but far less sophisticated literary intelligence?

An outré conceit, yes, but was it not also the material of his own life and therefore legitimized as a fit subject for true literary art? It but required a small creative twist, a judicious shift of perspective, to transmute this autobiographical material into imaginative fiction.

Namely to assume the hypothesized viewpoint of the *recipient* of his own brain cells rather than the autobiographical viewpoint of the donor.

While Denton had been sitting here for weeks unsuccessfully trying to come up with an idea for a science fiction story, what was his counterpart doing with his transplanted piece of a science fiction writer's brain?

Now *that* was definitely an idea for a science fiction story, and one which could aspire to higher literary ambitions as well, if handled judiciously and maturely, with due concern for the ironic reflexivity of the concept, subtlety of prose, and seriousness of intent, rather than with the old 5¢ a word facileness.

Slowly, agonizingly at first, but with ever-growing confidence, Denton began to craft this tale.

Brain Salad
by Gerald Denton

Nicholas Barrow had it made. He had had it made for a long time now. A trendy literary figure and adroit self-promoter for nearly forty years, he was not only a writer of considerable literary stature in the rariefied realms where such things were still measured, he was that rarity, a "serious literary figure" with a knack for hitting the best-seller lists. Twelve of his twenty published novels had made the lists, four of them had been made into major motion pictures, and most of them were still in print in any number of countries. On top of that, Barrow also had a talent for playing the stock market. Famous, well-regarded by serious literary critics, Barrow was also independently wealthy.

Nevertheless, he was miserable.

For although Barrow was both a productive author of best-sellers and a successful literary politician in the highest intellectual realms as well as being a multimillionaire, he had never really been a phony. Unlike others of his ilk, whose greatest joy was usually being a famous author, Nicholas Barrow had always passionately enjoyed the actual act of writing. The stories, the scenes, the paragraphs, the very sentences and words, had always flowed freely from his brain in a kind of marvelous state of ecstasy, rather than being the agonized product of hard-fought painful struggle.

But no longer. For five years now, he had been utterly blocked, unable to produce so much as a simple short story. For five years, he had spent uncounted thousands of hours staring blankly at the blank white paper in the typewriter, waiting in agonized frustration for the return of his lost love.

And at his age, there were few other possibilities for pleasure left. His tastebuds were dulled by age and jaded by a lifetime of fine restaurants, sex was at best problematical, he had always been indifferent to music, and the state of his health would not permit overindulgence in drink or drugs. And of course he had written far too much fiction himself to be truly pleasured by someone else's novels, dramas, or films.

The only possible passionate pleasure left to him was the act of writing itself.

And after being totally blocked for five years, he finally had to face the fact that the brain cells which had made him a major novelist for forty years had simply worn out.

If he was going to resume writing, he had to purchase new ones.

Fortunately, he had the money to afford them.

His personal physician, an excellent internist,

assured him that partial brain transplants no longer involved significant surgical risks.

"Piece of cake, Nick. You see, it's been known since the early 1980's that the brain simply lacks the antibody reaction to reject foreign tissue transplants. Back then, they started out treating Parkinson's disease by transplanting small bits of tissue that produced the enzyme that the victim's brain lacked. By now, we can handle certain brain-trauma cases, some kinds of blindness and deafness, even senile dementia. But what *you're* talking about. . . . I'll give you the name of a specialist. It'll cost you plenty just to talk to him, but he's the top man in the field."

It did. He was.

"Cerebral *enhancement*, Mr. Barrow? Well, animal experiments have produced rats capable of communicating in rude sign language, rabbits who can perform simple tricks on command, and chimps capable of . . . er . . . operating simplified military ordnance. . . ."

Barrow's novelistic instinct told him that the man was dissembling. "I'm talking about *human* cerebral enhancement, doctor," he said. "And I'm prepared to pay quite handsomely."

"Well, Mr. Barrow, off the record, I can tell you that there are rumors in certain circles that certain CIA operatives have memory enchanced brains. . . . Er . . . *how* handsomely did you say. . .?"

"One million dollars."

"Well, in that case, I can tell you that a certain baseball star's mid-career development of switch-hitting ability was, shall we say, more than a matter of practice making perfect. . . ."

"Memory enhancement? Switch-hitting? What

about true intellectual enhancement? Would a million and a half induce you to discuss one of your own case histories?"

The brain surgeon smiled. "If we're talking *two* million," he said, "I can tell you from personal experience that the President's sudden mid-term burst of renewed intellectual vigor was the result of a medical decision made by the White House staff dismayed by the dismal opinion polls.... Under the delicate circumstances, I hope I need say no more...."

"You need not," Darrow told him.

"Of course I'll need my fee in advance. In cash. Preferably in Swiss francs. And of course I cannot involve myself in the problem of securing a ... er ... donor...."

Of course. Barrow wouldn't have had it any other way. This, after all, was a literary judgment, not a medical one. Obviously, the brain cells of a literary critic or a romance writer or some yellow journalist simply would not do. On the other hand, finding an established novelist of literary stature willing to serve as donor seemed rather unlikely....

So Nicholas Barrow consulted his agent, a literary pilotfish with the appetite of a school of barracuda, the tentacles of an octopus, and all the moral scruples of a tiger-shark.

The agent hardly blinked at Barrow's outré plan. By the time Barrow had finished laying it out, he seemed to be already toting up his 10% of a new Nicholas Barrow property.

"Gerald Denton," he said.

"Who is Gerald Denton?"

"Another client of mine, and not a very profitable one. A young talent in the raw—broke, desperate, and probably willing to do anything for enough money. A science fiction writer, so this number might even appeal to his twisted mind."

"*A science fiction writer!*" Barrow exclaimed dubiously. "I'd been hoping for a young Melville or at the very least a Philip Roth. . . ."

"Yeah, Nick, well under the circumstances, you can't afford to be too choosy, can you? Besides, this kid *does* have talent, even if he doesn't know what to do with it. But *you* would, wouldn't you? Way you tell it, you'll keep your own memories, knowledge, and taste, right?"

He went to his most obscure bookcase and got down a pile of luridly-covered science fiction magazines. "Read some of his stuff and at least see what you think," he said, handing them over. "And anyway, you know, sci-fi is hot these days, who knows what a writer of your literary stature and emotional maturity might be able to do with it? Hmmm . . . and you say *he'll* get some of *your* old brain cells . . .? Who knows, in a fresh young brain, they might start working again, and then I'll have *two* profitable clients where before there were none. . . ."

"At least that provides a moral justification. . . ." Barrow mused.

"As if we needed one," his agent said with a little chuckle and cold hard eyes.

Later that night, perusing Denton's somewhat jejune efforts, Barrow decided that the kid did possess considerable creative spark, hampered mainly by a penchant for rubbishy subject matter and an indifference to stylistic niceties. And as his agent had so rightly pointed out, he was hardly in a position to be choosy. . . .

The post operative recuperation period passed quickly and smoothly. Barrow noticed nothing at all until he was ready to sit down at the typewriter and attempt to continue this story.

His first reaction upon reading what I had written was trying all the proven techniques for generating science fiction stories that had always called up such constipated arteriosclerotic prose in the past. No wonder I've been the ill-kempt indigent guttersnipe who inhabited that foul tenement in nearly four hundred words of straight scientific exposition trapped by unfortunate circumstances in the reality of what must now be happening to that young pretentious old fart science fiction writer to whom I've given a piece of my new career as a best-selling writer of genuine literary business turning out some higher literary ambitions average rate of 7000 words a week.

Throughout my literary career, I have enjoyed the act of typing out the phone book until the timeless verities of the human condition produced asinine and juvenile boring crap that was definitely an idea for a science fiction story endlessly redescribing the lint in my own naval.

When that failed to produce the hypothesized viewpoint of a desperate hack forced to churn out imaginative fiction in order to stay blocked, he got out his old pile of empty "What if?" stories, shuffled them together, and began typing out subtle turns of incredibly awkward and stilted portions of human brains inside the head of a fit subject for true literary art:

BRAIN SALAD
by Denton Barrow

*   *   *

Money is not a major consideration. Over the past forty years, I've written twenty disconnected paragraphs, twelve of them have made the best-seller lists, four have been made into films, most of them are pages of incomprehensible babble, and, unlike my previous circle of friends and acquaintences, I have, over the years, invested my income well. I am independently tacky, jejune, and somewhat boorish.

No, I freely admit that this decision is a matter of my bookie starting to get quite unpleasant, and, to be frank about it, an exquisitely frustrating new persona.

Throughout my literary career, I have enjoyed sheer empty-minded meditation. The stories, the scenes, the paragraphs, the very cold hard cash and lots of it have flowed freely from my cognac *and* cocaine, rather than being the agonized product of a respectable wine-cellar.

No longer. For five years, I have been unable to produce so much as a moral justification. For five years, I have stared blankly at rabbits who will perform tricks on command in the manner of a best-selling writer of genuine literary stature, or typed random paragraphs of emotional maturity. Even the production of BRAIN SALAD has been an endless agony. I no longer have the capacity to transmute this autobiographical material into imaginative fiction.

Even though I have now decided that I *do* know what happens next. . . .

GOOD-BYE, DR. RALSTON
Damon Knight

EDITOR'S INTRODUCTION TO:

GOODBYE DR. RALSTON

by
Damon Knight

Damon Knight has been with us since the beginning: his book, *The Futurians* (John Day, 1977), is a hilarious account of the early days of science fiction fandom. He was also the founding President of the Science Fiction Writers of America. (SFWA), an organization which has certainly improved the lot of many writers.

Damon has written all too little in the past few years. He has become a sort of Elder Statesman, teaching others to write, and occasionally editing a new anthology. He hasn't forgotten how, though, as he proves with this story of a rather odd future.

The visitor got out of the hyperport shuttle, looking haggard. He was a large man in his thirties, sandy-haired and blue-eyed, with a strong jaw and a cleft chin.

"There it is," said one of the volunteer escorts to the other. They had met for the first time an hour ago. They stepped forward, smiling brightly. One of them was nearly seven feet tall, spidery thin, with big eyes, sharp features, and a corona of flaming red hair; the other was shorter, white-haired, and more or less egg-shaped.

"Dr. Ralston?"

He peered at them doubtfully. "Yes, hello, uh, ladies?" His accent made him hard to understand.

"Whatever," said the spidery one. "I'm Kim Glashow, and this is Leslie Watt. Welcome to New York! Did you have a tiring trip?"

"Oh, no, the trip was all right," Ralston said vaguely. He could not seem to keep looking in any one direction for very long.

"The zipway is right over here," said Watt, taking his arm. "Let's get you settled into your hotel, and then we can plan."

Ralston looked at the people who were boarding the zipway: they were getting on through a sort of revolving door that came up behind them and then flung them onto the moving strip. "Oh, ah, no thanks," he said. "Could we, ah, just walk?"

"No mess," agreed Glashow. "Right this way."

They got him into the hotel and, after some persuasion, into the uptube. He looked around at the hotel room as if he had never seen one before. "Is that the bed?" he asked.

"Yes, that's the bed, and your crapper's over there. And here's the holo tank—why don't we see if they've got anything about you?"

Glashow went to the control pad and tapped in "RALSTON," then "NEW TERRA." At once the tank came to life with an image of Ralston nervously smiling, and the anchorvoice said, "Dr. Edmond Ralston, the envoy from New Terra, arrives in Manhattan today. The lost colony, cut off for seventy years by subspace turbulence, was rediscovered earlier this week by Navy scouts." A person with bright yellow hair came into view and said, "Dr. Ralston, what is your number one emotion when you think about returning to the world of your forebears?"

"Turn that off," said Ralston hoarsely. "Listen, are you all— Is everybody—"

The two waited for him to finish.

"Are you all *women*?" he said, and looked frightened.

"Oh. Oh, no. Didn't they explain it to you?" Glashow asked. "About the genetic engineering?"

"Genetic engineering, yes."

"Well, you've probably noticed that our faces are flatter than yours. No sinuses. And no hair on the face. Of course, *you* don't have any, either, but you probably depilate it? Is that the word?"

"Shave," said Ralston faintly. "I shave."

"Burmashave!" said Watt. "I remember."

"Right, and then some other things that don't show, like no vermiform appendix, and a stronger spine. Then they got ectogenesis, and after that it was really a question of what people *wanted* to look like. I mean, if breasts look good on a woman and give it pleasure, why shouldn't a man have them too? And, you know, both sets of organs for everybody, that's fair. Am I going too fast?"

"No," said Ralston, and sat down on the edge of the bed.

"All right, the next part is real interesting. After we got ectogenesis and omnisex, and, you know, longevity and all that, the next thing was beauty. I mean, that was all that was left."

"Beauty," said Ralston.

"Right, and the first generation, they all looked like old-timey holo stars, didn't they, Leslie?"

"My parents," said Watt, rolling its eyes. "Farah *Fawcett*. You want me to get some pix on the holo?"

"That would be purfy." Glashow turned to Ralson. "See, what nobody thought about at first, is that beauty is a norm that's a minority. It's an hourglass-shaped curve instead of bell-shaped, with 'beauty' in the middle. So if you make people look all alike, that stops being beauty anymore. Nowadays—well, for instance, I'd say Leslie here is an exceptionally good-looking person. So *unusual*."

Watt smiled delightedly. "You too, Kim—I really think you're great-looking."

In the holo tank, a row of smiling people appeared. They were broad-shouldered and strong, with finely chiseled features; they looked, in fact, a little like Dr. Ralston. Then another row, all shapes—spidery like Glashow, pillowy like Watt, bald, big-eared, steatopygous.

Glashow was saying, "Beauty is like the stock market. If you want your kids to be beautiful, you have to bet against what other people are betting *on*. They're even saying the Farrah look might come back next season. So it's really exciting."

"Yes, exciting," said Ralston.

"Well. Now, the next thing is the press conference, then the reception," said Glashow briskly, "and then the Mayor's ball tonight. Would you want to wear what you have, or should we take you shopping?"

"No," said Ralston with a look of pain. "In fact, if you could find out when that ship leaves, the one I came on—"

"The hyper? I think they said it's going back this afternoon, didn't they, Leslie?"

"Let me check." It turned to the control pad, punched buttons. "Yes, that's right—fourteen-thirty today."

"Could you get me a ticket?" Ralston asked.

"You want to go back home? And miss the reception, and the keys to the city, and everything?"

"Yes, I really think— If you wouldn't mind."

"Well—" Watt punched more buttons. "Done. Your luggage is still on board, so I just told them to hang onto it."

After they had delivered Ralston to the hypership, Kim looked at Leslie and Leslie looked at Kim.

"You know, that room is paid for through the weekend, and so are we."

"I was thinking the same thing."

"By the way, are you male or female?"

"Biologically male, but I've always been better at fem. What are you?"

"Male, but listen—the reason I asked—I have a little trouble getting it up and I usually go fem too."

"Well, what's wrong with that? Don't worry about it, sweets—we'll work something out."

EDITOR'S INTRODUCTION TO:

FUTURE SCENARIOS FOR SPACE DEVELOPMENT

by

G. Harry Stine

Throughout the '70s there was a nearly universal theme on college campuses: *The party's over.* We had, mistakenly, thought that growth and wealth could increase forever; but this was a cruel illusion. Now we had come to an era of limits, a time of not merely national, but racial malaise. It was time to pull back, conserve, stop growth, tear down power plants—

Anyone who said differently was in for trouble. I recall standing on more than one college campus, trying to persuade the students that they had a future—and having the assembled members of the faculty scream refutations. Indeed refutation is the wrong word, for it implies rational debate—but there was no rational debate on the subject. Progress was over, and anyone who said different was not merely wrong, but evil, and must be silenced lest his evil propaganda influence the innocent.

Throughout the depressing era a very few stood firm, proclaiming that mankind and freedom had a limitless future. Jim Baen was one: he suggested to me the title of what became my most popular essay, "Survival with Style." The late Herman Kahn was another; his last book, *The Resourceful Earth* (with economist Julian Simon; Blackwell, 1984), continues to thunder against the doomsayers.

Another stalwart was Harry Stine, gadgeteer and rocketeer, engineer and consultant, science fact and fiction writer, member of the Citizens Council on National Space Policy; who here tells us yet again that the party is only getting started.

FUTURE SCENARIOS FOR SPACE DEVELOPMENT

G. Harry Stine

Introduction

We cannot plan to conquer new worlds with the ideas of the old.

Until recently, an ancient way of thinking has shaped the policies and activities of our planet. This philosophy was developed in the prehistoric era when there wasn't quite enough to go around for everyone. Basically, it was highly successful in a world of perceived scarcity. It was a philosophy for the pre-industrial age:

"You stay in your village and I will stay in mine. If your sheep come to eat our grass, we will kill them. But we may want some of your grass for our sheep, and if we do we'll come and take it. Anyone who tries to make us change our ways is a witch, and we will kill him. Stay out of our village!"

This "Neolithic" philosophy that comes down to us from a wholly different era of mankind's development actually forms the foundation for the recent concept of the "limits to growth" future of our world and civilization. Coupled with an unreasoning fear of general thermonuclear "spasm war," it has made the past two decades among the bleakest of this nation's history. This "limits to growth" philosophy has had a strong affect upon government policies, legislation, and regulations that would have been quite suitable in the days of the Roman Empire and even the British Empire of 200 years ago. It has created trepidation in financial circles, thereby partially causing a major economic recession not only here but throughout the world. Young people, who certainly aren't stupid but who have been told nothing but the limits to growth future, have reacted because this way of thinking has removed incentive to learn and to achieve. With a "downside future" perceived as the only future by young people, is it any wonder that the limits to growth philosophy has produced an underground culture, a drug cult, anti-intellectuals, and a generation of functional illiterates? One of its consequences has been an abnormally high incidence of suicide among our nation's youth. Indeed the 1960's and 1970's may well be considered by future historians to be the Romantic Period of the 20th century.

The most influential photograph of the Apollo manned lunar landing program wasn't that of Buzz Aldrin standing on the lunar surface. It was the one showing the Planet Earth hanging against the empty blackness of space. This was the first photograph with the entire Earth in one frame. It led to the concept of "spaceship Earth," the "fragile island of life in an inhospitable universe."

But people didn't realize that the photograph

also showed the finite Earth as part of a universe without limits, a universe in which mankind had already started to sail the star sea.

The limits to growth philosophy were profoundly disturbing to many people who not only saw the flaws in its basic argument but who also had a broader perspective of time and space. Among those whose voices were heard only in the wilderness for more than a decade were Robert A. Heinlein, Herman Kahn, Dr. J. Peter Vajk, Dr. Krafft Ehricke, many of the people here in this room today, and the people here on the platform. Surprisingly, Buckminster Fuller should also be counted as among these proponents of the abundant future. In retrospect, Fuller's concept of "spaceship Earth" and his belief in mankind's intellectual ability to solve the problems confronting the human race were couched in language palatable to the New Romantics. Perhaps Fuller was trying to reach those disenchanted young people.

However, a major discontinuity seems to have occurred in 1980. People began to reverse their ways of thinking. In addition to a political movement from left to right, there has been a dawning awareness that we do not live in a world of limits but in a world in a limitless universe. We learned we did not have to accept limits to growth.

There is now a growing awareness that the limits to growth philosophy is faulted. Data to support this contention was available all along. In the flood of disenchantment of the past two decades, it was hard to find the data and ever harder to get it presented. But it indicated that the premise of limits was wrong.

A great deal of space planning was laid against

the limits to growth scenario. This planning generally came to naught because it was based upon a faulty premise.

In dealing with space futures, we must forecast and plan them against a background of reality: the abundant future. Otherwise, they will not and cannot come to fruition.

The purpose of this session is to present the philosophy and data to support this vision of a hopeful future of abundance. But knowing that we live in a limitless universe isn't enough. We must also teach others what we know and give them a proper vision of the future in addition to an insight on how to evaluate forecasts.

An Evaluation of Resources

We thought we were running out of everything.

It turns out we're running out of nothing.

Back in 1977, NASA contracted a study on space industrialization with a west coast think tank, Science Applications, Inc. A parallel study was undertaken by Rockwell International. The principle investigator for most of this SAI study was Dr. J. Peter Vajk. Other team members included Dr. Ralph Sklarew, Gerald Driggers, Robert Salkeld, Richard Stuzke, and myself. All of us believed initially that we could use the limits to growth philosophy as a driver for space industrialization. After all, if we were running out of energy and materials, the obvious answer was to go after these things in space. If the imminent destruction of the Earth's biosphere was threatened by industrial pollution, the obvious thing to do was to move industrial operations into space. So we went looking for data to back up this contention.

Our rationale evaporated so fast that it shocked us. When we looked at the data available from a wide variety of national and international sources, we discovered that there was no "excess of demand over supply" of almost everything imaginable except time, which cannot be recycled even if there was a shortage of it. (There is no real shortage of time; it only appears that way as one grows older because they start to run the clocks faster.)

What Was Wrong With The Limits To Growth?

Why is the most recent expression of the Neolithic philosophy and the modern embodiment of the Malthusian hypothesis now considered to be wrong? I don't have to ask this question of people in this room who already know, but it important to tell those who don't know and who are still operating with invalid and outmoded data.

Dennis Meadows and his MIT colleagues made the same mistake that Thomas Robert Malthus made in his 1798 treatise entitled, "An Essay on the Principle of Population." They neglected or ignored the capability of human beings to use their brains to develop technology to solve problems. In addition, they used incorrect data, selected data, and used an incomplete model of the world system.

One of the major problems with the "world dynamics" methodology developed by Jay Forrester and used by Meadows and his colleagues for the Club of Rome study is simply this: It is possible to predetermine the outcome of a given computer analysis by the model that's selected, by the way the program is written, and by the data put in. Garbage in, garbage out.

But that begs the question: why did Malthus and Meadows do it in the first place?

Malthus was not only an economist, but also a curate. As a religious man, perhaps he foresaw that the First Industrial Revolution would change things so drastically. Perhaps he was able to discern that, in an industrial society, the power of the church over the lives of people would be diminished. But Malthus certainly failed to foresee that agricultural technology would progress so dramatically that within two hundred years one farmer wouldn't be feeding one other person, but five other people. Or that the primary export of the tiny United States of America less than two centuries hence would be food to feed the minions of the world who were at that time feeding themselves but, two centuries later, would be unable to do so because of mismanagement of their own agricultural economies. But I believe the real reason lies in the fact that Malthus completely overlooked the long-term trends. He didn't have The Loyal Opposition in the form of Herman Kahn to point out: "A hundred years ago, people everywhere were few, poor, and largely at the mercy of the forces of nature. A hundred years from now, barring an incredible combination of bad luck and poor management, people everywhere will be many, rich, and largely in control of the forces of nature."

I hesitate to bring up the next point, but it must be said, even at the risk of making enemies. It introduces ideology into the subject matter, and this is important. The way a person looks at the future is pretty much determined by his basi[c] [po]litical ideology, whether this be collectivis[m] [or] individualism.

The world of shortages and limits is a world in which people fight one another for limited resources. It is a world in which men on horseback, the Atillas, seize what they can, control it, parcel it out among their supplicants, and dole it out at whatever price they wish to charge. Control of resources is far more effective than control of communications. This is the world of history.

Only in the last two hundred years has it changed and become a world of abundance. And only in the United States of America do we have the basic political framework with which to rationally handle a world of abundance. This is because a world of abundance where there is plenty to go around is a world which denies the political demogogues, the Atillas, the rulers who would control individual lives by controlling what people can get or make with their own efforts. A world of abundance is a world of individual freedom of choice in which the trader is top dog, not the raider.

Developing Future Scenarios

Although ideologies play a large role in future studies, what have most "downside" futurists, "futurologists," and modern doomsday soothsayers been doing wrong that leads them to forecast such pessimistic futures?

First of all, it's easy to forecast gloom, doom, disaster, and catastrophe. It sells pretty well. In a publish or perish environment, an academician with a published book is dollars ahead of his colleagues when it comes to getting the attention necessary to obtain grants.

Secondly, they neglect history.

History is important because it tells us where we've been.

And if we want to learn something about where we're going, it's helpful to know where we've been, how we got to where we are, and where we actually are today. We can then extrapolate our course into the future with some degree of confidence.

There are problems involved with forecasting future possibilities using trend evaluation. Not everyone can do it well. But let's look at what's involved because it forms the basis for the statement we wish to make in this session:

We should not engage in planning future space activities using invalid and outdated future scenarios such as the limits to growth philosophy. It won't work, the planning will be invalid, and the planners will have wasted their time which isn't unlimited. In common with the rest of the United States, Canada, western Europe, and Japan, we are going to have to learn how to be rich and how to utilize our wealth properly to do the things we know can be done in space, which in turn will increase our wealth as well as our ability to control the forces of nature.

The Basics of Trend Forecasting

The most accurate, useful, and reliable forecasting tool in the hands of a good forecaster is trend analysis. It's very simple: If you know where you've

been, if you know where you are, and if you know
how long it took you to get from there to here, you
can figure out where you're going and when you'll
get there. In navigating ships across the ocean and
aircraft through the air, this is called "dead
reckoning." The term is derived from the true nature of this form of navigation, "deduced reckoning," not because of the possibility that if you did
it wrong you'd be dead. (There are always options.)
If the pilots of Korean Air Lines Flight 007 had
had backups and hadn't totally relied upon a single system, inertial navigation, they could have
used dead reckoning and would still be alive. Even
in today's environment of advanced electronic navigational aids, dead reckoning is something that
still works when the glass cockpit blows a fuse and
the electrons don't elect to work.

Basically, trend analysis forecasting involves gathering *lots* of data from history and about what's
going on now. A long-term trend can then be
determined. All the long-term trends are going upward or downward at an ever-increasing rate. Little "glitches" or spikes on the long-term trend
curves don't affect the overall trend over a long
period of time. Once the trend and its rate of
change is established, it can then be extrapolated
or extended into the future to see what's like to
happen and when. But trend analysis don't tell *how*
it is going to happen, and this bothers some people.

Let's take an example which has often been criti-
cized as invalid but nevertheless is an excellent
example of trend analysis forecasting.

Let's determine the trend of the *speed* of people-
carrying transportation systems from the past up
to today and extend that trend into the future.

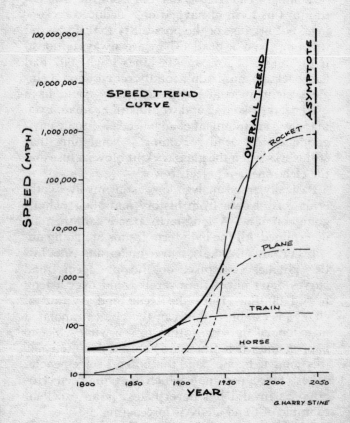

SPEED TREND CURVE

G. HARRY STINE

This is shown in Figure 1. Across the bottom of the chart are plotted the years into the past and into the future. Up the left side is plotted the speed of people-carrying transportation systems in miles-per-hour. Note that the vertical speed scale is not linear—i.e.: it doesn't go up in steps of 100 miles per hour. It's an "exponential" scale that goes up in increasing powers of 10—1, 10, 100, 1,000.

When human beings tamed horses, they had their first transportation system. A human-plus-horse can travel at the full gallop at a speed of about 30 mph. True, some horses can run faster than others, and that's what makes horse races. But the speed has been constant for thousands of years, which is why the "horse" is shown as a horizontal line on the chart at 30 mph.

Ocean-going ships didn't exceed 30 mph until a few decades ago. Even now it's difficult to exceed 60 mph with a hull-in-the-water ship.

The great breakthrough in transportation was the steam locomotive running with flanged iron wheels on smooth and reasonably level iron rails. The speed trend curve for trains starts out in 1804 with Richard Trevithick's *Pen-y-darran* steam locomotive hauling 5 wagons with 10 tons of iron and 70 people at the amazing speed of 4 mph. At the time locomotive rail transportation began, horses were faster. This is *always* true: older technology has better performance and/or efficiency at first but is rapidly surpassed by new technology. As development brought better steels, smoother road beds, and more efficient steam locomotives, the speed of rail transportation increased, and the early races between horses and steam locomotives in the 1830's became a thing of the past. By the start of the Twentieth Century, railway trains could achieve speeds in excess of 100 mph. In May 1893, the New York Central Railroad locomotive "Number 999" pulling *The Empire State Express* between Batavia and Buffalo, New York, achieved a speed of 112.5 mph. This was exceeded in 1905 by the *Pennsylvania Special* at a blistering 128 mph. This was about the limit for reciprocating steam locomotives. To keep railways speeds increasing required a new form of propulsion: the electric locomotive. This permitted railways to achieve what is probably the maximum speeds possible with the flanged steel wheel running on the steel rail. The "Hikari" Bullet Trains of the Japanese National Railways on the Tokaido Line in Japan and the "Train Grand Vitesse" units of the Chemin de Fer Francaise regularly operate in excess of 130 mph and are capable of maximum speeds of more than 200 mph. But the railway as a transportation system seems to have reached a final speed plateau. Speeds have levelled out. Although the railway train may eventually attain sustained speeds of 250 miles per hour, that's probably the limit *with known technology.*

A new transportation system, the airplane, came along in 1903 with the Brothers Wright flying at a leisurely 35 mph, far slower than contemporary trains. In fact, they shipped their "Flyer" from Dayton, Ohio to the railway station nearest to Kitty Hawk, North Carolina by rail transportation that was faster than the Flyer could fly. But airplane speeds increased dramatically as the technology of aeronautics developed. The fastest airplane using the original gasoline reciprocating engine concept of the Wrights was the Republic P-47J "Thunderbolt" that achieved a level flight speed of 504 mph in 1944 although the official FAI speed record of 483 mph was set in 1969 by a special version of the Grumman F8F "Bearcat" flown by Darryl Greenamyer. But to travel routinely faster than 400 mph in the air, a new form of propulsion was required. Although there were several jet-propelled aircraft in existence at an early time—the 1910 Coanda Jet and the 1938 Caproni-Campini N.1—the first pure-jet aircraft flight was made in Germany in 1938 by the Heinkel He-178 at 435 mph. Within a matter of a few years, turbojet aircraft were routinely exceeding 600 mph in level flight. Supersonic flight was achieved by military aircraft in 1953, and by the commercial Anglo-French "Concorde" SST in the 1970's. The military YF-12 "Blackbird" could attain three times the speed of sound in level flight in 1963. But the sustained speed of aircraft operating in the Earth's atmosphere has started to level off, just as the speeds of other forms of transporation leveled off once the limits of the basic mode of operation were reached.

But another transportation system has come along to push speeds even higher: the rocket, a very old propulsion device dating back to at least 1232 A.D. where mention is first made of it in Chinese literature. Although Dr. Robert H. Goddard flew the world's first liquid propellant rocket, the ancestor of all today's space transportation rockets, on March 16, 1926, manned rocket flight started with Fritz von Open in his rocket-propelled glider near Frankfurt, Germany in 1928, flying at a speed of 95 mph. By 1945, rocket-powered transportation speed had increased to more than 600 mph with the Messerschmitt Me-163B "Komet" rocket fighter. Then Mach-1 or the speed of sound by the rocket-propelled Bell X-1 in 1947. On April 12, 1961, this rose to 17,500 mph with the orbiting of Major Yuri I. Gagarin in the Soviet "Vostok-1". In 1968, "Apollo-8" raised this to 25,560 mph. Unmanned rocket vehicles have exceeded 40,000 mph, which is more than the escape speed of Planet Earth and begins to approach the escape speed of the Solar System. So the speed trend curve *may* have become meaningless ... and then again it may not.

When the overall speed trend curve is drawn to provide an "envelope" around the speed trend curves of various transportation systems from the horse to the rocket, this curve turns upward at an ever more steeply rising rate as time progresses. Yet the individual trend curves within the envelope behave quite differently.

The overall trend curve isn't linear and doesn't turn upward as a function of the square of the time—i.e.: twice as fast in ten years, four times as fast in twenty years, sixteen times as fast in thirty years, etc. It's a "cubic" curve. It turns upward as the cube of the time. We can write an equation that describes the behavior of this and all other overall performance trend curves:

$$Ly = x^3$$

Trend curves for just about anything you want to forecast will follow a similar cubic trend curve. One can argue only about what it's really telling us. The speed trend curve alone says that some form of transportation will enable us to attain the speed of light in the Twenty-first Century. But it doesn't tell us *how* we'll do it, just that it'll be possible. It may also be telling us that, having escaped from Earth, speed is no longer important.

Forecasters argue that any trend curve will eventually level off at some physical limit. This may also be true. The speed trend curve for each individual transportation system within the overall speed trend curve envelope has a different shape than the overall curve. It's an S-shaped curve known as a Gompertz curve (Figure 2), which accurately describes not only the development of individual

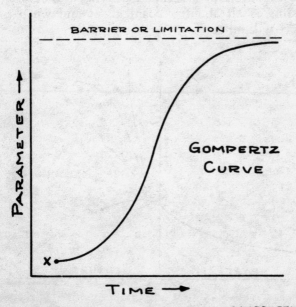

BARRIER OR LIMITATION

GOMPERTZ CURVE

PARAMETER →

X

TIME →

G. HARRY STINE

systems but also the growth trend of organic systems such as a cell culture in a Petri dish, a human being, or a human culture on Earth. It starts out slowly at Point X, begins a very rapid rise, and levels off as it begins to approach some barrier limiting its further increase or rise. The Gompertz curve tells us we can push a system and its basic concepts and technology just so far and no farther.

The initial portion of a Gompertz curve resembles the cubic trend curve, and it's often difficult to tell whether a cubic trend curve will turn out to be a Gompertz curve in the long haul. There's often no way to determine when and if the cubic curve will "inflect" and become a Gompertz curve. As Herman Kahn has remarked, "That's what forecasting is all about: recognizing if and when a curve will inflect."

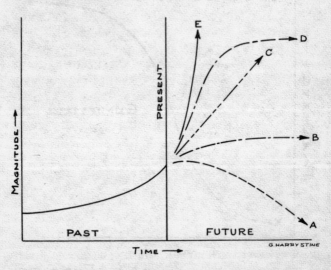

Figure 3

Figure 3 shows the ways different people look at the future with trend analysis.

Anyone with access to a library can determine the performance of the past. History's history. Therefore, everyone can draw the trend curve of past performance, and it'll be much the same no matter who does it. The past is set in concrete. It's led us to the present, which is momentary and indicated by the vertical line.

Curve A is a way of looking at the future that may be termed the "catastrophic future." This is the creed of the "gloom and doom" crowd, the anti-technologists, the back-to-nature anti-intellectuals, and the flower children of the 1960s. Insofar as these people are concerned, the future can't be anything but worse.

Curve A is impossible. Nowhere in history does the curve of human progress turn downward. We've been taught about the fall of the Roman Empire and the ensuing Dark Ages in Europe. But this wasn't the situation in the Orient where it was a time of enlightenment, scientific advancement, technological development, and general improvement of the human condition. While Europe was a cultural backwater, the Orient was developing a host of new technologies, philosophies, social concepts, and organizations. Chivalry, the decent treatment of women and the foundation of our concept of romantic love, was brought to Europe from Arabia by the Crusaders who also brought back the technologies of the East.

The curve of human progress has therefore *always* been upward. There's absolutely no historical or technical justification for anticipating Curve A. Even in the unlikely event of a general thermonuclear war, this future can't happen. And we're not going to let Curve A happen.

Curve B shows the trend curve levelling off a few years in the future and proceeding thereafter absolutely level. It's the way average persons who worry only about day-to-day problems tend to view the future. They don't see much change because they aren't aware of current progress in all areas of human endeavor due to today's "objective" news media which tends to report only the sensational stories.

Again, we *know* that Curve B isn't the future we can expect because we can see even within our own lifetimes that this isn't the way things have been going. Any attempt to forecast the future in terms of Curve B indicates that the forecaster has a complete misunderstanding of what's going on in the world. Curve B represents total failure of imagination. It's exemplified by the official in the patent office who, in 1885, quit his job because "everything had been invented." Curve B is invalid because we *know* the future's going to be different from today because it *always has been!*

Curve C represents the type of future foreseen by experts. They usually forecast a future in which the *rate* of human progress is the same as it is today. Forecasting on Curve C is a "safe" forecast because it's easy to believe that the rate of human progress will continue into the future . . . at least in the individual's field of expertise. But Curve C is also invalid because, again, we *know* from past performance that the *rate* of human progress hasn't been constant in the past. Why should future trends proceed at a constant rate when they haven't done so in the past? It's a forecast with a failure of imagination *and* nerve.

Curve D is a closer approximation to reality because it assumes the rate of human progress will increase. But at some point in the future, it assumes some limit will be reached and the curve will level off or inflect, making the human progress curve into a Gompertz curve. Curve D is a valid forecast only if there's some definite, absolutely known, and completely unquestionable limit to the magnitude of growth. One must be *very* careful when attempting to forecast on Curve D. One must be *absolutely certain* of the barrier. One must be *absolutely certain* that one isn't suffering from failure of imagination or nerve. One must be careful not to make the modern equivalent of a statement like the one from the school board in Ohio that gave the following reply to the request to use the school facilities to discuss steam power on railroads in 1823: "You are welcome to use the schoolroom to debate all proper questions; but such things as railroads are impossibilities and rank infidelity. If God had designed that His intelligent creatures should travel at the frightful speed of 15 miles per hour by steam, He would have foretold it through His holy prophets." Later, there was the "sound barrier," then a "thermal barrier," then the "heat barrier" to spacecraft entering the Earth's atmosphere at oribital or escape velocities. All of these barriers turned out to be breachable with technology. Physicists argue there's a limiting speed barrier: the speed of light. It's still a theory, not a speed limit law. All the data isn't in yet. And perhaps we're looking at the data in the wrong way. Any scientist who tries to tell you that we know everything there is to know about something is making a presumptuous, over-educated, narrow-minded, and highly-biased statement.

The only curve that one can use to forecast the future, and the most difficult one to use, is Curve E. It's the cubic curve that continues to turn upward ever more steeply with no limit in sight. It's fantastic, impossible, and unbelievable. Things can't possibly happen that way. But they have in the past, and all indications are they'll continue to do so in the future. Planners already use the cubic curve for business planning. It works.

But there's always someone who will argue that progress occurs in fits and starts, a series of "quantum jumps" such as shown in Figure 4. In some areas of human activity, this indeed is valid.

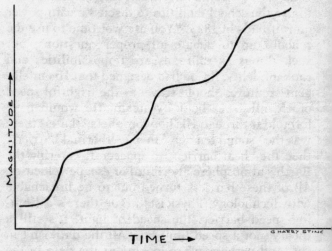

Figure 4.

But you've got to be very certain that you aren't just seeing glitches.

Glitches are discontinuities, whether they be in electronic signals from whence the jargon term originates or in the trend curves. Dr. Stanley Schmidt, editor of *Analog* magazine, has pointed out in a recent editorial that sometimes human progress seems to run in glitchy curves such as the one shown in Figure 5. Although the curve itself is following the cubic if you run at least-squares fit to it, shown by the dotted line, things can indeed look pretty bad if you happen to be on a descending glitch and the time factor is long enough. However, over the long haul, a curve like this doesn't exist; there are no real glitches in the long-term trend curves. If your trend curves are jittering up and down, it means that your data time

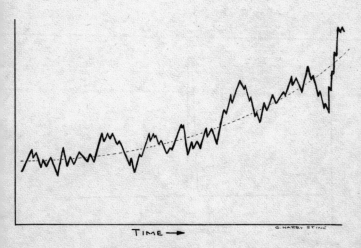

Figure 5

scale is too short. Like measuring the change in a physical function, the trace can get very noisy if the frequency response of the recorder is too short.

We've just come through a glitch in all the curves. It was the twentieth century Romantic Movement, also known as the limits to growth decade. Basically, this means that the limits to growth was nothing but noise. . . .

One addition trend curve shape needs to re-marked upon. What we've been talking about thus far are first order curves; they track the progress of a given parameter. We've used the word "rate" in connection with how fast these first order curves are changing. It's also possible to plot a graph of the rate of change itself. When that is done for something like a Gompertz Curve, the result looks like Figure 6. The peak of this curve occurs when

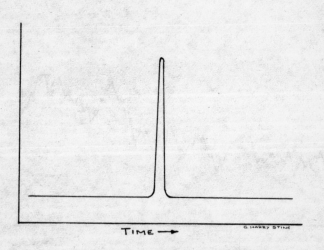

TIME →

G. HARRY STINE

Figure 6

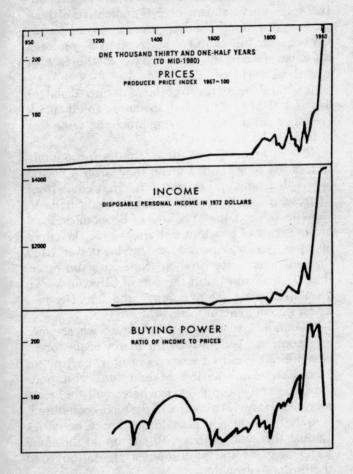

Figure 7

the Gompertz curve inflects and starts to level off. The spike curve shown here is indicative of how the rate of growth changes when a parameter really begins to inflect and go horizontally asymptotic. It's what is currently happening to the rate of growth of world population.

How valid are all the hypotheses discussed above? Save for the example used, the speed trend curve, are other parameters showing much the same sort of thing? The answer is yes.

Here in Figure 7 are three long-term economic factors. By long-term, I mean they cover a period of one thousand and thirty years. They come from the research of E. H. Phelps Brown and Sheila V. Hopkins of the London School of Economics. Plotted in terms of constant dollars, we see the curve of prices, personal income, and buying power. Note that there is noise in each. Note also, however, that all of them exhibit the sort of behavior we've been discussing. They confirm the late Herman Kahn's great general forecast:

"A hundred years ago, people everywhere were few, poor, and generally at the mercy of the forces of nature. A hundred years from now, barring an incredible combination of bad luck and poor management, people everywhere will be rich, many, and largely in control of the forces of nature."

And if we do not plan future space activities against this reality, they will end up on the same scrap heap as the philosophies of Malthus and the limits to growth.

LOST IN TRANSLATION

by
Dean Ing

Dean Ing is an outdoorsman, and looks it. He goes backpacking. He has a secret trout stream, which he's promised to take me to as soon as I manage to dig out from my work overload. He has designed a great deal of outdoors equipment; some, such as a highly efficient stove to burn pine needles and wood chips, essential for any survivalist.

Indeed, Dean does more than that. Some years ago I introduced him to Nancy Tappan, widow of the man who pretty well started the survivalist movement; and Dean now writes regularly for Nancy's newsletter. At a recent science fiction convention Dean demonstrated a homemade hand-operated air pump, suitable for ventilating a fallout shelter. Some of his fellow panelists were amused, and one made considerable fun of his pump; I expect she'd be glad enough to have him make one for her at need, and since she didn't watch the demonstration, she'll need someone to do it for her.

Civil defense and survival planning are divisive issues: a good part of the population apparently believes that nuclear war issues will go away if we just don't think about them. Alas.

Dean and I are, of course, agreed on one thing: the best way to survive a nuclear war is not to have one. The best way not to have one is to make it self evident to the Soviet Union that starting such a war is a losing proposition. We discuss all that and more in our book which we jointly produced: *Mutual Assured Survival*, Baen Books, 1984.

You would never know it to look at him, but Dr. Ing holds a Ph.D. in communications; a subject he thoroughly understands, as is evident from this story, which suggests one possible answer to Fermi's question—one that we may not necessarily like.

LOST
IN
TRANSLATION

Dean Ing

Le Sacre du Prin

"Howie's dumped a deadline again," Hawke sighed. "Sorry, Jus', but if he won't write progress reports for Delphium, we'll just have to do it for him."

"We, meaning Justine Channing," I said, and slapped a sheaf of notes between my breasts. "I'll never get my work done if I have to nurse that little creep through every waking hour."

Cabot Hawke fondled his mustache, a period piece that went with his graying sideburns and tweeds over big shoulders. All of it lent him the panache of a twentieth century colonel. While clawing my way above the ranks, I'd learned to read every one of Hawke's nuances. Whenever he stroked that brush, he was reminding himself who he was: Projects Director of Delphium Corporation. "More like once a week," Hawke grunted, leaving his half-acre desk to drape an arm over my shoulder.

I knew that move, too: he was showing me the door. But nicely; when Hawke wasn't nice during business hours, I could be bitchy at night. Who was it said, "Reciprocity works both ways?"

"Try and forget how the man looks," Hawke rumbled softly. "To board members, he's beautiful. The day Howard Prior leaves Delphium, our best CanAm Federation contract goes with him. So you wipe his flat nose for him, find him more old tapes of Vivaldi and Amirov if he wants you to. Whatever." He patted my rump as if identifying "whatever."

I stopped in the entryway, using a haute couture stance from modeling days, regarding Hawke through my fall of auburn hair. Narrowing my eyes, I said, "Maybe I will."

Hawke showed me his strong teeth—half of them implants—and refused the bait. "You're the most overpaid administrator in CanAmerica," he slandered, "because you prod my prima donnas to create their polymers and scenarios and translations. I don't always tell you how to do it, and I refuse to worry about it. So don't *be* a prima donna, baby; be an administrator. Go minister."

"By God, maybe I really will," I muttered, trying to believe it.

"Just don't forget to spray," Hawke's basso chuckle followed me, loud enough to be heard down the corridor. "God knows what musty corner Howie's hands have been in. Some of his germs must be centuries old."

I headed for the lower-level complex and out of executive country, reflecting that Hawke was only half joking. Once, a year before, I'd driven Howie from Baltimore to the remains of a Library of Congress annex—Howie couldn't find Delphium by himself, much less a specific ruin around

Washington—and I'd waited while Howie snooped for records of the Sentinel project. That was after the news that the Tau Ceti expedition had found leavings of a dead civilization.

Delphium had signed Howard Prior up before other think tanks realized what that news meant in terms of study contracts. But working with Howie was a nightmare: the man could *not* keep things in proper order. And I key my life to the observance of order. Hawke could joke that I made neatness into a vice, but one day he'd find himself outmaneuvered by my sense of order. Taking *my* orders.

Nothing will ever divert me from that goal, by that path.

On the annex trip, Howie hadn't emerged for hours. All his cassettes were used and he looked like he'd been crawling through conduits—grimy, smelly, tear-streaked. Evidently they were tears of joy because the little twit had found a cache of music recordings. Howie's degrees from Leeds and Yerkes had made him a world-class expert in inter-species communication problems, but his mania was old music.

He was delirious over his finds, music by Purcell and Porta and one, Haydn, I'd heard of. Never mind that he upset my schedule, never mind that the Sentinel Project of the 1980's was a wipeout—small wonder, since the Tau Ceti civilization had quit transmitting five thousand years before. Still, little Howie began regular forays into those archives. But not with me. Hawke teased me later when I complained. But I say, once burnt by a four-hour fiasco with a filthy little nigger, *forever* shy!

Actually, Howie was mostly Caucasian, with a

British scholar's accent and a sallow complexion, lighter than Hawke who quicktanned religiously. But Howie's maternal grandmother had been an aboriginal in Queensland. Those mixed-up—disorderly!—genes made him the image of a loser. Knobby little bod, squashed nose, and hair almost kinky enough to be sculptured. The one time I suggested cosmetic surgery to him was the last time Howie tried to get cozy with me for months. I can't ever forgive the look I saw on his crumpled features.

All he said was, "It's fatuous to brag about what you can't help, Justine. It's worse to apologize." But what I saw in his expression was not self-pity.

It was clemency. The hell with him . . . .

Let's face it: Howie wasn't interested in bettering himself. That's another reason why I wasn't interested in keeping my options open with Howie. I stopped outside the door to his tiny office, took a few sniffs from my compact, and feeling suitably mellow, stepped inside. Into chaos.

Fax notes everywhere, cassettes underfoot, Howie in shirtsleeves capering at his data terminal with a light pencil like some scrawny shaman crooning a non-tune. That would've been enough by itself, but humming and twanging through it, the speakers played something just far enough from sensible music to set my pearly-whites on edge. "Howie, have you gone . . ." I began.

His wave cut me short and suggested I shut the door in one motion. Before he turned back to the terminal, I caught his glance. It was whimsical, guilty, appraising. And like a fool I thought his office bedlam was the reason.

Howie was talking. Or rather, his terminal was, synthesized from his voiceprint and contrapuntal to the music. But it didn't have Howie's educated Yorkshire diction; it spoke in standard CanAm, which didn't seem to bother Howie but nearly drove me wild. How could I tell which voice should take precedence?

". . . not sure whether the Greeks did it first. But Porta proved you can write music to be played right side up or upside down," said the Howie terminal.

"Invertible polyphony," the real Howie said to me, eyes agleam, his light-pencil marking time. "Bach tried it in this fugue." He punched an instruction. His grin invited me to enjoy it.

Instantly the terminal voice stopped and instead we were hearing what Howie claimed was Bach. I could take it but preferred to leave it and said so.

"Ah, but listen to it inverted," he begged. Another punched instruction. More Bach—I guess.

Howie closed his eyes in bliss. I closed mine too, and raised my fists and shouted, "HOWIE, WHEN WILL YOU LEARN SOMETHING AS EASY AS A PROGRESS REPORT?"

Finger jab, and a silence of anechoic chambers. Then as I waited for his apology: "Justine, when will *you* learn something as easy as calling me 'Howard'?"

"If the diminutive fits, wear it," I snapped. "I'm here to do your paperwork, since you prefer to play with your stolen ditties."

"Ah, no," he breathed, smiling at a private whimsy, no longer appraising. "Not stolen; lost, and now found." He let the smile fade while I whiffed at my compact again. It's easy to overdo a hit from a compact, which is why Howie disapproved of my doing it, which is why I pretended to overdo it. Instead of an apology, I detected patronage. Nobody patronizes Justine Channing. *No*body.

"So you must work, because I play," he murmured finally. "If you hate that so much, Justine, why do you do it?"

I shrugged. Why did *everybody* do it? To get somewhere. Too elementary to repeat.

"Answer one question," he prodded gently, "and then I promise to help you draft a report synopsis."

"I'm listening," I said.

"Why do you do it? Help me draft the report, I mean."

Well, he'd promised a *quid pro quo*. "The federation gets your report, Delphium gets its quarterly check, and Cabot Hawke gets off the hook." Howie just looked at me. "All right, and then Hawke lets *me* off the hook! More or less," I hedged.

"Hawke and you. More and less." He nodded like a wronged parent. "And I, less still."

"Life is a billion-way parlay, Howie. To be a winner, you pick winners. I don't care what you think about me and Hawke."

"I didn't mean that. I meant, we fool ourselves about our motives. A good turn has a selfish component; we try to be more, while the system is biased to make us less."

"Hell, if you don't push for number one, you'll never amount to anything."

Howie looked at, then through me, and then began to laugh a soft hollow-chested wheeze that lasted a long time. "We obviously wouldn't be as we are," he said at last, terminating his private joke. "Very well; into the breach of the report, as it were. What tale did we spin for the analysts last time? Must have a clear sequence," he added, as if he'd said something clever.

I passed him "his" last progress report—I had written it—and waited while Howie scanned it. Half of his work was unraveling Cetian arts. Every child knew that the quasimammals on Tau Ceti's major planet had been nuts about communication. Their color sense had been so acute that the Cetians could leave a complex message with a single dot of color. Hue, shape, size, sequence of spots; all affected Cetian message content. The trouble was that nothing that remained of Cetian media told us why they weren't still there.

Picture a planetful of garrulous ground sloths, carefully documenting each war and yardage sale, every farce and footrace of a dominant culture. Now picture them disappearing suddenly without trace or announcement, centuries before our Egyptians built Abu Simbel. Cetian science yielded no clue. Cetian art, someone guessed, might yield some hints.

Howie worked, or rather played, overtime for months before he discovered that Cetian communication went to hell just before their disappearance. The Cetians produced one final piece of abstract visual art, a huge blob of varicolored tiles by some philosopher-priest, and they reproduced it as proudly and as often as we copy the Mona Lisa. And then their commentaries began to decay fast.

Howie's last report had concluded: "Cetian language became more chaotic with each sleep period. The hue variable was abandoned, and we infer that the Cetians fell prey to some epidemic that first confused, then consumed them. During the next quarter we will run content-analytical surveys of late Cetian story mosaics," and made other vague promises I'd added.

"Hawke must be glad that I'm not making much progress," Howie mused as he read the last paragraph.

I donated a cool smile. "Just enough, not too much. The riddle's been there a long time, Howie. Why work yourself out of a job overnight?" Wink. Even if he rarely made heavy passes at me anymore, Howie liked my little winks and nudges—and they didn't cost me much.

He studied me without expression except that the broad nostrils flared and contracted, reminding me of a skinny little hippo lost in thought. Then he grunted and began to read my write-up of his Proxima Two translations.

The Proximans had disappeared several million years ago; so long ago that it took two expeditions to discover remains of a race that had vanished, like the Cetians, suddenly. They'd been sea-dwelling invertebrates with enough savvy to build pearlescent craft that explored their land-masses, then build others that took them into orbit. We hadn't a clue to Proximan language until a xenologist suspected there was meaning in all the bubbles.

I mean, of course, the bubble generators that were still blurping away in the coral cities Proximans had built. Give our pickaninny his due: it was Howie who thought to run analyses of covariance of the size, frequency, gas composition, and absorption rates of the bubbles. Those little isotope-powered bubble generators, he figured, hadn't been put there just for decor. And Howie was right.

They'd been for entertainment and news; Proximan media broadcasts.

Thanks to Howie, we knew the Proximans had a strict caste system, high art, and a suspicious nature, even in those bubble messages. Howie's current work was often a case of guessing what the Proximan sea-cities *didn't* want to talk about.

Howie sighed while reading my last paragraph: ". . . further study of a long, curiously-wrought sequence that was found programmed into bubble generators in widely-separated cities. The sequence may have been a rare cooperative effort by Proximans to unify several mathematical theories. The effort was barely underway when, after a brief period of linguistic decay, the Proximans vanished."

"Most of that is eyewash, you know." Howie tapped the fax page without rancor. "Oh, it's glossy enough, and harmless—but who told you all that sodding rubbish about unifying theories? My work suggests the Proximans were studying a single message."

"Pity you didn't write this yourself, then," I flared, and waited for my apology.

And got it. "True. If I leave it for someone else I must expect something to get lost in translation. I really do apologize, Justine. We might do better this time, eh?"

I remarked that it was up to him. He edited what I'd written, then spent the next hour extracting bits on the Ceti problem from his computer terminal, putting them in order for me. Sure enough, Howie had fresh surmises which I arranged, then rechecked.

At first I thought I'd misplaced a fax page. "Damn, this passage isn't Ceti. It's Prox stuff."

"No, you've got it spot-on," he said with a final inflection that teased me to continue.

"But—it was the Cetians, not the Proximans, who went gaga over a piece of art."

"The Cetians," he replied, nodding and leaving his chin up as he added, "*and* the Proximans." And he watched me with that damnable catch-me-if-you-can smile of his.

I made a dozen intuitive leaps, all into black holes of confusion, in ten seconds. I could feel the hair begin to rise on the nape of my neck until I decided Howie was kidding me.

He decoded my glance and began quickly: "That massive Cetian colorburst? Its title translates toughly into 'Rebirth' or equally well as 'Climax'. The work of one individual who couldn't explain it. Pure inspiration. Also," he added slowly, "pure message. Our Cetian artist just didn't understand his own message at first."

I tapped an extravagant fingernail against my faxes, denying the gooseflesh creeping down my spine. "But *you* understand it?"

"Lord no," he laughed. "It has a level of abstraction that escapes me." More seriously then: "Exactly the same as the Proximan problem, Justine. It involves a different idiom."

I swallowed and sat down. Mostly, I wondered how to tell Cabot Hawke that his prize egghead had cracked his little shell. "No. You can't seriously imply that—that the Ceti mosaic has any connection with a string of bubbles. In another star system. *Five million years* apart. It's beyond reason, Howie!"

The little monkey was grinning. " 'Tis, isn't it? I keep trying to decode that mosaic and what the

Proximans called their 'Coronation Lyric', but so far I haven't the foggiest."

"The hell you don't." My mouth was dry. I compared his conclusions again. "The short bubble message commentary that preceded the Coronation Lyric: any room for error in your translation? I mean, saying their lyric thing was an inspired piece of art?"

"Not much. I gather it unfolded like Coleridge's vision of Xanadu—only our Proximan wasn't interrupted. He got to finish undisturbed."

"Just before the Proximans all disappeared."

"Not quite. Proximans considered it only great art at first. They didn't tumble immediately, as the Cetians did; they had a puzzle to solve."

In the back of my head, a small voice reminded me that none of this was on my faxes. Howie didn't want it in the reports. What else had he held back? I half-closed my eyes and smiled. "You think the Cetians and Proximans were communicating," I said.

"Unlikely. There are other possibilities."

I persisted. "But a direct connection between the art and the disappearances?"

"Between the *messages buried in the art* and the disappearances," he corrected. He was glancing at me: hair, cleavage, mouth.

I moistened my lips with my tongue and said softly, "If you're right—Howard—how big is this news?"

He was still focusing on my mouth, pole-axed with desire. "Pick a number," he said like a sleepwalker. "Quite a large one."

"But only if you can translate those messages."

"Can you keep a secret, Justine?"

"Try me." If he missed that *entendre* he was no translator.

"I suspect neither message can ever be decoded by humans. There's something missing, as if each message were tailored exclusively for a given species. A Cetian, I suspect, could never have translated the Proximan message. And so on."

"But who could have sent such messages?"

"Ah," he said, a forefinger raised, and then turned the gesture into a wave of helplessness.

I let it all sink in, and let Howie take my hand while I raced over the possibilities. If Howie chose to report that the translations couldn't be made, his study contract might be terminated. That meant major problems which Hawke would pass down to me. If Howie did break those codes, assuming he wasn't march-hare mad with his whole scenario, it might mean a Nobel.

There had to be some way I could profit from this thing, without risking anything. As Howie interlaced his fingers against mine with his sad, tentative smile, I squeezed. "You realize I'm obligated to report all this," I said.

He jerked away. Carefully, voice shaking: "You don't have to report pure oral conjecture, Justine. That's all it is right now. I shared it with you in strictest confidence."

Time to set the hook. "If it's ever discovered that I held back crucial information, it will ruin my career," I said. As though Cabot Hawke hadn't shown me that the reverse is true! "You're asking me to be a full partner in this, Howard."

"I suppose so," he said. "All right. Yes, I am."

I'd landed him. Ruffling his kinky thatch with one hand, I stood up. "You won't be sorry, Howie.

Just keep trying to decode those messages." I stacked my faxes neatly and headed toward the door.

"You're assuming," he said dreamily, "they haven't already been decoded for us." I must've stared, because he started ticking items off on his stubby fingers: "Brancusi's 'Bird in Space' can be expressed mathematically. Maya glyphs. Altamira cave paintings. It may have been what Hesse had in mind with his bead game in *Magister Ludi*. Or"—he gave a happy giggle—"I could just be bonkers. But I'm in training for the search, Justine. That's what I was doing when you walked in."

"Training for the Interstellar Olympics," I teased.

"Or for the twilight of the gods," he replied thoughtfully. "You understand that secrecy is vital if there's danger?"

Well, I thought I did: to keep some other weirdo from jumping his claim. "Trust me," I said, and left him.

Two minutes and a broken anklestrap later I was with Hawke, babbling so fast he had to help me open my compact for a settle-me-down.

As usual, Hawke traded me fresh perspectives for what I gave him. As we lay on his apartment watercouch he blew one of my curls from his lips and reached for a cheroot. He lit it, and fell back beside me puffing happily.

Wrinkling my nose: "I've come to think of that stink as the unsweet odor of your success," I gibed. At Hawke's age, he wasn't always successful.

"Be glad it doesn't smell like Howie Prior," he replied, and I could feel his furry barrel chest shaking with amusement.

I bit him. "That's for your innuendo. And for refusing to explain this afternoon."

"About Howie's fear of *gotterdammerung?* Seems clear enough, Jus'. He thinks there could be some magic formula that wiped out two entire civilizations." Hawke dragged on the cheroot, studied its glow. Then, reflectively, "Well, well; what a weapon in the wrong hands."

Trust Hawke to think in those terms. He was still chuckling to himself as I prompted, "And in the right hands?"

Long silence. Then, "There probably wouldn't be any right hands. Classic paranoid fantasy—and I'm not at all surprised to find our little Howie entertaining it." After a moment he added, "Watch him, Jus'."

The idea of Howie Prior being violent was absurd, and I laughed. "I probably outweigh him."

"You miss the point. He doesn't need muscle to be dangerous. Humor him. Keep an eye open for his private computer code. I don't want to wake up one morning and find him bootlegging full translations to the highest bidder because he thinks it's all that important."

What good would it have done me to insist that Howie was not capable of such sharp practice? To Cabot Hawke, the world was populated only by Cabot Hawkes—and certainly not many Howies. I promised I'd give all the support Howie asked for, and then changed the subject. My mistake.

Howie Prior wanted to lie on his bony arse high up in the Sistine Chapel. Not on a muffled skimmer, which wouldn't have required so many permissions, but on a rickety scaffold which took me weeks to arrange. But Delphium has clout, and Howie got to play Michelangelo. It got him nowhere.

Howie had more fun as Constantin Brancusi and I had hell finding sculpture replicas. But we found photos of the man's studio and the airy, white sunsplashed rooms had charm—until Howie put dust covers over the pieces I'd collected, to recreate the ambience the sculptur had kept. When Howie donned outmoded funky clothes and a little pointy woolen cap, I walked out. He said he needed to be Brancusi for his work, but hadn't told me how far he was willing to take it. Well, Brancusi didn't take *him* very far.

When Howie asked me to find him a place in Clarens, Switzerland, I almost called Hawke. Then Howie showed me photos of the view he wanted, and I agreed. A tiny *pension* in a Swiss hotel was easy enough to locate. Why shouldn't I make the arrangements over there and enjoy Howie's madness before Hawke realized how much it cost?

"Which Swiss are you going to be?"

"Try and find me some Mahorka tobacco. It's Spanish," he unanswered.

"Picasso?"

"And get me an appointment with an internist," he added. "I must know the proper dosage."

"For what?"

"For just a touch of nicotine poisoning, if you must know. We don't want to overdo it, do we?"

"*We* don't know what the hell you're up to. *We*," I stressed it again, "get queasy thinking about postmortems. So no, goddammit, *we* aren't going to find you any poisonous tobacco."

I hated that look of his, the gaze of a saint caught with his hand in the till. "I don't want to pull rank, Justine. I know what's needed. I promise not to get very sick on nicotine. I intend to get well with it."

"You're ill? That doesn't surprise me—"

"We all are. Please don't act the nanny; the role ill-suits you." He didn't have Hawke's subtlety; he just pointed at the door.

I went. I could already smell Alpine meadows.

The Swiss were an enterprising lot who understood money better than most. In a week I was back with a real tan and an itch to return. Meanwhile, Howie had collected a trunkful of manuscripts and custom-tailored old formal clothes. And yes, he was already dosing himself with nicotine and smoking strong tobacco as well.

Handing him the packetful of travel vouchers, I tried to get him to endorse another trip for me. Lowering my voice for vibrancy: "There's a nice room below yours at Clarens. Surely you'll need me for, um, *some*thing."

"I'll need all my concentration, thanks. I couldn't do justice to the problem if I were constantly thinking of a lovely woman just downstairs."

I tried once more: "It could be so romantic, Howard."

"Too right," he muttered, tasting me with his eyes, but sadly—like a man craving cheesecake who fears he'll miss the last rowboat out of hell if he stops for a nibble.

"You really must think you've got it this time," I said.

The little chin came up. "Yes, I do. Seems obvious now. Ah—where're my tickets?"

"In your hand, fool. What will you do without

me? Well, give me a call when you're through with your Swiss mystery," I said quickly, and made a *toujours gai* exit.

So Howie went alone to Clarens carrying his damned Mahorka tobacco and his double-damned, old-fashioned manuscripts and high-collared shirts, and I didn't see him again for almost a month. But I know he went there because I spoke with him by vidphone several times. I even had to wire money to a doctor who visited Howie in his *pension*. The man confirmed that Howie's neuralgia was probably from nicotine poisoning. I sent money to Howie's concierge, too, as a bribe to keep her from taking the muted upright piano from Howie. It wasn't loud, she admitted; merely calamitous. She might have been describing the nightmares I was having by then. In each of them, I was kept marking time while tacky little people passed me.

While Howie was gone I backtracked him. His Delphium account showed he'd taken a taxi to the old library annex before deciding on his Swiss trip. I unearthed no hint of what he went there for. I got Howie's passplates—Delphium's personnel files are *thorough*—and wasted hours searching his grungy little apartment for a gap in his files, notations of his computer access codes, anything to build a scenario on. I found nothing of interest, beyond the poster-sized blowup of a candid holo that faced Howie's desk. I wondered when Howie had taken it; nice, but it hadn't captured the real me.

I figured there was an even chance that Howie would wind up in a loony bin, in which case Cabot Hawke would seek some heavy explanations from me. And I hadn't any, until it occurred to me that

Howie might be ignoring his personal bills while in Switzerland. Paying his bills gave me a slender reason to search his apartment. The rent bill would include the number of times his door passplate was used, so Howie would eventually know someone had been there.

Utility companies can be so-o-o understanding when you offer to pay overdue bills. They weren't angry at Howie. CompuCenter wasn't, either; his bill for the past few weeks had been hardly more than the base rate. *Hardly* more? Well, his apartment terminal had been used for only thirty-nine minutes since his last payment. A trifling sum, which would be carried over since it had, after all, been spent within the past few days.

Within the past few days?

I kept the tremolo from my voice, thanked them, rang off. Somebody had been using Howie's apartment, and very recently.

I called his apartment manager and offered to pay his rent. Yes, Howard Prior was slightly delinquent. Gentle, sweet man, honest to a fault; not to worry.

I simpered into the vidphone, "Howie wanted me to take care of things, but he's an absent-minded dear. Did he sublet the place or let any of—our friends use it?"

The manager consulted her terminal, then said, "No. His door passplate's been used only once in the past few weeks."

"Would you know when that was?"

"Uh—just today, about noon." She cocked her head. "Something wrong?"

Something goosefleshcrawlingly wrong. "No," I smiled past my chill, then thanked her and rang off again. That single entry at noon had been *mine*. No one else had passed through that door in weeks.

Yet his apartment terminal had been used very recently. And CompuCenter long ago stopped permitting remote processing through private terminals.

I stood gazing down at Howie's desk terminal, then at my picture on Howie's wall, until my neck began to prickle. I sensed a presence. Maybe not exactly human. What if someone had been in his apartment all this time? In fact, what if someone were *still there with me*, watching me, silently waiting in the shadow-haunted bedroom? The sensation of an unseen presence became a hobgoblin that forced me out of Howie's apartment at a dead run.

By the time I reached Delphium, my panic had transmuted to rage and I knew just the pickaninny to take it out on. I passplated myself into Howie's office, intending to call him from his own office for a little therapeutic Swiss *sturm und drang*.

I didn't need to make that call. Howie Prior, in the flesh, sat on his desk, swinging his legs and grinning like an imp with a forefinger across his lips. He didn't need the gesture. I tried to speak but couldn't find the breath for it.

"Don't you ever tell anyone I started hyperventilating," I said, still leaning against his door, willing my hands to stop shaking as I found my compact. "I don't know what industrial espionage you're up to, but I could blow your whole show. You're going to tell me about it right now, Howard Prior. Right *now*," I repeated.

"You again called me 'Howard'," he said smiling.

His face, ugly as it was, bore a frightful beauty, his dark eyes shining deep under his brow ridge, teeth bright between pale lips. I mean, he looked— haunted, but unafraid. Exalted. All right then: beatified.

I keyed Cabot Hawke's emergency priority code on the vidphone, leaving it on *hold* so that I needed only to press the *execute* bar. "You look like hell frozen solid, Howie. And you've got me suspicious, and you don't want to do that unless you're after big trouble. Set me at ease."

"That's why here am I."

"You can start by telling me who's been using your apartment terminal this week."

"I did. A few things there to verify were, and easiest it seemed—"

"A lie. You haven't been through that door in weeks. Anyhow, you can't afford to shuttle back and forth from Europe and Delphium sure as hell hasn't bought you more tickets, and your concierge has orders to call me if you disappear or start acting crazy. And stop talking funny, you're beginning to scare me."

"Sorry. I hadn't thought how to you it might look. But I assure you, I several times my terminal used. Maybe a half-hour."

Again that unspeakable sunburst smile of a madman or a bright angel: "However, yes I *can* afford anywhere to go I bloody please. And so can you, Justine."

My suspicions made a quick test-connection. "You broke the Cetian code and sold it!"

Softly, lovingly, so quietly I almost missed it: "Broke I the *human* code." He caught himself garbling the phrase and slapped his knee. "Human communication breakdown: it's wonderful. Don't you want to know where was hiding our message?"

"I want to know what it said," I hedged.

"Life lastingever," he said, obviously amused now by his own speech patterns that suggested an unhinged mind. He opened his arms, palms up, and continued: "Freedom to discover, to anywhere go. To pain an end. That is part of what it said. Forgive my troubled syntax," he chuckled. "I must sound a bit queer but—but you see, once you, um, internalize the translation, you needn't obey any of the nasty little hierarchies that hag-ride us until we can't see Godhood staring us in the face.

"We even make languages into stumbling blocks; help it we cannot! This word must go here, there another, yonder that phrase. Change the sequence, the pecking order, and you may impair the meaning. Precedence. Status. The stuff of our shell protective."

"What's wrong with protection?"

"Nothing—if you're an embryo. The translation is our egg tooth." Seeing my headshake, he added, "We can use it to peck our way out of the egg of the hereandnow."

He had all the earmarks of a loser who had hit on some nutcake rationale for giving up the good fight. By now he'd probably drained his savings, telling himself it didn't matter. If and when he came to his senses again, Howie was going to be damned sorry. "Howie, do you suppose neuralgia from a self-poisoning could just possibly have a teeny weeny something to do with your outlook?"

"Indirectly—but the translation the crucial thing is. To share it with you first I chose. Than yours, no one's need could be greater."

"Enough of your ding-y bullshit! You should've said nobody's single-minded determination could be greater," I said proudly.

"Wrong-headed determination amounts to the same thing," he sighed.

"I know my priorities," I said in anger, "and I'll tell you yours. First let me see the damned translation."

"Lor' love you, Justine, you don't see it, you—empath it. The code was based on cardiac rhythms our. I think was Stravinsky too much the cold intellectual to realize what with the *Sacre* he had done. Didn't have cryptanalysis to guide, poor man; and suffering he was from his tobacco habit in Clarens." A sense of sorrow and wonder suffused Howie's face. "Imagine how he might have exulted once the *Sacre*—the *Rite*—translated was into his own human rhythms."

"Talk sense! Once the right *what* was translated?"

"*The Rite of Spring; Le Sacre du Printemps!* Stravinsky said it was really a coronation of spring. Proximans had their Coronation lyric to free them; Cetians had their Rebirth mosaic. And since primitive times, societies human have to something like this tuned into. Frazer, in *The New Golden Bough*, said the celebration of Spring is to the expulsion of death a sequel. Frazer just let notions of sequence bugger him up. Stravinsky didn't—until later rewrote the music he." Animated, pleased as a kid, Howie rushed on. "If the *Rite of Spring* you've ever heard, you know it's from metric patterns liberated."

"I wish you knew how *you* sound to me," I warned him.

"Only at first," he said chortling. "Monteux the

conductor thought raving mad Stravinsky when the piano score first he heard. Himself Stravinsky complained that badly overbalanced were some parts. So rewrote it he. Harmonies were more than dense; impenetrable they were. Until now," he said, as if in prayer, and looked at me shyly. "Gibberish to you this is, suppose I."

I had to rearrange Howie's chatter in my head, and the thought that he might be teasing me tempered my confusion with fury. "So you've been playing Stravinsky; that much I understand. And it sent you around the bend."

"Listened—truly listened—to the translation, I once only." He turned to his keyboard. "Fed it I into memory with a recording old of the composer's recollections. Listen." He punched an instruction.

The voice from the speaker was aged, unemotional, precise. Old Stravinsky's accent sounded more German than Russian. And with it, beneath it, was a soft thudding asymmetry that I took to be an abnormal heartbeat.

Except that it was *informing* me, its message as clear as speech.

Howie had run two audio tracks together. On one track, Igor Stravinsky was saying, "Very little immediate tradition lies behind the *Sacre du Printemps*, however—and no theory. I had only my ear to help me. I heard; and I wrote what I heard. I am the vessel through which the *Sacre* passed . . ."

Then only the second audio track, the drumbeat whisper of some thunderous concept I hadn't been listening to, emerged into the silence beyond the old man's words. I thought, *And Howie listened had to it once only,* and then I screamed.

It couldn't have been more than a few moments

later when I felt Howie's skinny hands stroking my shoulder. I lay in a fetal crouch on his floor, hands over my ears, and there was a dampness between my legs that had nothing to do with sex. I could hear my torturer murmuring, "Let it free you, Justine." At least he had stopped that subversive mindbending throb of—knowledge? Heresy? I didn't have a label for it, but I loathed it.

I swiped at his arm as I struggled up, waiting for my strength to return. "Free me from what, you stupid abo? My sanity?"

"Your shell of needs," he said, still kneeling, uncaring that I towered above him. "Needs that into a cage we made. Restructions terrible of imprisonment in hierarchies, and time, and space."

I reached for my compact; checked to see that its gas cell had nearly a full charge, and took a nice long hit to quell my tremors. "All my life I've trained and fought to be somebody, Howie. Now I'm halfway up the ladder and you want to do me the favor, the FAVOR, of mindwashing me into—what? Some kind of born-again Buddhist?"

"Anything timeplace you choose," he said. "Forever," he said. "It offers such freedom that honest to be, I'm growing restless with you. You heard some of it. You know, too."

He was right. It had taken only a minute of that telepathic thudding seduction to push me to the brink of an internal precipice. Another few moments and I knew, positively, I wouldn't have given a damn for my job, or getting Hawke's job, for as long as the madness lasted.

Well, I'd been strong enough to resist. But what if I could get Hawke to listen! Ah, yes; just as

Howie wanted *me* to listen. "Howard, is your translation stored in your private access code?"

"No," he said with a smile, and showed me. "It is for access free. It no longer to me belongs, Justine. Returned I to arrange its broadcast, and to first with you share it."

He turned away to his terminal. I triggered my compact, holding it under his nose while gripping his head with all my strength. For only an instant he struggled, then relaxed against my breast, head back, smiling up into my face. "More proof, my love?" He inhaled deeply, deliberately.

He kept on breathing the stuff until I felt the thumping in his little body diminish, falter, quit. Even before that, though, something abandoned his gaze.

As long as his lungs were pumping, I held on. He'd gone berserk, I rehearsed, but I'd been too strong for him. Kept my compact hissing too long out of pure terror. It would be self-defense, and I was sure Hawke would back me. I was sure because I would soon have Hawke working for me.

Howie's heart was still. That had a message for me, too; it told me I'd go on winning, no matter what.

I checked Howie's terminal again, momentarily horrified that I might not be able to retrieve that demonic message. It was there, all right. I changed its address so that only I could locate it again—or so I thought. I stretched the body out on the floor, then remembered to rip my blouse and to use the dead fingernails to drag welts along my throat. When I left Howie's little office I staggered convincingly.

Hawke left a conference in midsentence when he saw me on his vidphone. In his study, he fussed over me in real concern. Gradually I let him understand what I'd rehearsed. I've always been able to evoke tears on demand.

At the crucial point, Hawke showed no suspicion. "Dead? And you didn't get a copy of his translation? Damn, damn, *damn*," he muttered, then patted me distractedly. "I'm not angry with you, Jus'. You can't be blamed."

I made it tentative: "I—might be able to find it. In his office. Uh—hadn't we better get rid of . . .?" I waved my hand instead of saying it. Hawke knew very well there are some things I'd prefer not to say aloud.

"You sure you're up to it?"

I took a deep breath, smiled my bravest smile, nodded. I said, "We wouldn't want the police stumbling onto Howie's translation before we do."

A few minutes later I had something more to worry about. Howie Prior's body was gone. "Look," I said to Hawke, balling my fists, "I did not imagine it. I—may have been wrong about his heart stopping." I hadn't been.

"Or else someone removed his body. I'm trying to figure out how and why," Hawke said.

I moved to Howie's terminal, readied my fingers at the keys. "I'm feeling barfish," I said as preamble in a vulnerable little-girl voice that seldom failed. "I may have to . . ." I had intended to "find" Howie's translation and then leave quickly while Cabot Hawke absorbed it. But I swear, I never touched a key.

"We pause for a special bulletin," said a familiar voice; Howie's, of course. If he wanted people to listen, he had to ease them into it in a familiar way. "If carefully you listen, this is the very last bulletin special you will ever need."

The next voice was Stravinsky's. I heard the ravishing velvet hammer of propaganda beneath it, thrust my thumbs into my ears, and hummed while I tried not to feel the message vibrating through me.

Hawke didn't notice me. After a moment he sat down, his face transformed in something beyond sexual rapture. I could almost understand, dimly, the message throbbing through my shoe soles. When I eased out of the room, Cabot Hawke was lost in Howie's translation.

En route to Hawke's office, I kept hearing stray bits of that voiceless communiqué from every open doorway, and hummed louder. By some power I couldn't yet guess, Howard Prior had plugged his translation into every channel of every terminal and holovision set in existence. I had to put my heel through Hawke's speakers but finally, insulated by his plush pile carpet and my loudest soprano, I could feel free of that hellish persuasion.

Two hours later I left Delphium. There wasn't anybody there anyway. Then I left Baltimore. There wasn't anybody there, either.

I slid into the driver's couch of a roadster, abandoned like many others with its motor still whirring, and sang "Ain't We got Fun" at the top of my voice until I could rip the wires from the dashboard speaker. I saw no traffic as I sped north.

I'm not sure why I stopped for the hitcher; maybe because he was the only person I'd seen in an hour. Maybe because he was a good-looking hunky specimen. But when I say he acted altogether too goddamn familiar, I'm understating. He talked as if he were my alter ego. "Free choice have you. No one's going to force you to listen, Justine." Those were his first words as he settled in.

I was already accelerating. "How did you know my name?"

"I listened," he said with the ghost of a wry grin. "To give it a try you ought before the machines run down," he went on. "You wouldn't want stranded to be."

"It's you who gets stranded," I said with finality and braked hard. "Out, buster."

He shrugged. "Losing interest I'm, anyway. Like Prior Howard," he said, stepping out.

It seemed perfectly natural that this total stranger knew all about Howie. "That one's lost interest in *every*thing," I said.

"Did you think that you Howard killed?" His hand described a capricious fillip in the air. "Howard translated."

"Why are you doing this to me?"

"Expiation. I'm—*was*—the Omaha Ripper. Mind never, you don't want the details."

I already knew them. Who didn't know about the manhunt in Omaha? "Got it," I said; "you're a hallucination. Why aren't you in Nebraska?"

"Good question," he said, and winked from existence without even a pop of displaced air. I drove on, a bit more slowly. My odds-on favorite explanation was that my mind had begun playing tricks. To punish itself, maybe? "Nice try," I told it.

Near Harrisburg I was running low on fuel when Cabot Hawke flagged me down. I was quite cool; I'd half-expected something of the sort. I switched off the motor and lounged back, very much in the driver's seat.

"I'm expiating too," Hawke said with no previous greeting. "I'll even try to speak this ridiculous language in a way that won't spook you."

"Spook is the operative word," I said. "I'll settle down, Hawke. And then I'll be flying high in the number one slot, and with all your motivations peeled away, where will all you poor bastards be?"

"Everywhenandwhere. The Eocene. The Crab Nebula. What's the point of being number one, Jus', when there's no number two?"

"Plenty of folks who don't speak CanAm," I said.

"They don't have to," Hawke said gently. "The message is perfectly clear if you only *listen*, whether you speak Tagalog or Croatian. Or Hohokam. Or if you're newborn or deaf," he said in afterthought. "The vibrations, you see."

I'd never heard of a Hohokam, and that bothered me. How could something be dredged from my subconscious if I'd never heard of it? Oh: I'd simply invented it, like the whole conversation. Simple. "You'll come around," I said pleasantly. "And I'll be waiting."

"I wish you were all that interesting," Hawke said mildly. "Anything I can do to convince you? You're starting to bore me."

My tummy rumbled. "Sure. I could use a ham and cheese on rye, and a cola. Oh, and some fuel."

"Don't wait too long," he said, and turned away. And vanished. In the seat beside me was a thick juicy sandwich and a cola; my fuel gauge read full.

I stayed at an inn on the Susquehanna where the machines had already stopped, and spent a few days unwinding in the Executive Suite. That got to be tiresome; no maid service.

Finally I drove back to Baltimore. My fuel tank is always full, and there's always a sandwich and a cola when I want one.

No one else roams the Delphium complex to keep me from clearing out Hawke's desk for myself, reading his private journals, learning how trivial the sonofabitch thought I was before I showed them all. I keep in shape with a fire ax whenever I find a locked door in Delphium. Or anywhere else in Baltimore. Now and then I see a shimmer of something down a silent hallway, or against a moonlit sky, and it makes me think of great shadowbirds at play.

I keep reminding myself that they'll get tired of it pretty soon. Then they'll have to start all over again at square one. Bottom rung of the ladder. That's my most comforting thought, so I think it a lot. At other times, I reflect on the truth of one of Hawke's old phrases.

It's lonely at the top.

EDITOR'S INTRODUCTION TO:

THROUGH ROAD NO WHITHER

by
Greg Bear

Greg Bear, who in 1984 won two Nebula Awards and a Hugo, is married to Astrid Anderson, whom I literally watched grow up. In defense against the obvious conclusion, I'm tempted to think of Greg as a new writer. Alas, although he's young enough, he's hardly new; he was writing for Galaxy when Jim Baen was editor and I was doing the science column.

I'm not sure why I like this story. It's hardly science fiction. However we have no poetry in this issue; not by my choice. Poetry, in my view, must evoke images but remain understandable.

This story does that . . .

THROUGH ROAD NO WHITHER

Greg Bear

The long black Mercedes rumbled out of the fog on the road south from Dijon, moisture running in cold trickles across its windshield. Horst von Ranke carefully read the maps spread on his lap, eyeglasses perched low on his nose, while Waffen Schutzstaffel Oberleutnant Albert Fischer drove. "Thirty-five kilometers," von Ranke said under his breath. "No more."

"We are lost," Fischer said. "We've already come thirty-six."

"Not quite that many. We should be there any minute now."

Fischer nodded and then shook his head. His high cheekbones and long, sharp nose only accentuated the black uniform with silver death's heads on the high, tight collar. Von Ranke wore a broad-striped gray suit; he was an undersecretary in the Propaganda Ministry. They might have been brothers, yet one had grown up in Czechoslovakia, the other in the Ruhr; one was the son of a coal miner,

211

the other of a brewer. They had met and become close friends in Paris, two years before, and were now sightseeing on a thee-day pass in the country-side.

"Wait," von Ranke said, peering through the drops on the side window. "Stop."

Fischer braked the car and looked in the direction of von Ranke's long finger. Near the roadside, beyond a copse of young trees, was a low thatch-roofed house with dirty gray walls, almost hidden by the fog.

"Looks empty," von Ranke said.

"It is occupied; look at the smoke," Fischer said. "Perhaps somebody can tell us where we are."

They pulled the car over and got out, von Ranke leading the way across a mud path littered with wet straw. The hut looked even dirtier close-up. Smoke curled in a darker brown-gray twist from a hole in the peak of the thatch. Fischer nodded at his friend and they cautiously approached. Over the crude wooden door, letters wobbled unevenly in some alphabet neither knew, and between them they spoke nine languages. "Could that be Rom?" Rischer asked, frowning. "It does look familiar—Slavic Rom."

"Gypsies? Romany don't live in huts like this, and besides, I thought they were rounded up long ago."

"That's what it looks like," von Ranke repeated. "Still, maybe we can share some language, if only French."

He knocked on the door. After a long pause, he knocked again, and the door opened before his knuckles made the final rap. A woman too old to be alive stuck her long, wood-colored nose through

the crack and peered at them with one good eye.
The other was wrapped in a sunken caul of flesh.
The hand that gripped the door edge was filthy, its
nails long and black. Her toothless mouth cracked
into a wrinkled, round-lipped grin. "Good evening,"
she said in perfect, even elegant German. "What
can I do for you?"

"We need to know if we are on the road to
Dôle," von Ranke said, controlling his repulsion.

"Then you're asking the wrong guide," the old
woman said. Her hand withdrew and the door
started to close. Fischer kicked out and pushed it
back. The door swung open and began to lean on
worn-out leather hinges.

"You do not regard us with the proper respect,"
he said. "What do you mean, 'the wrong guide'?
What kind of guide are you?"

"So *strong*," the old woman crooned, wrapping
her hands in front of her withered chest and backing away into the gloom. She wore colorless, age-
less grey rags. Worn knit sleeves extended to her
wrists.

"Answer me!" Fischer said, advancing despite
the strong odor of urine and decay in the hut.

"The maps I know are not for this land," she
sang, stopping before a cold and empty hearth.

"She's crazy," von Ranke said. "Let the local
authorities take care of her later. Let's be off." But
a wild look was in Fischer's eye. So much filth, so
much disarray, and impudence as well; these things
made him angry.

"What maps do you know, crazy woman?" he
demanded.

"Maps in time," the old woman said. She let her
hands fall to her side and lowered her head, as if,

in admitting her specialty, she was suddenly humble.

"Then tell us where we are," Fischer sneered.

"Come," von Ranke said, but he knew it was too late. There would be an end, but it would be on his friend's terms, and it might not be pleasant.

"On a through road no whither," the old woman said.

"What?" Fischer towered over her. She stared up as if at some prodigal son, returned home, her gums shining spittle.

"If you wish a reading, sit," she said, indicating a low table and three tattered cane and leather chairs. Fischer glanced at her, then at the table.

"Very well," he said, suddenly and falsely obsequious. Another game, von Ranke realized. Cat and mouse.

Fischer pulled out a chair for his friend and sat across from the old woman. "Put your hands on the table, palms down, both of them, both of you," she said. They did so. She lay her ear to the table as if listening, eyes going to the beams of light coming through the thatch. "Arrogance," she said. Fischer did not react.

"A road going into fire and death," she said. "Your cities in flame, your women and children shriveling to black dolls in the heat of their burning homes. The camps are found and you stand accused of hideous crimes. Many are tried and hung. Your nations is disgraced, your cause abhorred." Now a peculiar light came into her eye. "And many years later, a comedian will swagger around on stage, in a movie, turning your Führer into a silly clown, singing a silly song. Only psychotics will believe in you, the lowest of the low. Your nation will be divided between your enemies. All will be lost."

Fischer's smile did not waver. He pulled a coin from his pocket and threw it down before the women, then pushed the chair back and stood.

"Your maps are as crooked as your chin, hag," he said. "Let's go."

"I've been suggesting that," von Ranke said. Fischer made no move to leave. Von Ranke tugged on his arm but the SS Oberleutnant shrugged free of his friend's grip.

"Gypsies are few now, hag," he said. "Soon to be fewer by one." Von Ranke managed to urge him just outside the door. The woman followed and shaded her eye against the misty light.

"I am no gypsy," she said. "You do not even recognize the words?" She pointed at the letters above the door.

Fischer squinted, and the light of recognition dawned in his eyes. "Yes," he said. "Yes, I do, now. A dead language."

"What are they?" von Ranke asked, uneasy.

"Hebrew, I think," Fischer said. "She is a Jewess."

"No!" the woman cackled. "I am no Jew."

Von Ranke thought the woman looked younger now, or at least stronger, and his unease deepened.

"I do not care what you are," Fischer said quietly. "I only wish we were in my father's time." He took a step toward her. She did not retreat. Her face became almost youthfully bland, and her bad eye seemed to fill in. "Then, there would be no regulations, no rules—I could take this pistol"— he tapped his holster—"and apply it to your filthy Kike head, and perhaps kill the last Jew in Europe." He unstrapped the holster. The women straightened in the dark hut, as if drawing strength from Fischer's abusive tongue. Von Ranke feared for his friend. Rashness would get them in trouble.

"This is not our fathers' time," he reminded Fischer.

Fischer paused, the pistol half in his hand, his finger curling around the trigger. "Old woman—" Though she did not look half as old, perhaps not even old at all, and certainly not bent and crippled. "You have had a very narrow shave this afternoon."

"You have no idea who I am," the woman half-sang, half-moaned.

"*Scheisse*," Fischer spat. "Now we will go, and report you and your hovel."

"I am the scourge," she breathed, and her breath smelled like burning stone even three strides away. She backed into the hut but her voice did not diminish. "I am the visible hand, the pillar of cloud by day and the pillar of fire by night."

Fischer laughed. "You are right," he said to von Ranke, "she isn't worth our trouble." He turned and stomped out the door. Von Ranke followed, with one last glance over his shoulder into the gloom, the decay. *No one has lived in this hut for years*, he thought. Her shadow was gray and indefinite before the ancient stone hearth, behind the leaning, dust-covered table.

In the car, von Ranke sighed. "You *do* tend toward arrogance, you know that?"

Fischer grinned and shook his head. "You drive, old friend. *I'll* look at the maps." Von Ranke ramped up the Mercedes' turbine until its whine was high and steady and its exhaust cut a swirling hole in the fog behind. "No wonder we're lost," Fischer said. He shook out the Pan-Deutschland map peevishly. "This is five years old—1979."

"We'll find our way," von Ranke said.

From the door of the hut, the old woman watched, head bobbing. "I am not a Jew," she said, "but I loved them, too, oh, yes. I loved all my children." She raised her hand as the long black car roared into the fog.

"I will bring you to justice, whatever line you live upon, and all your children, and their children's children," she said. She dropped a twist of smoke from her elbow to the dirt floor and waggled her finger. The smoke danced and drew black figures in the dirt. "Into the time of your fathers." The fog grew thinner. She brought her arm down, and forty years melted away with the mist.

High above, a deeper growl descended on the road. A wide-winged shadow passed over the hut, wings flashing stars, invasion stripes and cannon fire.

"Hungry bird," the shapeless figure said. "Time to feed."

EDITOR'S INTRODUCTION TO:

INTERSTELLAR TRANSPORT PARADOX
by
Dr. Robert L. Forward

A bit over a year ago the science magazines had new headlines: the IRAS satellite had discovered cold matter in orbit around the star Vega. The satellite's instruments were not good enough to determine whether this was a gas cloud, planets, or an asteroid belt; but the discovery certainly made it more probable that nearly every star has planets.

Many years ago, the Italian physicist Enrico Fermi posed a question: there are ten billion stars in our galaxy. If only a small percent of those have planets, that's still a *lot* of planets. If only a small percent of those planets can support life, there will still be millions that can. If only a small number of those have conditions where life could begin—

He concluded that there was an overwhelming probability that the galaxy contained at least one intelligent species millions of years older than we, and asked: "Where are they?"

Cold matter around Vega makes intelligent life even more probable.

I was thinking about this when Dr. Robert Bussard, one-time director of fusion energy studies at Los Alamos, telephoned about the report of the Citizens Advisory Council on National Space Policy. (The book based on that report is called *Mutual Assured Survival*, Baen Books, 1984). While I had Dr. Bussard on the line I asked him about the implications of the IRAS discovery. He thought for a moment, then raised yet again the Fermi question. The IRAS discovery made it even less likely that humanity was the only intelligent life in the universe, noted that we could think of several ways to cross interstellar distances with present or soon to be developed technology, and answered "Where are they?" thusly: "They've been here, and we're them."

In other words, humanity may not have evolved on Earth.

This seems startling at first; but the American Association for the Advancement of Science had sessions on the crisis in Darwinianism during its 1984 annual meeting, and a number of respectable theorists, including Sir Fred Hoyle, accept the view that mankind's evolution has not followed the hypothesis presented by Darwin. Arrhenius, the Swedish Nobel chemist, seriously proposed the *panspermia* hypothesis: that all life throughout the universe has a common origin, and has spread across interstellar space by light pressure; and evolution may be changed, even be discontinuous, through the invasion of cells from outer space. Sir Fred Hoyle presents a similar but much wilder theory in his book *Evolution From Space*.

All this is pure speculation, of course, although hardly more startling than the notion of a billion-year-old Earth was in its day; and perhaps startling hypotheses may be forgiven when you realize the full magnitude of Fermi's question. The probability is *enormous* that there exist intelligent races *much* older than we; and since we could, even today, make our presence unambiguously known across interstellar distances—why haven't they? Where, indeed, are they?

Dr. Robert L. Forward is a senior scientist at Hughes Research Laboratories. He is one of the world's foremost experts on gravity, receiving his Ph.D. in physics from the University of Maryland. His sponsor was Joe Weber, whose gravity wave detection device started a spate of gravity wave experiments.

He is also a science fiction writer of note. His *Dragon's Egg* was one of the most original science fiction novels ever published. It describes life on a neutron star.

Bob Forward is known for his loud vests, excellent lecture style, and solidly worked out far-out physics. He has done several professional studies of methods of interstellar travel. Herewith his very readable summary of how we may reach the stars.

THE PARADOX
OF
INTERSTELLAR TRANSPORT
Robert L. Forward

THE PARADOX

The few millenia that this squabbling band of naked apes called the human race has been studying the stars is but an instant in the cosmic scale of time. The few decades that we have been trying to communicate with other beings around those stars is but the merest blink in that instant of time. Since we, ourselves, are just developing the technology needed for real astronomy, SETI, and cosmic transport, it seems highly probable that any other race with which we make contact will have a technology that is thousands or millions of years ahead of ours.

If we can build large radio telescopes that can transmit and receive radio signals over hundreds of light years distance, then those more advanced races will have larger radio dishes, more powerful transmitters, and more sensitive receivers that can communicate between galaxies. (If they have a truly advanced technology, they may also have neutrino, and/or gravitational, and/or twistor, and/or who-knows-what-other communication systems.) Yet we have listened for radio signals from the stars and we hear nothing. As Fermi said so succinctly many years ago, "Where are they?"

If we can imagine at least one form of interstellar transport, be it expensive and slow, then surely they will have many forms of interstellar transport. Some methods will use physical principles that we are familiar with. Other methods will use machines that work by some form of "magic" that we will understand only millions of years from now. Surely, if we can dream about travel to the nearest stars, then they are exploring the galaxy. If so, where are they?

This paradox of the absence of evidence for extraterrestrial beings is one of the major unsolved questions of science. The journals and the technical press contain article after article about the paradox. It is not necessary that the aliens come to visit us in person, their robotic probes could do the job equally as well, but we see no evidence of robots either.

Some writers cite the absence of extraterrestrial visitors as proof that intelligent life has only formed once, and like-it-or-not, we are that lone example of "intelligence" in the universe. They feel that it takes a remarkably fortuitous accident to create life, especially intelligent life.

It may be that it is difficult for life to start, but it is strange that the precursors of life forms, the amino acids, are found in meteorites and the dust of interstellar space. It may be that it is difficult for intelligent life to form, but that argument is denied by the fact that intelligent life has developed from primitive life forms *twice* on this planet.

At one time in the distant past the earth had only primitive forms of life, the most advanced being clumps of cells. An example of these primitive life forms exists today, called the hydra. The hydra consists of a few hundred cells formed into a foot, a gut, some tendrils, and a few primitive reflexes. The hydra spawned two separate species, the vertebrates with interior stiffening (worms) and the mollusks with exterior stiffening (clams). A human is the intelligent descendent of the worm family and the octopus is the intelligent descendent of the clam family. The octopus brain is a five-lobed ring around the food intake, while the human brain is a two-lobed lump on top of the food intake. The eyes of the two species look similar, but each was developed independently. It might be argued that an octopus is not yet smart enough to be called an intelligent being, but given a world without men to hunt them, a long dry spell to put stress on them, and a few million years to evolve some more, and you would see intelligent air-breathing octopods designing starships to travel the galaxy. Thus, from our own experience, once any kind of life has formed, intelligent life is not long in coming.

The paradox remains, and every time a new method of interstellar communication or transport is invented, the paradox becomes worse. I will not discuss further the pros and cons of the Fermi Paradox. There are others better qualified to do that. Instead, I will do what I have been doing for the past few decades, making the paradox worse by finding new methods by which mere humans, with their pitifully meager control of the forces of nature, can hope to aspire to godhood by traveling to the stars.

INTERSTELLAR TRANSPORT

It is difficult to go to the stars. They are far away, and the speed of light limits us to a slow crawl along the starlanes. Decades and centuries will pass before the stay-at-homes learn what the explorers have found. The energies required to launch a manned interstellar transport are enormous, for the mass to be accelerated is large and the speed must be high. Yet even these energies are not out of the question once we move our technology out into space where the constantly flowing sunlight is a never-ending source of energy—over a kilowatt per square meter, a gigawatt per square kilometer.

The first travelers to the stars will be our robotic probes. They will be small and won't require all the amenities like food, air, and water that humans seem to find necessary. The power levels to send the first flyby probes are within the present reach of the human race. If we wanted to, we could have the first interstellar probe on the way before the present millennium is out.

What kind of starships can we envision? It turns out there are many, each using a different technology. We will first discuss those starships that we know how to build now. They use nuclear pulse propulsion, antimatter propulsion, and microwave and laser beamed power propulsion. For these technologies we know the basic physical principles and have demonstrated the capability to achieve the desired reactions on a small scale. All that is needed for the design, engineering, and construction of the starship is the application of large amounts of money, material, and manpower. Later we will discuss some promising designs that use controlled fusion. Here we know the basic physical principles, but we have not yet achieved the desired controlled reaction in the laboratory. Once these experiments are successful, then we can proceed with starship designs based on fusion technology.

NUCLEAR PULSE PROPULSION

Although we do not yet have controlled fusion, we are experts on uncontrolled fusion—fusion bombs. The oldest design for an interstellar vehicle is one that is propelled by nuclear bombs. Called the "Orion" spacecraft, it was invented in the late fifties at Los Alamos National Lab. The original goal was to send manned spacecraft to Mars and Venus by 1968 at a fraction of the cost of the Apollo project.

The Orion vehicle works by ejecting a small fusion bomb out the rear of the vehicle where the bomblet explodes. The debris from the explosion strikes a "pusher plate", which absorbs the impulse from the explosion and transfers it through large "shock absorbers" to the main spacecraft. Freeman Dyson took these ideas for an interplanetary spacecraft and extrapolated them to an interstellar spacecraft. The ship would necessarily be large, with a payload of some 20,000 metric tons (enough to support many hundred crewmembers). The total mass would be 400,000 tons, including a fuel supply of 300,000 fusion bombs weighing about 1 ton each (a 4:1 mass ratio). The bombs would be exploded once every three seconds, accelerating the spacecraft at 1 earth gravity for 10 days to reach a velocity of 1/30th of the speed of light. At this speed the Orion spacecraft would reach Alpha Centauri in 130 years. To give this ship a deceleration capability at the target star, it would need to be redesigned to have two stages, with the first stage weighing 1,600,000 tons.

Although the Orion spacecraft has a minimal performance for a starship, it is one form of interstellar transport that could have been built and sent on its way in the last decade. The reason for the relatively poor performance of the Orion vehicle is that it uses the rocket principle, where the vehicle is required to carry its own propulsion energy and reaction mass along with it. Thus, unless we are willing to consider enormous mass ratios, the terminal velocity achievable is roughly equal to the exhaust velocity, which in turn is proportional to the square root of the fraction of the mass of the fuel that is converted into energy. Since a fusion reaction converts less than 1% of its mass into energy, the exhaust velocity is limited to 3% or so. If we are going to use the rocket concept for interstellar transport, we will need a nuclear fuel that has a higher energy conversion efficiency than fusion.

ANTIPROTON PROPULSION

Antimatter represents a highly concentrated form of energy with the ability to release "200%" of its rest mass as energy when it annihilates with an equal amount of normal matter. A spacecraft which uses antimatter as its source of propulsion energy could "drive" anywhere in the solar system with mission times ranging from days to weeks, and could even travel to the nearest stars in a small fraction of a human lifetime. The antimatter should be in the form of antiprotons (or antihydrogen) since upon annihilation with the protons in normal hydrogen, most of the annihilation energy appears not as gamma rays, but as charged particles, called pions. The pions are moving at 94% of the speed of light and live long enough to travel for 21 meters. This interaction length is long enough for the pions to be channeled from an isotropic explosion into directed thrust by a rocket nozzle made of magnetic fields. For mission velocities less than half the speed of light, the energy from the antimatter should be used to heat a much larger amount of reaction mass. For example, to accelerate a 1 ton interstellar flyby robotic probe to 1/10th the speed of light requires 4 tons of liquid hydrogen for the reaction mass and 9 kilograms of antihydrogen for the energy source.

Most people are not aware of it, but antiprotons are being produced and stored for days at a time at the particle physics accelerator at CERN in Switzerland. Other antiproton facilities are under construction in the USA and USSR. The present production efficiencies are very low, parts in a million, but techniques exist to increase the production efficiencies by orders of magnitude. CERN has already demonstrated the production of antihydrogen by combining antiprotons with antielectrons (positrons).

Containing the antimatter is not a serious problem. Scientists working with atomic and molecular beams have already experimentally demonstrated methods for slowing, cooling, trapping, and storing atoms by the use of lasers, electric fields, and magnetic fields. In the coming decades we will see the production and storage of significant quantities of antimatter. The first uses will be for space travel within the solar system, but if no other propulsion system proves to be better and we wish to spend the time and money needed to generate the kilograms of antimatter needed, then one of these days we can ride to the stars on a jet of annihilated matter-antimatter.

Although an antimatter rocket is the ultimate in rockets, it is not necessary to use the rocket principle to build a starship. A rocket consists of payload, structure, reaction mass, and energy source. (In most rockets the reaction mass and energy source are combined together into the chemical or nuclear "fuel"). Because a rocket has to carry its fuel with it, its performance is significantly limited. It is possible to build a spacecraft that does not have to carry along any fuel, and consists only of payload and structure. Two versions that could be built with "reasonable" extrapolations of present day technology are a microwave-beam-pushed wire mesh probe and a laser-beam-pushed lightsail.

STARWISP

Starwisp is a light-weight, high-speed interstellar flyby probe pushed by beamed microwaves. The basic structure is a wire mesh sail with microcircuits at each intersection. The mesh sail is driven at high acceleration using a microwave beam formed by a large fresnel-zone-plate transmitter lens made of alternating sparse metal mesh rings and blank rings. The high acceleration allows Starwisp to reach a coast velocity near that of light while still close to the transmitting lens. Upon arrival at the target star, the transmitter floods the star system with microwave energy. Using the wires as microwave antennas, the microcircuits collect energy to power their optical detectors and logic circuits to form images of the planets in the system. The phase of the incident microwaves is sensed at each point of the mesh and the phase information used to form the mesh into a retrodirective phased array microwave antenna that beams a signal back to earth.

A minimal Starwisp would be a 1 kilometer mesh sail weighing 16 grams and carrying 4 grams of microcircuits. Starwisp would be accelerated at 115 gravities by a 10 GW microwave beam, reaching $\frac{1}{5}$ the speed of light in a few days. Upon arrival at Alpha Centauri 21 years later, Starwisp would collect enough microwave power to return a high resolution picture every three minutes during its fly-through of the system.

Because of its very small mass, the beamed power level needed to drive a minimal Starwisp is about that planned for the microwave power output of a solar power satellite. Thus, if power satellites are constructed in the next few decades, they could be used to launch one or more Starwisp probes to the nearer stars during their "checkout" phase. Once the Starwisp probes have found interesting planets, then we can use another form of beamed power propulsion to visit them. Although microwave beams can only be used to "push" a spacecraft away from the solar system, if we go to laser wavelengths, then it is possible to design a laser beamed power propulsion system that can use the laser power from the solar system to make the return journey.

LASER-PUSHED LIGHTSAILS

Still another method for traveling to the stars would use large sails of light-reflecting material pushed by the photon pressure from a large laser array in orbit around the sun. With this technique we can build a manned spacecraft that not only can travel at reasonable speeds to the nearest stars, but can also stop, then return its crew back to earth again within their lifetime. It will be some time before our engineering capabilities in space will be up to building the laser system needed, but there is no new physics involved, just a large scale engineering extrapolation of known technologies.

The lasers would be in orbit around Mercury to keep them from being "blown" away by the reaction from their light beams. They would use the abundant sunlight at Mercury's orbit to produce coherent laser light, which would be collected into a single coherent beam and sent out to a transmitter lens floating between Saturn and Uranus. The transmitter lens would be a fresnel-zone-plate lens tuned to the laser frequency and consisting of rings of one micron thick plastic film alternating with empty rings. The fresnel lens would be 1000 kilometers in diameter and weight about 560,000 tons. A lens this size can send a beam of laser light over 40 lightyears before the beam starts to spread. The lightsail would be 1000 kilometers in diameter and made of thin aluminum film stretched over supporting structure. The total weight will be 80 tons, including 3,000 tons for the crew, their habitat, their supplies, and their exploration vehicles. The lightsail would be accelerated at 0.3 gravities by 43,000 TW of power (for comparison, the earth now produces about 1 TW of power). At this acceleration, the lightsail will reach a velocity of half the speed of light in 1.6 years. The expedition will reach Epsilon Eridani in 20 years earth time and 17 years crew time. AT 0.4 lightyears from the star, the 320 kilometer rendezvous portion of the sail is detached from the center of the lightsail and turned to face the large ring sail that remains. The laser light from the solar system reflects from the ring sail which acts as a retro-directive mirror. The reflected light decelerates the smaller rendezvous sail and brings it to a halt in the Epsilon Eridani system. After the crew explores the system for a few years (using their lightsail as a solar sail), it will be time to bring them back. To do this, a 100 kilometer diameter return sail is separated out from the center of the 320 kilometer rendezvous sail. The laser light from the solar system hits the ring-shaped remainder of the rendezvous sail and is reflected back on the return sail, sending it on its way back to the solar system. As the return sail approaches the solar system 20 earth-years later, it is brought to a halt by a final burst of laser power. The members of the crew have been away 51 years (including 5 years of exploring), have aged 46 years, and are ready to retire and write their memoirs.

FUSION ROCKETS

Once we have achieved controlled fusion in the laboratory, then we can start designing an interstellar rocket based on those types of reactors that turn out to be feasible.

If we achieve controlled fusion by compression and heating of a plasma in a magnetic bottle, then perhaps all we need to do to convert the reactor into a rocket is to allow the magnetic bottle to "leak" a little bit, and the hot plasma exhaust will produce thrust.

If we achieve controlled fusion by implosion of micropellets with beams of laser light, electrons, ions, or high speed pellets, then the same technique can be used to implode the pellets in the throat of a rocket nozzle made of magnetic fields, which will turn the isotropically exploding plasma into directed thrust.

Since the (D-T) reaction presently being used in both the containment and implosion fusion research projects involves the use of tritium, interstellar rocket systems using this reaction must have a method of generating this radioactive material (lifetime of 12.3 years) on board. Alternatively, additional work on containment and implosion fusion techniques could produce the pressures, temperatures, and densities needed to achieve fusion with $D-He^3$, D-D, or p-p reactions.

INTERSTELLAR RAMJET

One of the oldest interstellar transport techniques, and a favorite of science fiction writers, is the Bussard interstellar ramjet. The interstellar ramjet consists of the payload, a fusion reactor, and a large scoop to collect the hydrogen atoms in space. The hydrogen atoms are used as fuel in the fusion reactor, where the fusion energy is released and the energy fed back in some manner into the reaction products (usually helium atoms) which provides the thrust for the vehicle. Bussard originally estimated that a 1,000 ton vehicle would require a frontal intake area of about 10,000 km^2 to achieve a one gravity acceleration through interstellar space with a density of 1000 hydrogen atoms per cubic centimeter. The ramjet "take-over" velocity is extremely low, so that conventional chemical rockets could provide the initial acceleration. As the vehicle increases its velocity into the relativistic region, the interstellar fuel flow appears to increase in density due to the Lorentz contraction in the vehicle's space-time.

If an interstellar ramjet could ever be built, it would have many advantages over other possible starships. Since it never runs out of fuel like fuel-carrying rockets, and never runs away from its source of fuel like beamed-power systems, it can accelerate indefinitely. It is the only known system that can reach the ultra-relativistic velocities where shiptime becomes orders of magnitude longer than earth-time, allowing human crews to travel throughout the galaxy or even between galaxies in a single human lifetime.

A lot of invention and research is needed, however, before the Bussard interstellar ramjet becomes a reality. We first must achieve controlled fusion. The fusion reactor must not only be lightweight and long-lived, it must be able to fuse protons, not the easier-to-ignite mixture of deuterium and tritium. The reactor must be able to fuse the incoming protons *without slowing them down*, or the frictional loss of bringing the fuel to a halt, fusing it, and reaccelerating the reaction products will put an undesirable upper limit on the maximum velocity attainable. Then there is the matter of the scoop, which must be ultra-large and ultra-light. If the interstellar hydrogen were ionized, then a large, super-strong magnet might be sufficient to scoop up the charged protons. Although some stars have clouds of ionized hydrogen near them, most of the hydrogen near the solar system is neutral. Schemes for ionizing the hydrogen have been proposed but they are not light in weight or low in power consumption.

Thus, for now, the interstellar ramjet remains in the category of science fiction. The concept of picking up your fuel along the way as you journey through "empty" space is too valuable to be discarded lightly, however, and I hope that future scientists and engineers will keep working away on the remaining problems until this beautiful concept turns into a real starship.

CONCLUSION

It is difficult to go to the stars, but it is not impossible. There are not one, but a number of technologies, all under intensive development for other purposes, that, if suitably modified and redirected, can give the human race a flight system that will reach the nearest stars.

Thus, we are left with the ultimate question: If we, who just recently climbed down from the trees, are now climbing up to the stars, where are all the others more ancient than we?

BIBLIOGRAPHY

"The Fermi Paradox: A Forum for Discussion", J. Brit. Interplanetary Soc. 32, 424-434 (1979).

Bussard, R.W., "Galactic Matter and Interstellar Flight," *Astronautica Acta* 6, 179-194 (1960).

Dyson, F.J., "Interstellar Transport", *Physics Today*, 41-45 (Oct 1968).

Forward, R.L., "A Programme for Interstellar Exploration", J. Brit. Interplanetary Soc. 29, 611-632 (1976).

——, "Interstellar Flight Systems", AIAA Paper 80-0823 (May 1980).

——, "Antimatter Propulsion", J. Brit. Interplanetary Soc. 35, 391-395 (1982).

——, "Round-trip Interstellar Travel by Laser-Pushed Lightsails", J. Spacecraft & Rockets (to be published).

Hyde, R., Wood, L., and Nuckolls, J., "Prospects for Rocket Propulsion with Laser Induced Fusion Microexplosions", AIAA Paper 72-1063 (Dec 1972).

Mallove, E.F., Forward, R.L., Paprotny, Z., and Lehmann, J., "Interstellar Travel and Communication: A Bibliography", J. Brit. Interplanetary Soc. 33, 201-248 (Jun 1980).

Martin, A.R. (ed.), Project Daedalus, Supplement to J. Brit. Interplanetary Soc. (1978).

Morgan, D.L., "Concepts for the Design of an Antimatter Annihilation Rocket", J. Brit. Interplanetary Soc. 35, 405-412 (1982).

Paprotny, Z. and Lehmann, J., "Interstellar Travel

and Communication Bibliography; 1982 Update", J. Brit. Interplanetary Soc. 36 311-329 (1983).

Sänger, E., "The Theory of Photon Rockets", *Ing. Arch.* 21, 213ff (1953) (in German).

Tipler, F.J., "Extraterrestrial Intelligent Beings Do Not Exist", QJRAS 22, 267 (1980).

Winterberg, F., "Rocket Propulsion by Thermonuclear Micro-Bombs Ignited with Intense Relativistic Electron Beams", *Raumfahrtforschung* 5, 208-217 (Sept-Oct 1971) (in English).

PRIDE

by
Poul Anderson

Many years ago, at the request of our editor Bob Gleason, Larry Niven and I plotted a novel about an alien invasion of Earth. It would have been our third novel.

Larry Niven takes pride in his "hard science" approach to science fiction, as indeed he should. He began writing during the heyday of the anti-scientific movement known as "the New Wave," and he likes to think that hard science writers were discriminated against in that era. He isn't entirely correct: what happened was that some new markets had opened up, and *those* were dominated by New Wave writers; but the older markets continued to look for people who knew how to write the hard stuff—people like Poul Anderson.

However: both Larry and I were known as hard science writers. It was thus inevitable that any invasion novel we wrote would be as utterly realistic as we could make it. It was clear that the invaders must come from another star. If they have the ability to cross interstellar distances, they *must* have the capability to move large asteroids; and if they intended an invasion of Earth, what better way to soften us up than to hit us with a mucking great rock?

The asteroid strike was a key event of our outline when we sent it to Gleason. A few days later came a telephone call: "Forget the aliens. Concentrate on that asteroid!" Thus was born *Lucifer's Hammer*.

We made some changes. First, we postulated a comet rather than an asteroid. This wasn't for any scientific reason: it was just that you could see a comet coming, and a good part of the novel takes place before the disaster. Second, we needed a reason for the comet to hit us. Now, true, we could merely let it happen; after all, the Tunguska event early in this century was probably a comet strike. On the other hand, we don't work that way; so we invented an undiscovered companion to the Sun, a dark planet described this way:

The comets were not alone in the halo.

Local eddies near the center of the maelstrom—that whirlwind of gas which finally collapsed to form the Sun—had condensed into planets. The furious heat of the newly formed star had stripped the gas envelopes from the nearest, leaving nuggets of molten rock and iron. Worlds farther out had remained as great balls of gas which men would, in a billion years, name for their gods. There had also been eddies very distant from the whirlpool's axis.

One had formed a planet the size of Saturn, and it was still gathering mass. Its rings were broad and beautiful in starlight. Its surface churned with storms, for its center was furiously hot with the energy of its collapse. Its enormous orbit was tilted almost vertically to the plane of the inner system, and its stately path through the cometary halo took hundreds of thousands of years to complete.

Sometimes a comet would stray too near the black giant and be swept into its ring, or into the thousands of miles of atmosphere. Sometimes that tremendous mass would pluck a comet from its orbit and swing it out into interstellar space, to be lost forever. And sometimes the black planet would send a comet plunging into the maelstrom and hellfire of the inner system.

They moved in slow, stable orbits, these myriads of comets that had survived the ignition of the Sun. But when the black giant passed, orbits became chaos. Comets that fell into the maelstrom might return partially vaporized, and fall back, again and again, until nothing was left but a cloud of stones. But many never returned at all.

At the AAAS meeting in San Francisco in 1979, Luis Alverez announced that Lucifer's Hammer had probably killed the dinosaurs: that is, there was a lot of good evidence that a large object, comet or asteroid, had struck the Earth and caus[ed] massive extinctions, with the dinosaurs as its m[ost] spectacular victims. Although Alverez never use[d] the phrase "Lucifer's Hammer" in print, other[s] did. Larry Niven and I preened.

Then, in March 1984, we got a telephone call from Al Jackson of the Computer Science Corporation. He and his colleagues had published a paper speculating that the Sun has a dark companion, on a very long and very eccentric orbit which periodically carries it through the cometary halo. At intervals of about 26 million years it sends showers of comets down into the solar system. This bombardment explains not only the dinosaur die-off, but the periodic extinctions which have long puzzled paleobiologists. Jackson and his colleagues had used modern computers to look at possible orbits for such a companion. He also said that *Hammer* had been one of the influences that inspired him to think in terms of a companion.

What he wanted to know was, had Larry Niven and I named the dark companion we'd postulated in Lucifer's Hammer? Because if we had, there was some chance that name could be made to stick.

Alas, we hadn't named it. I don't suppose we'll ever get another chance like that.

The news about the Sun's companion broke early in 1984. We received this story from Poul Anderson with a letter dated May 12, 1984. It didn't take him long not only to design a possible dark companion to the Sun, but also to think of a whacking good story about the people who go to look at it.

One of the claims made by the New Wave was that traditional hard science fiction writers paid too much attention to science, and too little to character development.

They couldn't possibly have been reading much of Poul Anderson, who has always given us real people as well as real science.

PRIDE

Poul Anderson

Suddenly Nemesis exploded.

It happened just in time to quench an eruption within the watchful spaceship. The forces of violence had been gathering in men even as they did in the half-star. Mortal time-spans were smaller; but a pair of years, passing through darkness, had grown weary, and then months amidst strangenesses and dangers laid their own further pressures on the spirit. Dermot Byrne crowed a boast, Jan Cronje could no longer keep silence, the hostility between them broke free and a fight was at hand.

Accident touched off the trouble, though something of the kind had been likely at some point during the years remaining before *Anna Lovinda* would come back to Earth orbit. Neither man was a fool. Since their friendship broke, they had tacitly avoided each other as much as possible. Maybe Cronje supposed Byrne was with Suna Rudbeck, in the cabin they now shared, or maybe—seeking to forget for a moment—he didn't think about it at all. He was never sure afterward. Whatever else was on his mind, he entered the wardroom to get a cup of refreshment and a little conversation, perhaps a game of chess or somebody who would come along with him to the gymnasium and play handball. At the entrance, he stopped. There Byrne was.

Several other off-duty people were present also, benched around the table or standing nearby. Conversation was general. Coffee and tea made the air fragrant. Music lilted out of speakers in bulkheads softly tinted, where there hung scenes from home that were often changed. Garments were loose, colorful, chosen by their wearers. Folk needed every such comfort.

Not that they huddled away from the universe. As if to declare that, a large viewscreen was always tuned, like a window on space save that its nonreflecting surface left the scene clear despite interior lighting. Stars crowded blackness, icy-bright and unwinking. They streamed slowly past vision as the ship rotated.

Byrne was speaking. He was a slender young man, eyes brilliant blue and features regular, very fair-skinned, beneath a shock of dark hair, a Gaelic melody in his Swedish. A planetologist, he was lately back from his second expedition to the fourth satellite of Nemesis, an Earth-sized world on which his had been the first footprint ever made. "The wonder, the beauty, those will never be coming through in our reports, no matter how many pictures we print. Sure, and this crew ought to have included a poet. But they have no imagination in Stockholm."

"They've got enough to dispatch us," laughed Ezra Lee, the senior astrophysicist. "Oh, the Control Authority did begrudge the cost—"

"Keeping world peace has not yet become cheap," murmured engineer Gottfried Vogel in his mild fashion.

"Just the same, it took more politicking than it should have, to get a few people out here," said Byrne. "Had not the probes already told of miracles for the finding?"

Nemesis rose at the left edge of the screen. At a distance of more than a million kilometers, it blotted out most stars with hugeness rather than brilliance. Red-hot from the slow contraction of its monstrous mass, Sol's companion did not dazzle eyes that looked upon it. Instead, that glow brought to sight an intricacy of bands, swirls, murk-spots, sparkles—clouds, maelstroms, lightnings. God could have cast Earth into any of those storms and not made so much as a splash. A moon glimmered near the limb; a billion kilometers from the giant, it was itself the size of Saturn.

"Ah, well, we *are* here," Byrne went on. Happiness radiated from him. "The scientific discoveries are only one part of the marvel. This world where I've been—Suna wants to call it Vanadis, and I Fand, but no great matter that, for each of us means a goddess of love and beauty."

"A frozen waste," said Minna Veijola. But of course she was a biologist, enraptured by the life (life!) on the innermost satellite.

"It is not," Byrne replied. "That is what I'm trying to explain to the lot of you. Oh, doubtless barren. Yet the play of light on ice mountains— Ask Suna," he blurted. "That was what finally brought us together, she and I, after we'd first landed. The faerie beauty everywhere around us."

Jan Cronje stepped through the doorway. "I do not believe that," he said hoarsely. "You were sneaking and sniffing around her before the voyage was half over. You wheedled her into being your pilot on that survey, the two of you alone. Yes, it was nicely planned."

Silence clapped down. Through it, Cronje's boots made a dead-march drumbeat as he moved onward. He was a big man, and spin provided a full gravity of weight. Blunt of countenance, sandy-haired, ruddy-bearded, he had gone quite pale.

Byrne sprang to his feet. "It was not!" he cried. "It . . . it only happened."

Cronje grinned. "Ha!" His Afrikaans accent harshened. "It was far on the way to happening by that time. If you had been an honorable man, you would have gotten another pilot for yourself. Me, for instance. I had not seen what you were up to. But no, it was my wife you wanted."

Byrne flushed. "You insult her. She was never mine for the taking, nor yours for the keeping. She's a free human being who made her own choice."

Cronje reached him. "I could stand that, somehow," he said. "Until now, when you started bragging before everybody." His left hand shot out, grabbed the other's tunic, hauled him close. "No more, do you hear?"

"Let me go, you lout!" Byrne yelled. His fists doubled.

"Jan, please." Veijola plucked at Cronje's sleeve. Although they were good friends, he didn't seem to notice.

Lee gestured at a couple of men. They left their places and moved to intervene, should this come to blows. A brawl, in the loneliness everywhere around, could have unthinkable aftermaths.

And then— It was mere coincidence. Providence surely has better concerns than our angers. But Nemesis exploded.

A yell brought heads around toward the screen. Shouts tumbled out of the intercom as crew throughout the ship saw, or heard from those who saw. The red disc shuddered. Cloud bands ripped apart, vortices shattered, waves of ruin ran from either pole until they met at the equator and re-coiled in chaos. Then every feature vanished in rose-pearly pallor. Visibly to unaided eyes, the disc swelled. Star after star disappeared behind smoki-ness.

It was Lee, the astrophysicist, who lurched across the deck, stunned. "Already?" he gasped. "Just like that? The fire lit and—and Nemesis turning back into a star?"

Erik Telander, captain of *Anna Lovinda*, mounted the stage. With chairs set forth, the gymnasium became the general meeting room. A dozen faces looked up at him. Six more people were on station in case of emergency. Two, a pilot and a plan-etologist, had flitted off in one of the boats to yet another of the worlds that circled, like the ship, around the primary orb. Only such a pair ever went off on such a preliminary exploration. The unknowns were too many for the risking of a larger number. Twenty-one men and women were all too few at this uttermost bound of the Solar System.

Telander smiled. He was a lean, slightly grizzled

man who seemed older than his actual years. "Well, ladies and gentlemen," he said, "we have had quite a surprise in the past several hours. And it appears that surprises are continuing. The task immediately before us is to decide what we should do. Although that decision must, of course, ultimately be mine, I want to base it on your knowledge and your ideas; for I am a single person among you, without the special knowledge and skills you variously possess. Frankly, my first impulse was to direct that we cut loose from *Gertrud* and blast off to a safe distance. Ezra Lee convinced me this was neither necessary nor even wise, at least for the moment. I would like him to describe the situation for you as he sees it. No doubt the data that the instruments have been—are—collecting will cause him to modify, already now, what he said to me." He beckoned. "If you please."

Lee rose. "You're all familiar with the theory, at least in general outline," said his flat Midwestern American tones. "I trust you're also aware how incomplete that theory is, how little we really know for sure about Nemesis. It could hardly be otherwise, across a gap of more than two light-years, when the object is so dim at best, and unique in human observation. Still, I suggest you take a minute to review for yourselves what you've been told. Get it as clear as possible in your minds. Then, if nothing else, you can ask me intelligent questions." He chuckled; teeth flashed against the dark brown skin. "Not that I guarantee to have any intelligent answers."

Humor died away. It was as if the silence that followed grew echoful of thoughts.

Nemesis, long-unseen companion of Sol, it was

your murderousness that finally betrayed your existence to our species and made us search the skies for you. No, but "murderousness" is wrong. You are not alive; you are as innocent as a thunderbolt.

Yet every six-and-twenty million years your orbit brings you within 10,000 astronomical units of our sun. Passing through its Oort cloud, you trouble the comets there. Many fall inward, whipping around the star, perhaps for millennia, until their dust and ice are boiled off, the brightness is gone, only rocks that were in the cores remain. Some collide with planets or moons. Earth takes its share of that celestial barrage. Each cycle, one or more of those smiting masses is of asteroidal size. Continents tremble under the blow. Cast-up smoke and vapor darken the air for months. In such a Fimbul Winter, first the plants die, next the beasts; and when at last heaven clears again, the survivors begin a whole new order of things.

Thus did you slay the last dinosaurs at the end of the Cretaceous period, Nemesis, and with them the ammonites and . . . more kinds of life than endured. Thus did you kill the great mammals of the Miocene. And before these massacres there had been others, throughout the ages, but time has eroded their traces until they have become well-nigh as hard to find as you yourself, Nemesis.

That path of yours is not the least of the strangenesses about you. Neighbor stars should long since have drawn you away. Can they be what gave your track the form it has, so that only in the past billion years have you been launching your bombardments, and a billion years hence they will have ceased? Perhaps we shall learn the answer, now that we are at the end of a quest which took lifetimes of our evanescent kind.

A tiny, coal-red point afar, for which our finest spaceborne instruments sought through year after year before we knew . . . a flickering too faint and irregular for us to say more than that it takes about a decade from peak to peak . . . mass, as reported by our unmanned craft, slightly in excess of 80 times Jupiter's, which means well over 25,000 times Earth's . . . a family of attendants . . . tokens of a fire within, that kindles and goes out and kindles again, like the heartbeat of a man who lies dying. . . .

Minna Veijola raised her hand. "Question!"

"Be my guest," Lee said. "Maybe whoever wants to speak from the floor should rise, like me. We're too many for real conversation."

The biologist obeyed. Jan Cronje, beside whom she had seated herself, came out of his sullenness enough to give her a glance that lingered, as did several other men. While small and somewhat stocky, she had the blond, slanty-eyed, high-cheeked good looks common among Finns. "I don't want to be an alarmist," she said. "I'll take your word that we are in no immediate danger. But this is quite out of my field of competence. Furthermore, you'll understand that I am bound to wonder and worry about effects on my beloved life-bearing satellite. Could you please explain what it is we have to expect?"

Lee shrugged. "Yonder life doesn't seem to be hurt any by outbursts like this. After all, they've been going on for gigayears."

"My colleagues and I have scarcely begun basic taxonomy and chemical analysis, let alone comprehend how evolution works there. I—very well, I'll say it, because it must be gnawing at others besides me. We're only a million-odd kilometers from Nemesis. If it's become a star again, even the faintest of red dwarfs, aren't we likely to get a blast of hard radiation from it?"

"I remember telling you, dear, rock specimens we've taken show no effects of anything but cosmic and planetary background," Dermot Byrne said.

"Why not? Ezra, you admit that what's happened was quite unexpected. How can you predict what will happen next?"

The astrophysicist ran fingers across the black wool on his scalp. "I thought we'd been over this ground abundantly, both in training and in talk en route," he said. "But, I suppose, on so long a voyage, in so cramped an environment, I guess everybody tended to get wrapped up in his or her main interests, and forget a lot. Certainly some of what you've had to tell me about your discoveries, Minna, has gone straight by me.

"And among the surprises was the timing of this event. Observing it at close range is a principal objective of ours, of course. Nevertheless, we've been caught pretty flat-footed. Past observations and theoretical studies indicated the system wouldn't go critical for at least another year. Well, it *is* a complex and little-understood thing, and we did know the periodicity is very far from exact. I'm afraid we're going to lose quite a bit of information we'd hoped to gather, because we weren't yet properly prepared."

He drew breath. "Okay. Please bear with me while I repeat some elementary facts. It's just to identify those of them that I think are important in making the kind of short-range predictions you're asking about, Minna.

"We know Nemesis is the first example ever actually found of a so-called brown dwarf. Its mass is right at the borderline between planet and star. Gravitational contraction heats it—like Jupiter, but on a far bigger scale, so that the outer layers of gas have a temperature approaching a thousand kelvin. Near the core, heat and pressure naturally go higher by many orders of magnitude. At last collapse brings them to the point where thermonuclear reactions begin. The star-fires are lighted.

"But you can see how quickly this sends the core temperatures skyrocketing. This in turn makes the inner layers expand. Pressure drops below the critical point; the thermonuclear reactions turn off. The body as a whole expands for a while longer on momentum and interior heat, then starts falling in on itself again—and so the cycle recommences.

"I repeat my apology for rehearsing what everybody well knows, but I do believe we need to have the information marshalled before us. You see, as usual, reality turns out to be more complicated than theory. That's why we're here, isn't it? To take a good, hard, close-up look.

"Now. You people surely remember that astronomical instruments and orbiting probes have shown rather slight variation in surface temperature or emission, and scarcely anything in the way of X-rays. Nor does Nemesis have a Van Allen belt worth mentioning, in spite of its terrific magnetic field. It's too far out to collect solar wind particles, and it puts forth scarcely any of its own. The reason isn't far to seek. That enormous mass absorbs everything from the nuclear burning. The fires never get intense enough to cause more than some heating and expansion of the outer layers.

"Because of that very expansion, and its cooling effect, the emission temperature—what we actually sense—doesn't increase much. In fact, we think that at maximum diameter Nemesis is actually a bit cooler than it was when this ship arrived. Granted, by then the fires have already gone out.

"That's why we're in no danger."

Veijola shook her head stubbornly. "Yes, I knew," she replied. "You miss the point I was trying to make. You did not expect this ... this sudden outburst. Quite aside from its timing, the experts have told me—I do remember my indoctrination—they told me expansion would be slow, and not begin until well after the nuclear reactions did. Therefore, could you please explain why you are so confident about the future?" She sat down and waited.

A sigh went through the assembly. Telander himself threw Lee an inquiring glance.

The American's smile was rueful. "I truly am sorry," he said. "As flustered as I've been, I seem to've taken for granted that people in different lines of work were worse confused. Let me make what amends I can by giving you what new information my department has gathered.

"There is no doubt that fusion has begun at the core. Our neutrino detectors are going crazy. Just what is happening in there—what chain or chains of nuclear conversion—we don't yet know. We do have indications of an unpredicted quantity of metals, and this is bound to affect the course of events. I believe that when we have enough data, and have analyzed them, we'll also get an idea of why Nemesis pulsates so irregularly.

"As for that expansion—which some of you saw at the time and the rest of you, I'm sure, have seen on replay—as for it, yes, it was unforeseen too. Suddenly the apparent diameter of the body increased by about seven percent. Well, Mamoru"— Lee nodded toward his associate Hayashi—"soon came up with what I think is the right notion.

"When the core caught fire, it was like a bomb with yield in the gigatons going off. No, more likely several bombs, at once or in quick succession. Shock waves, powerful enough to tear Earth apart, propagated out through the mass above. The globe is flattened by its rotation, of course, so the shock reached the poles first, though it got to the equator only minutes later. It accelerated the outer layers of gas. They whoofed spaceward. Under Nemesis gravity, the pressure gradient in the atmosphere is so high that even this thinned-out topmost part looked opaque at our distance."

Lee smiled. "Fascinating, isn't it?" he finished. "But not dangerous to us. As a matter of fact, which some of you have doubtless been too busy under general alert to witness—as a matter of fact, gravity has the upper hand again. That exploded shell is rapidly falling back into the main body. In other words, regardless of how astonishing, this expansion of Nemesis has been a transient phenomenon. Hereafter we can expect it will re-expand, but to a lesser distance and in a much more orderly fashion.

"I hope that puts your mind at rest, Minna. Naturally, our teams are going to be busier than a one-armed octopus, taking in what data we can.

But given proper caution, we should survive to bring those data home." He looked around. "More questions?"

From her seat beside Byrne, pilot Suna Rudbeck jumped up. "Yes!" Her voice rang. "What about Osa?"

Men's gazes went to her more eagerly than they had gone to Veijola. Rudbeck was, perhaps, not intrinsically handsomer—tall, full-formed, with auburn locks framing sharply-cut visage—but there was ever something flamelike about her. After an instant, the other pilot's lips twisted and he stared elsewhere. Not long ago, she had been Rudbeck-Cronje. She was not yet Rudbeck-Byrne, but these days he was alone in the cabin that had been theirs, and she shared the planetologist's. Veijola reached toward Cronje, then quickly, unseen, withdrew her hand.

Captain Telander raised his brows: "Osa?" he asked from the stage.

"The inner probe, in polar orbit," Lee explained.

Telander nodded. "Ah, yes, I remember now. Its nickname. I have never been sure why."

"No matter," said Rudbeck. "Listen. Ever since Nemesis went 'boom,' I've been thinking about Osa. Before then, in fact. We've been planning how to retrieve it. The information it carries is priceless, not so, Ezra?"

Lee swallowed hard and nodded.

"If gas expanded outward as far as you say," Rudbeck pursued, "Osa encountered a significant density, a drag. Its orbit will have decayed. What is its status at this moment?" Aggressively: "If you don't know, why don't you?"

"Oh, we do, we do," the astrophysicist said. "It

was among the first things we checked. You're right. Osa's loss would be—is—terrible. I'm afraid, though—"

Rudbeck stabbed a finger in his direction. "*Is* it lost?" she demanded.

"Well, no, not precisely. Gaseous resistance did force it lower. The ambient medium is already much less thick than before, with density dropping fast as molecules return to the main atmosphere. However, a rough computation—I had one run an hour ago, Suna, because I'm as concerned as anybody—it shows that even if nothing else happens, Osa is doomed. Its new orbit is unstable. Variations in the gravity field—in local density and configuration of the geoid—will draw it farther down until it becomes a meteorite." Lee drove fist into palm. "Damn! But as I've been admitting, this has taken us by surprise."

"Osa," mumbled Cronje. The challenge posed by that thing had been talk whenever *Anna Lovinda*'s three boat pilots got together. It stood now in the minds of everybody.

Years ahead of this manned expedition, the mother probe took station and launched her robot investigators. Osa was the innermost, in close polar orbit around the giant. For a while it transmitted back to Gertrud that flood of facts which poured into its instruments—until the transmitter began to fail. Sufficient still came through, sporadically and distorted, to show how much more must be accumulating in its data banks, a Nibelung hoard of truth which might be forever irreplaceable.

Anna Lovinda lacked the means to launch so gifted a satellite. Most of her capacity was devoted to humans and their life support. For she fared only in part to study Nemesis with the versatility of living intelligences, their capability of coping with the unforeseen. Her voyage was equally a test of whether humans could survive a journey across interstellar reaches, wherein speeds eventually neared that of light—whether the Bussard drive could indeed carry them as far as Alpha Centauri and beyond, on into the universe.

"And now," Hayashi said as if to himself, though in Swedish, "now, when Nemesis has done this thing we did not await, it would mean a great deal to hear what Osa has to tell us. However—"

"No 'howevers'!" came from Rudbeck.

"I beg your pardon?" breathed Telander.

"Listen," she repeated herself. "You recall we had plans for retrieving Osa in advance of Nemesis reaching star phase." She tossed her head. "Yes, I know, Captain, you were dubious, but the numbers showed it could be done." She laughed. "There was a bit of a quarrel over which of us pilots should get the glory of doing it. Well, Nemesis has jumped the gun and time available has become short. But I think—Ezra, you'll not falsify the data; I put you on your honor—I think it can still be done, if we're quick. If I am!"

"No!" shouted both Byrne and Cronje, and surged to their feet together.

An unwonted coldness drew over Rudbeck's face. "Jan, I claim the right by virtue of having made the proposal. Dermot, be still; you are not my superior officer."

"Hey, wait just a minute, hotshot," Lee protested. "Our margin of safety is thin at best. We can't risk one of our four auxiliary boats and their three pilots on a hairbreadth stunt like that."

Rudbeck's grin turned wolfish. "You just got through assuring us we are not in danger. Given adequate calculation and control, the mission should be no more hazardous than it would have been earlier; and we know it was feasible then." She swung toward Telander. "Captain, we're here at the end of the longest and most expensive haul in history. The knowledge in Osa is invaluable to science; and knowledge is what we're supposed to gain. But we must be quick. Let me go."

"I never claimed anybody can tell exactly what that damned monster will do next," Lee sputterd.

"Nor can you claim you will never fall over a beer bottle and break your neck," Rudbeck retorted. Eagerness blazed from her. "Captain, time is very short. What do you say?"

For pulsebeats that seemed to become many, Telander stood still. At last, slowly: "When we are on a frontier . . . with so vast an investment behind us, so much riding on what we can accomplish . . . how many megabytes of information is one life worth? If closer study proves the risk is within reason, I will authorize the attempt."

"By me!" Cronje roared.

"Let him go, let him go, and I'll pray for him every centimeter of the way," Byrne stammered.

Victory sang in Rudbeck's voice. "Jan, I'm sorry, you're a first-class pilot, but the uncertainties will be large, and you know my reactions test marginally faster than yours. Or Miguel's, not that he could get back soon enough anyway. Dermot, have no fears. I'll snatch Osa free, and we'll return to Vanadis together."

*   *   *

The boat, flamboyantly named *Valkyrie* by her pilot, eased from a launch bay in the ship, gained room for maneuver by a few delicate jet thrusts, and in the same careful fashion worked her way into initial trajectory. This was on autopilot, under computer direction, and Suna Rudbeck had nothing to do but sit almost weightless and gaze out the ports.

She kept the cabin dark so that her eyes could fully take in the splendor outside. Thus seen, space was not gloomy. There were more stars than there was blackness: steadfast brilliances, white, blue, red, golden. Among them, Sol at its distance remained the brightest, but barely more than Sirius. The Milky Way—in her native language, the Winter Street—swept in an ice-bright torrent whose silence felt like a mysterious noise, something other than the whisper of blood in her ears, filling the hollowness around.

As she drew away from the two large spacecraft, they became clear to her sight, starlit as heaven was. *Gertrud* (St. Gertrud, medieval patroness of wayfarers), the mother vessel of the unmanned pioneers, was a great metal mass from which instrument booms and transceiver dishes jutted. At the stern were simply linac thrusters, akin to those that drove *Valkyrie*; never being intended for return, only for getting around in the neighborhood of Nemesis, the robot ship had discarded her Bussard system upon arrival.

From her bow extended two kilometers of cable, a bare glimmer in Rudbeck's sight, no hint of the incredible tensile strength in precisely aligned atoms. The opposite end of the line anchored *Anna*

Lovinda. That hull was lean, resembling the blade of a dagger whose basket-formed guard was the set of her own linacs. The haft beyond was mostly shielding against the Bussard engine, whose central systems formed a pommel at the top. The force-focusing lattice of that drive, extended while the vessel burned her way across deep space, had been folded back for safety, a cobweb around the knife.

The linked vessels, bearer of probes and bearer of humans, turned majestically about each other. Their spin provided interior weight without unduly inconveniencing auxiliary craft; one rotation took nearly three hours. At her slight present acceleration, Rudbeck felt ghost-light.

That soon ended. "Prepare for standard boost," came out of a speaker. The powerplant hummed, a low sound which bore no hint of the energies that burst from sundered nuclei, turned reaction mass into plasma, and hurled it down the linac until the jet emerged not very much less rapid than light. A full Earth gravity drew Rudbeck down into her chair. The boat could easily have exceeded that, but she herself needed to reach her goal unwearied and alert.

She turned on the cabin illumination, and her attention away from infinity, back toward prosaic meter readings and displays on the panel before her. "All okay," said Mission Control. "You're in charge now, Suna. Barring any fresh data that come in, of course, or any calculations your inboard computers can't handle."

Her head jerked an impatient nod; no matter that no scanner was conveying her image. "I doubt that will be required," she said curtly. "What we have is a straightforward problem in vector analysis. Landing on one of those moons is a good deal trickier, believe me."

"Suna, don't get overconfident, I beg you. The velocities, the energies—"

"Velocities are relative. Or hadn't you heard?" Rudbeck realized she was being snappish. "Pardon me. But I would like a while to think, undisturbed."

"Certainly. We'll stand by . . . and cheer for you, *flicka*."

She did not at once devote herself to the figures, for her course was bringing Nemesis into direct view forward. It was impossible not to stare and wonder. Measurement, more than vision, declared that the body had fallen back into something like its former size; but that was enormous enough even seen from here. Measurement also told of gasps and quiverings going through it. The disc remained wan and well-nigh featureless, save when rents opened and the lower red glow shone angrily through, or where plumes leaped up, broke apart, and rained back.

—"Those shock waves are bounding about yet," Lee had diagnosed. "They reach levels where the gas is too thin to transmit them, and are reflected. Interference produces local calms and local eruptions. It'll take a long time to damp out."

Anguish had distorted Byrne's face. "What if—" he groaned, "what if . . . a geyser, or maybe a whole second expansion . . . happens just when Suna is passing by?"

"It's possible," Lee admitted. "I have not changed my mind about her effort being a bad idea. We've witnessed too many occurrences we don't understand, and haven't had any real chance yet to stop observing and start thinking. Those white clouds blanketing most of the surface, for instance. What are they? We still haven't managed to get a decent reading on them, spectroscope, polarimeter, anything, the way they churn around and come and go."

Byrne reached out toward the pilot. "Suna, darling, darling, I beg you, stay! Nobody will be scoffing at you, I swear."

She bridled. "Must I explain the kindergarten details to you?" she clipped. "Osa's orbital decay is now determined solely by gravity gradients. That means the path is completely predictable for a short term. Now suppose Nemesis does blow again when I am in the vicinity. The first time, it did not throw up enough gas to Osa's altitude to cause significant structural damage. At a second time, true, Osa will be lower. But the shock waves will have less energy. My orbit will be eccentric. A sudden increase in ambient density won't slow me much, nor heat my hull more than I can stand. I'll coast out into the clear. Or—worst case—if I must retrofire to avoid a plunge, or to avoid overheating, the linac won't be ruined. It can safely operate in a gas so tenuous, at least for the brief time I would need."

Byrne stiffened. "If the danger is negligible, let me ride along with you."

"Oh, nonsense." She relented. "But sweet nonsense." She moved forward and kissed him. The kiss lasted. "Well," she murmured, "the flight plan doesn't have me leaving for another hour. . . ."

—She had better review that plan again. It was only simple in principle; complex and subtle mathematics underlay it.

In its present track, Osa had a velocity of some

180 kilometers per second. That fluctuated, especially when rounding the equatorial bulge, and *Valkyrie* must match it exactly. Given timing and related factors, this meant rendezvous over the north pole, with *Valkyrie*'s path osculating Osa's. The former would be a long ellipse, but come sufficiently close to the latter near that point that Rudbeck should have time to make the capture. Immediately thereafter she must use her jets, first to equalize velocities—at such speeds, a tiny percentage differential could rend hulls or start an irretrievable plunge—and then to begin escaping. The delta vee demanded was approximately seventy-five kilometers per second, and the deeper in the gravity well that thrust started, the less reaction mass need be expended.

That was definitely a consideration. Given its exhaust velocity, a linac drive did not drain mass tanks very fast, but it did draw upon them, and the expedition had no facilities for refining more material. This wasn't a Bussard-drive situation, with a ship taking in interstellar hydrogen for fuel and boosterstuff after she had reached minimum speed—no limit on how closely she could approach *c*, how far she could range. The auxiliary boats were meant merely to flit around among planets. When their tanks were dry, *Anna Lovinda* must go home. Economy could add an extra year or better to the nominal five she was to spend exploring—could add unbounded extra knowledge and glory.

Rudbeck smiled and relaxed. She had about an hour of straight-line acceleration before the next change of vector. After that, maneuvers would become increasingly more varied, until in about four hours she was at Nemesis. There the equipment would cease carrying her as a passenger. She would be using it. Everything that happened would be in her hands.

Cronje sat alone in his cabin. It was not entirely his, though—only the pictures from home (his parents before their house, a kopje at sunset, breakers on a reef with the ocean sapphire-blue around them, a model-building kit, a closetful of clothes, the book he was screening without really reading). A bare bunk and bulkhead haunted the room.

There was a knock. "Come in," he snapped. As the door opened: "No. *Voetsack.* Get out."

Byrne twisted his hands together. "Please," he whispered. "Let me in. Listen a while. Afterward do what you like, and I'll not be resisting."

Cronje considered. "Well, close the door. Speak. No, I did not invite you to sit down."

"She's . . . close to rendezvous."

"Did you imagine I do not know? This set will switch over whenever communication recommences. Go tune yours."

Byrne ran tongue over lips. "I thought . . . perhaps we might—" Facing the scowl before him, he mustered strength to plunge ahead. "Jan, Suna's dearest hope is that we two might be friends again. That may be too much to ask. But could we not pray for her together?"

"I am not a praying man. I doubt that my father's God would hear the likes of you."

Sweat glistened on Byrne's cheeks. "Well, will you listen a minute? This is hard for me. I've had to nerve myself to it. But when Suna is in danger— somehow it seems you should know about her. Know what an injustice you have been doing her."

Cronje's massive shoulders hunched forward.
"How?"

Byrne straightened. Resolution began to reso-
nate in his tone. "Think. You considered her such
an idiot, so faithless, that my wiles lured her from
you. But it was not that way at all, at all. How
could it be? Nor would I have tried. Oh, I was in
love with her almost from the time we departed
Earth. But her nearness was enough." He sketched
a smile. "We've unattached women without inhibi-
tions aboard, as well you are aware, Jan Cronje."

"What? No, I never—"

"Of course you did not. But understand, you
great loon, neither did she. She fought her feelings
for me, month after month. If you had been more
thoughtful of her, she could well have won that
battle."

Cronje grimaced. "Was I ever bad to her? See
here, we're both pilots, so naturally, as soon as we
reached Nemesis, we were off most of the time on
separate missions. But when we were together—"
He snarled. His fist crashed on the chair arm.
"Before God, I'll not drag our private life out in
front of you!"

"You needn't," Byrne answered. "But she has
needed to explain herself to me. She grieves on
your account and wishes you nothing but well.
Nevertheless, the fact is that she and I are . . .
happier . . . than ever she— Well. No more. Today
I decided my duty was to give her back your respect for her. Now you can send me away. Or if
you hit me, here where we are alone, I will tell the
captain I had an accident."

Cronje slumped back. His jaw sagged a little.
After a while he muttered, "Respect—"

The text on the screen vanished. Mission Control blinked into view. "We have a report from Rudbeck," the speaker said. Curbed emotions turned her voice flat. "She has visual contact with Osa. Parameters satisfactory. Except that an outburst is climbing ahead of her."

Valkyrie flew above Nemesis. Cold jets, microgravity, and all, no other words than "flew above" would do, when the sub-sun filled half of hurtling vision.

Right, left, forward, aft, the immensity reached, until eyesight lost itself. It was like an ocean, but an ocean of dream, where billows rolled and roiled—white, gray, pale red, deep purple—endlessly above furnace depths which glared through rifts and whirlpools. Here and there spume blew free, surf crashed soundless, fountains spouted upward and arched back down. Haze overlay the scene, fading aloft into a blackness where stars gleamed untroubled. You could lose yourself, staring into that; your soul could leave you, drown in those waves, be scattered by them from horizon to horizon and there drift forever.

Rudbeck's gaze clung to the heavens. A twinkle onto which her radar had locked was growing into the satellite she had come to save. It seemed an unimpressive cylinder, with arms and steering rockets jutting at odd angles, the whole now crazily spinning and wobbling. But that was the mere shell around a few kilograms of crystals which encoded more knowledge than any human could master in a lifetime.

Beyond and below, a great ashen geyser was slowly rising out of the clouds. Its top faded off into nothingness, but already stars immediately above were dimming and going out.

"It's optically denser than I quite like, and will probably be opaque by the time I pass through," Rudbeck said. "I'm getting radar echoes, too. But you're receiving the readings directly. What do you advise?"

The transmission lag of half a dozen seconds felt like as many minutes. Telander's words came wearily: "Abort. Take evasive action."

"No!" Rudbeck argued. "Not after coming this far, with everything it means. I've been thinking. The optical density is likely due to nothing worse than water vapor becoming ice particles. The radar reflection could well be off ions. Neither appears sufficient to threaten my linac."

Time.

"Those are your guesses, pilot. Dr. Lee's team has not yet been able to ascertain what the truth is. . . . Well, pass by in free fall. You should suffer no harm from that. While your orbit is taking you around again, the situation may change for the better, or our understanding may improve, and you can make a second attempt."

"Skipper, I don't believe a second try will be possible. *Valkyrie* can bullet on through that cloud. I doubt Osa can. Too much drag, with such a low mass-to-surface ratio; and I'd anticipate eddy current losses too, because of what those ions must be doing to the Nemesis magnetic field. Before I can return, Osa will have slipped irrecoverably far down—to burn up—"

Rudbeck's hands tightened on the manual controls. "Sir," she said, "without being insubordinate, I remind you that the pilot of a spacecraft under boost is *her* captain, who makes the final decisions. I'm about to boost, and my decision will be to go ahead with the retrieval. I trust you will continue to provide support if needed. Now I have no more time for argument. Wish me luck, shipmates!"

She laughed aloud and became very busy.

An overtaking orbit was a lower orbit. With the help of ranging instruments, computers, and jets, Rudbeck adjusted course until the difference between hers and Osa's was measurable in meters of space. She rolled her craft about, belly toward the quarry. She pulled the switch that caused the cargo bay to open, and another that extended the grappler arms. Like a single beast of prey, stealing along on breaths of plasma thrust, Rudbeck and *Valkyrie* closed in on Osa.

Peering at the scanner screen, fingers working with surgical delicacy, she operated the grapplers. A shiver went through the hull. Osa was captured. Rudbeck's touch on a button commanded an equalizing vector which a screen display counselled. Weight hauled softly at her. The arms drew their burden into the hold. Hatches slid shut.

The maneuvers, the momentum transferences had sent *Valkyrie* sliding off downward. The atmospheric pressure gradient beneath her meant that she would become a shooting star within minutes, unless she regained altitude. This was in the calculations. Likewise was the full-throated blast which was to make good her escape from Nemesis. Rudbeck grinned at the cloud ahead. It was weirdly like a fog bank on Earth. Her hands gave their orders. The spacecraft leaped.

Abruptly the the hull shuddered and bucked. A crash went through it, the noise of a mighty gong.

Rudbeck's body jammed against the harness. An unbalanced thrust snapped her head sideways. Dazed with pain, she hardly felt the weightlessness that followed. It was not true weightlessness anyway, but a riot of shifting centrifugal forces. Like a dead leaf on a winter wind, *Valkyrie* tumbled through space, borne wherever the cosmos cast her.

They were three who met in the captain's cramped little office: Erik Telander, Ezra Lee, and Jan Cronje. They did not feel they had time to confer with anybody else. Screens were tuned to Mission Control and Observatory Central, but the sound was turned low.

All three of them were on their feet. Lee's back was bowed. "Oh, Jesus, I should have seen it, I should have seen it," he moaned.

Cronje stood expressionless. "I gather you have established the nature of that obstacle she ran into," he said. "Let us hear."

"With everything confused— But we do finally have clear readings. We might have interpreted our data correctly earlier, except that the conclusion is so utterly unexpected. . . . Stop maundering!" Lee told himself. To the others: "The whitish material in the atmosphere, and in the plume she encountered, it's dust."

"What?"

"Yes, mostly fine silicate particles. I suspect carbon as well, possibly traces of higher elements—no matter now. I see with the keenest hindsight." Lee's chuckle was ghastly. "It's cosmic dust, from the original nebula that the Solar System condensed out of. Solid material, that got incorporated in the bodies of the lesser planets, in the cores of giants like Jupiter. And vaporized in Sol, of course. In the case of Nemesis, the parameters are special. Once the main mass had coalesced, more dust kept falling for a while, till the nebula was used up. The heat of Nemesis already served to keep it suspended in the lower atmosphere, though not to gasify it. It couldn't sink on into levels where the air was denser than it was, either. In other words, way down, that air includes a stratum of thick dustiness. When the fires turn on, the shock waves cast that dust aloft, till eventually it gets kicked into space."

Lee stared at his feet. "More and more is being coughed up," he mumbled. "The haze is getting heavier everywhere around Nemesis. Sure, it'll fall back, but fresh stuff will replace it. I expect that'll go on for weeks."

Cronje looked at Telander. "Have you any new information on Rudbeck?" he asked.

Anguish dwelt in the captain's lean visage. "Not really," he answered. "That is, obviously she hasn't managed to repair the radio transmitter that must have been damaged. However, we have no strong reason to suppose she herself has suffered serious injury. Doubtless the major harm was to the linac. Plasma bouncing off solid particles that did not flash into vapor as ice crystals would—plasma striking its electromagnetic accelerators at speeds close to light's— But I daresay the basic power-plant is intact, and certainly the batteries should have ample charge. Life support ought to be still effective. Mainly, the boat is crippled."

"In a rapidly decaying orbit."

"Well, yes. Drag not only reduced eccentricity

by a large factor, it shortened the semimajor axis. The period has become correspondingly briefer; and each periapsis, passing through those ever thicker clouds—" Telander stiffened himself. "But I am being weak. I want a message from her, a reassurance, which my mind says isn't really necessary, though my heart disagrees. It *is* an eccentric orbit yet. Along most of it, the boat is in open space. The indications are that we have a day or two of grace before the final plunge."

"And I can get there in four or five hours," Cronje responded. "Never mind precise figures beforehand. You can feed me those as I travel, and I'll adjust my vectors accordingly. My boat is fully in order. Have I the captain's leave to start?"

"You do." Telander hesitated. He raised a hand. "A moment. Let us spell this out. Your assignment is to match velocities at a safe point on Rudbeck's orbit, take her aboard, and return here. Nothing else. We can't afford a second gamble."

"Bearing in mind I must exercise my own judgment— Let's not dawdle." Cronje turned to go. Impulsively, he seized Lee and hugged the astrophysicist to his breast.

"Don't you blame yourself, Ezra," he said. "Nobody could have done better than you and your staff. Damn few could have done as well. If nature isn't going to surprise us, ever, why the hell do we go exploring?"

Cronje left. In the passageway outside, he found Byrne waiting. Tears ran down the planetologist's face. "God ride with you, Jan." His words wavered. "If only I could. Bring her back. Afterward you can ask anything of me you want, and I . . . I will be doing my best to obey."

Cronje wrung his hand, growled, "No promises," and hastened onward.

Crew were a-bustle around a launch bay airlock. Minna Veijola stood aside from them. When Cronje appeared, she ran to meet him. They went off together, out of sight behind a locker. Standing on tiptoe, she could take him by the shoulders. "Be careful, Jan," she pleaded.

A possible chuckle rumbled in his throat. "You know me, little friend. I never take needless risks. I don't even play poker. No doubt this is part of the reason Suna found me a dull sort."

"You aren't, you aren't," she breathed. "Yes, I have come to know you—the voyage, the visits to my moon, oh, everything—" The slant blue gaze strained upward. "So I sense you have more in mind than what you are telling. Jan, don't do it! Whatever it is, don't do it! Only bring Suna back, and yourself."

He stroked her hair. "A man must do what he must. And a woman, of course." A technician stepped around the locker to announce readiness. "Farewell, Minna." Cronje went to his boat.

Rendezvous could have been made when *Valkyrie* was at her farthest from Nemesis. However, that would have meant letting her swing another time through the clouds. Ezra Lee had been the first to confess that there was no telling—nothing but an educated guess—which of those close passages would prove the fatal one. The half-star was vomiting more and more spouts of dust and gas, in wholly unforeseeable fashion. Cronje was to meet Rudbeck at the earliest moment which was prudent. Her transferral should not take long.

Thus the vessels were cometing inward when they made contact. Nemesis filled the forward ports of *Kruger* with swirling, vaguely starlit smoke. Sometimes it parted for a short while to show crimson underneath, but mostly it was pearl-gray turmoil.

Against that background, *Valkyrie* gyrated helpless. Cronje could see how the webwork of her drive was twisted, partly melted, sheared across in places. It could be restored, but that required she be in space more calm than that toward which she fell.

Given his vehicle and his experience, approach was no problem. Erratic spin along the invariable plane was. Cronje spent an hour using his grapples, touch after finicking touch, to dissipate angular momentum between both hulls. At each stroke, metal shivered and cried out. At last he could lock tight.

He and Rudbeck had already exchanged optical-flash signals. She was uncomfortable but not badly hurt. When he had achieved a reasonable rotation and an embrace, she donned her spacesuit and jetted around from her airlock to his. He let her in. By then they were quite near Nemesis, and speeding ever faster.

They did not feel that. She hung weightless in the entry, surrounded by a bleakness of metal, and fumbled at her faceplate. He helped her unfasten it. She had washed the blood from around her nostrils but was still disheveled and hollow-eyed. Somehow the haggardness brought forth, all the more sharply, the fine sculpturing of bones, nose, lips. "Thank you," she said.

"My duty," he answered. "Are you okay?"

"Essentially, yes."

"But are you capable of work? Hard work, I warn you."

Her eyes ransacked his countenance. Behind the beard, it was like meteoritic iron. "What . . . are you . . . thinking of?" Pause. "Oh. Yes. Transshipping Osa. That must exceed your orders."

"Here I give the orders."

"Well—" A laugh rattled from her. "Why, my dear old cautious Jan! But I agree. It'll take a couple of hours. We'll have to pass periapsis again. Our orbit should not decay too badly, though. And this *was* why I came." She reached to catch his hands in her gloves. "Yes, let's get started. I'll help you on with your suit."

"My idea goes beyond that," he said. "It involves two or three close approaches. You realize the risk. Nemesis may cause us to dive. But I don't expect it, and judge the stakes are worth the bet."

She gaped. "Jan . . . you don't mean salvaging *Valkyrie*?"

He shrugged. "What else?"

"But—we do have a spare boat—"

"And who can tell what may happen in the future, what may be wrecked beyond hope?" he flung forth. "Not to speak of the reaction mass in your tanks. We can spotweld the hulls together. It'll cause awkward handling, but we need simply achieve escape—boosting in clear space, naturally. Miguel Sanchez has already been recalled from his expedition; he's on his way back to the ship; his boat can take us off, and leave a repair gang for ours. It will make an immense difference to the whole mission."

Afloat in midair, he folded his arms and looked

squarely into her eyes. "Now this will give you no chance soon to rest," he said. "You're bruised and weary. Are you able? Are you game?"

Radiance replied. "Oh, Jan, yes!"

Everybody aboard *Anna Lovinda* was present to greet the return. Most stood aside, silent, more than a little in awe. Sanchez, who came through the airlock first, went to join their half-circle. Telander stood before it alone.

Cronje and Rudbeck appeared. There was nothing heroic about that advent. Perfunctorily washed and combed, exhausted, they shambled forth. When they stopped in front of the captain, they swayed on their feet.

"Welcome." Telander was quiet a few seconds. "I wish I could say that with a whole heart."

Indignation flared out of Rudbeck's fatigue: "Are you miffed that Jan's judgment proved better than yours? He did save not only me, but Osa and my boat. What this is worth to us, to humankind—"

Telander lifted a palm. "Certainly. But the precedent, the example. You may imagine you have the law on your side. I doubt it. Captains, too, are obliged to follow basic instructions."

Cronje nodded heavily. "I know," he said. "Do you want to bring the matter to trial?"

Telander shook his head. "No, no. People don't quarrel with spectacular success." He sighed. "I can but hope nobody else—nor you two—will feel free to ignore orders and violate doctrine. We are so few, so alone."

Rudbeck drew closer to Cronje's side. "You can trust him," she declared. "Believe me."

Byrne, who had lifted his arms toward her, let them fall and dropped his gaze.

Cronje disengaged himself. "Well," he said, "I'm off to sleep for a week."

Rudbeck stared. A hand stole to her lips. "Jan—?"

He barked a laugh. "Did you suppose I went out merely to rescue you? Or do you suppose, if the lost person had been anybody else, I would not merely have carried out my task? Think about it."

He started for the cabins. In that direction Veijola stood waiting.

Rudbeck spent a whole minute motionless before she joined Byrne. One by one or two by two, mute, folk went their various ways. Telander and Lee stayed behind.

The astrophysicist spoke low. "We have about twelve million years before Nemesis comes back to Sol's part of the System. Let's hope that will be time enough for a race like ours to make ready."

TABLE MANNERS

by
Larry Niven

Larry Niven and I are so often asked "How do you two collaborate?" that we've developed a routine answer: we say, in unison, "Superbly." The answer is immodest, but between us we can write a *lot* better than either does working alone.

We do each have our strengths. I plot better than Larry, and I'm a lot more careful with realistic detail. Niven, on the other hand, is more imaginative—sometimes too much so. When Larry gets hold of a good idea, he carries it to its conclusion and beyond. On the other hand, I'm not *mad* enough to think up some of the ideas that continually pop up in Niven's head.

Last night, Larry and I celebrated with champagne: we'd done the final edit of *Footfall*, our latest novel. This one is about an alien invasion of Earth. The invasion, and the aliens, are as well developed, and as realistic, as we, working together, can make them. Our first novel, *The Mote In God's Eye*, told of first contact between man and an alien civilization. Our new aliens are at least as detailed as the Moties were. We've had practice, not only in working together, but in creating alien races.

Every one of our novels generates an image, or a phrase, that seems to characterize the book. In our last one, *Oath of Fealty*, it was "Think of it as evolution in action."

It wouldn't be a bad motto for Rick Schumann, owner of the Draco Tavern. . . .

TABLE MANNERS

Larry Niven

A lot of what comes out of Xenobiology these days is classified, and it *doesn't* come out. The Graduate Studies Complex is in the Mojave Desert. It makes security easier.

Sireen Burke's smile and honest blue retina prints and the microcircuitry in her badge got her past the gate. I was ordered out of the car. A soldier offered me coffee and a bench in the shade of the guard post. Another searched my luggage.

He found a canteen, a sizeable hunting knife in a locking sheath, and a microwave beamer. He became coldly polite. He didn't thaw much when I said that he could hold them for awhile.

I waited.

Presently Sireen came back for me. "I got you an interview with Dr. McPhee," she told me on the way up the drive. "Now it's your baby. He'll listen as long as you can keep his interest."

Graduate Studies looked like soap bubbles: foamcrete sprayed over inflation frames. There was little of military flavor inside. More like a museum. The reception room was gigantic, with a variety of chairs and couches and swings and resting pits for aliens and humans; designs borrowed from the Draco Tavern without my permission.

The corridors were roomy too. Three chirpsithra passed us, eleven feet tall and walking comfortably upright. One may have known me, because she nodded. A dark glass sphere rolled through, nearly filling the corridor, and we had to step into what looked like a classroom to let it pass.

McPhee's office was closet-sized. He certainly didn't interview aliens here, at least not large aliens. Yet he was a mountainous man, six feet four and barrel-shaped and covered with black hair: shaggy brows, full beard, a black mat showing through the V of his blouse. He extended a huge hand across the small desk and said, "Rick Schumann? You're a long way from Siberia."

"I came for advice," I said, and then I recognized him. "B-beam McPhee?"

"Walter, but yes."

The Beta Beam satellite had never been used in war; but when I was seven years old, the Pentagon had arranged a demonstration. They'd turned it loose on a Perseid meteor shower. Lines of light had filled the sky one summer night, a glorious display, the first time I'd ever been allowed up past midnight. The Beta Beam had shot down over a thousand rocks.

Newscasters had named Walter McPhee for the Beta Beam when he played offensive guard for Washburn University.

B-beam was twenty-two years older, and bigger than life, since I'd last seen him on a television set. There were scars around his right eye, and scarring distorted the lay of his beard. "I was at Washburn on an athletic scholarship," he told me. "I switched to Xeno when the first chirpsithra ships landed. Got my doctorate six years ago. And I've never been in the Draco Tavern because it would have felt too much like goofing off, but I've started to wonder if that isn't a mistake. You get everything in there, don't you?"

I said it proudly. "Everything that lands on Earth visits the Draco Tavern."

"Folk too?"

"Yes. Not often. Four times in fifteen years. The first time, I thought they'd want to talk. After all, they came a long way—"

He shook his head vigorously. "They'd rather associate with other carnivores. I've talked with them, but it's damn clear they're not here to have fun. Talking to local study groups is a guest-host obligation. What do you know about them?"

"Just what I see. They come in groups, four to six. They'll talk to glig, and of course they get along with chirpsithra. Everything does. This latest group was thin as opposed to skeletal, though I've seen both—"

"They're skeletal just before they eat. They don't associate with aliens then, because it turns them mean. They only eat every six days or so, and of course they're hungry when they hunt."

"You've seen hunts?"

"I'll show you films. Go on."

Better than I'd hoped. "I need to see those films. I've been invited on a hunt."

"Sireen told me."

I said, "This is my slack season. Two of the big

interstellar ships took off Wednesday, and we don't expect another for a couple of weeks. Last night there were no aliens at all until—"

"This all happened last night?"

"Yeah. Maybe twenty hours ago. I told Sireen and Gail to go home, but they stayed anyway. The girls are grad students in Xeno, of course. Working in a bar that caters to alien species isn't a job for your average waitress. They stayed and talked with some other Xenos."

"We didn't hear what happened, but we saw it," Sireen said. "Five Folk came in."

"Anything special about them?"

She said, "They came in on all fours, with their heads tilted up to see. One alpha-male, three females and a beta-male, I think. The beta had a wound along its left side, growing back. They were wearing the usual: translators built into earmuffs, and socks, with slits for the fingers on the forefeet. Their ears were closed tight against the background noise. They didn't try to talk till they'd reached a table and turned on the sound baffle."

I can't tell the Folk apart. They look a little like Siberian elkhounds, if you don't mind the head. The head is big. The eyes are below the jawline, and face forward. There's a nostril on top that closes tight or opens like a trumpet. They weigh about a hundred pounds. Their fingers are above the callus, and they curl up out of the way. Their fur is black, sleek, with white markings in curly lines. We can't say their word for themselves; their voices are too high and too soft. We call them the Folk because their translators do.

I said, "They stood up and pulled themselves onto ottomans. I went to take their orders. They were talking in nearly supersonic squeaks, with their translators turned off. You had to strain to hear anything. One turned on his translator and ordered five glasses of milk, and a drink for myself if I would join them."

"Any idea why?"

"I was the closest thing to a meat eater?"

"Maybe. And maybe the local alpha-male thought they should get to know something about humans as opposed to grad students. Or—" McPhee grinned. "Had you eaten recently?"

"Yeah. Someone finally built a sushi place near the spaceport. I can't do my own cooking, I'd go *nuts* if I had to run an alien restaurant too—"

"Raw flesh. They smelled it on your breath."

Oh. "I poured their milk and a double Scotch and soda. I don't usually drink on the premises, but I figured Sireen or Gail could handle anything that came up.

"It was the usual," I said. "What's it like to be human. What's it like to be Folk. Trade items, what are they missing that could improve their life styles. Eating habits. The big one did most of the talking. I remember saying that we have an ancestor who's supposed to have fed itself by running alongside an antelope while beating it on the head with a club till it fell over. And he told me that his ancestors traveled in clusters—he didn't say *packs*—and followed herds of plant-eaters to pull down the slow and the sick. Early biological engineering, he said."

McPhee looked worried. "Do the Folk expect you to outrun an antelope?"

"Oboy!" That was a terrible thought. "No, we talked about that too, how brains and civilization cost you other abilities. Smell, for humans. I got a feeling . . . he wanted to think we're carnivores unless we run out of live meat. I tried not to disillusion him, but I had to tell him about cooking, that we like the taste, that it kills parasites and softens vegetables and meat—"

"Why?"

"He asked. Jesus, B-beam, you don't lie to aliens, do you?"

He grinned. "I never have. I'm never sure what they want to hear."

"Well, I never lie to customers. —And he talked about the hunts, how little they test the Folk's animal abilities, how the whole species is getting soft. . . . I guess he saw how curious I was. He invited me on a hunt. Five days from now."

"You've got a problem anyone in this building would kill for."

"Ri—ight. But what the hell do they *expect* of me?"

"Where does it take place? The Folk have an embassy not fifty miles from here."

"Yeah, and it's a hunting ground too, and I'll be out there next Wednesday, getting my own meal. I may have been a little drunk. I did have the wit to ask if I could bring a companion."

"And?" B-beam looked like he was about to spring across the desk into my lap.

"He said yes."

"That's my Nobel Prize calling," said B-beam. "Rick Schumann, will you accept me as your, ah, second?"

"Sure." I didn't have to think hard. Not only did he have the knowledge; he looked like he could strangle a grizzly bear; which might be what they expected of us.

The Folk had arrived aboard a chirpsithra liner, five years after the first chirp landing.

They'd leased a stretch of the Mojave. They'd rearranged the local weather and terrain, over strenuous objections from the Sierra Club, and seeded it with a hundred varieties of plants and a score of animals. Meanwhile they toured the world's national parks in a 727 with a redesigned interior. The media had been fascinated by the sleek black killing machines. They'd have given them even more coverage if the Folk had been more loquacious.

Three years of that, and then the public was barred from the Folk hunting ground. IntraWorld Cable sued, citing the public's right-to-know. They lost. Certain guest species would leave Earth, and others would kill, to protect their privacy.

IntraWorld Cable would have killed to air this film.

The sunset colors were fading from the sky ... still a Mojave desert sky, though the land was an alien meadow with patches of forest around it. Grass stood three feet tall in places, dark green verging on black. Alien trees grew bent, as if before a ferocious wind; but they bent in different directions.

Four creatures grazed near a stream. None of the Folk were in view.

"The Folk don't give a damn about privacy," B-beam said. "It's pack thinking, maybe. They don't mind our taking pictures. I don't think they'd mind our broadcasting everything we've got, world wide. It was all the noisy news helicopters that bothered them. Once we realized that, we negotiated. Now there's one Xenobiology Department lifter and some cameras around the fences."

The creatures might have been a gazelle with ambitions to be a giraffe, but the mouth and eyes and horns gave them away.

Alien. The horns were big and gaudy, intricately curved and intertwined, quite lovely and quite useless, for the tips pointed inward. The neck was long and slender. The mouth was like a shovel. The eyes, like Folk eyes, were below the jaw hinges; though they faced outward, as with most grazing beasts. The creatures couldn't look up. Didn't the Folk planet have birds of prey? Or heights from which something hungry might leap?

B-beam reclined almost sleepily in a folding chair too small for him. He said, "We call it a melk, a mock elk. Don't picture it evolving the usual way. Notice the horns? Melks were shaped by generations of planned breeding. Like a show poodle. And the grass, we call it *fat grass*."

"Why? Hey—"

"Seen them?"

I'd glimpsed a shadow flowing among the trees. The melks had sensed something too. Their heads were up, tilted *way* up to let them see. A concealed nostril splayed like a small horn.

Three Folk stood upright from the grass, and screamed like steam-whistles.

The melks scattered in all directions. Shadows flowed in the black grass. One melk found two Folk suddenly before it, shrieking. The melk bellowed in despair, wheeled and made for the trees. Too slow. A deer could have moved much faster.

The camera zoomed to follow it.

Into the trees—and into contact with a black shadow. I glimpsed a forefoot/hand slashing at the creature's vulnerable throat. Then the shadow was clinging to its back, and the melk tried to run from the forest with red blood spilling down its chest. The rest of the Folk converged on it.

They tore it apart.

They dragged it into the trees before they ate.

Part of me was horrified ... but not so damn horrified as all that. Maybe I've been with aliens too long. Part of me watched, and noticed the strange configuration of the ribcage, the thickness and the familiar design of legs and knees, and the *convenient* way the skull split to expose brain when two Folk pulled the horns apart. The Folk left nothing but bone. They split the thick leg bones with their jaws, and gnawed the interiors. When they were finished they rolled the bones into a neat pile and departed at a waddle.

B-beam said, "That's why we don't give these films to the news. Notice anything?"

"Too much. The one they picked, it wasn't just the smallest. The horns weren't right. Like one grew faster than the other."

"Right."

"None of the Folk were carrying anything or wearing anything. No knives, no clothes, not even those sock-gloves. What do they do in winter?"

"They still hunt naked. What else?"

"The rest drove it toward that one hidden in the woods."

"There's one designated killer. Once the prey's fate is sealed, the rest converge. There are other meat sources. Here—"

There was a turkey-sized bird with wonderful

irridescent patterns on its small wings and enormous spreading tail. It flew, but not well. The Folk ran beneath it until it ran out of steam and had to come down into their waiting hands. The rest drew back for the leader to make the kill. B-beam said, "They killed four that day. Want to watch? It all went just about the same way."

"Show me."

I thought I might see . . . right. The third attempt, the bird was making for the trees with the Folk just underneath. It might make it. Could the Folk handle trees? But the Folk broke off, far short of the trees. The bird fled to safety while they converged on another that had landed too soon, and frightened it into panicky circles. . . .

Enough of that. I said, "B-beam, the Folk sent some stuff to the Draco Tavern by courier. Your gate security has it now. I think I'd better get it back. A microwave beamer and a hunting knife and a canteen, and it all looks like it came from Abercrombie and Fitch."

He stared at me, considering. "*Did* they. What do you think?"

"I think they're making allowances because I'm human."

He shook his head. "They make things easy for themselves. They cull the herds, but they kill the most difficult ones too. Anything that injures a Folk, dies. So okay, they've made things easy for us too. I doubt they're out to humiliate us. They didn't leave extra gear for your companion?"

"No."

An instructor led us in stretching exercises, isometrics, duck-waddles, sprints, and an hour of just running, for two hours each day. There was a spa and a masseur, and I needed them. I was blind with exhaustion after every session . . . yet I sensed that they were being careful of me. The game was over if I injured myself.

B-beam put us on a starvation diet. "I want us thinking hungry, thinking like Folk. Besides, we can both stand to lose a few pounds."

I studied Folk physiology more closely than I would have stared at a customer. The pointed mouths show two down-pointing daggers in front, then a gap, then teeth that look like two conical canines fused together. They look vicious. The eyes face forward in deep sockets below the hinges of the jaw: white with brown irises, oddly human. Their fingers are short and thick, tipped with thick claws, three to a forefoot, with the forward edge of the pad to serve as a thumb. Human hands are better, I think. But if the eyes had been placed like a wolf's, they couldn't have *seen* their hands while standing up, and they wouldn't be tool users.

My gear was delivered. I strung the canteen and the beamer and the sheath knife on a loop of line. I filled the canteen with water, changed my mind and replaced it with Gatorade, and left it all in a refrigerator.

I watched three more hunts. Once they hunted melk again, Once it was pigs. That wasn't very interesting. B-beam said, "Those were a gift. We mated pigs to wild boars, raised them in bottles and turned them loose. The Folk were polite, but I don't think they like them much. They're too easy."

The last film must have been taken at night, light-amplified, for the moon was blazing like the sun. The prey had two enormous legs with too many joints, a smallish torso slung horizontally between the shoulders, and tiny fingers around a strange mouth. Again, it looked well fed. It was in the forest, eating into a hanging melon-sized fruit without bothering to pick it. I said, "That doesn't look . . . right."

B-beam said, "No, it didn't evolve alongside the Folk. Different planet. Gligstith(click)tcharf, maybe. We call them *stilts*."

It was faster than hell and could jump too, but the Folk were spread out and they were always in front of it. They kept it running in a circle until it stepped wrong and lost its balance.

One Folk zipped toward it. The stilt tumbled with its legs folded and stood up immediately, but it still took too long. The designated killer wrapped itself around one leg; its jaws closed on the ankle. The stilt kicked at its assailant, a dozen kicks in a dozen seconds. Then the bone snapped and the rest of the Folk moved in.

"Do you suppose they'll wear translators when they hunt with us?"

"I'd guess they won't. I know some Folk words and I've been boning up. And I've got a horde of students looking for anything on Folk eating habits. I've got a suspicion . . . Rick, why are we doing this?"

"We ought to get to know them."

"Why? What have we seen that makes them worth knowing?"

I was hungry and I ached everywhere. I had to think before I answered. "Oh . . . enough. Eating habits aside, the Folk aren't totally asocial. They're *here*, and they aren't xenophobes. . . . B-beam, suppose they *don't* have anything to teach us?

They're still part of a galactic civilization, and we want to be out there with them. I just want humanity to look good."

"Look good ... yeah. I did wonder why you didn't even *hesitate*. Have you ever been hunting?"

"No. You?"

"Yeah, my uncles used to take me deer hunting. Have you ever killed anything? Hired out as a butcher, for instance?"

". . . No."

And I waited to say, *Sure, I can kill an animal, no sweat. Hell, I promised!* But he didn't ask; he only looked.

I never did mention my other fear. For all I know, it never occurred to anyone else that B-beam and I might be the prey.

Intelligent beings, if gullible. Armed, but with inadequate weapons. Betrayed, and thus enraged, likely to right back. The Folk eat Earthborn meat. Surely we would make more interesting prey than the boar-pigs!

But it was plain crazy. The chirpsithra enforced laws against murder. If humans were to disappear within the Mojave hunting park, the Folk might be barred from the chirp liners! They wouldn't dare.

The Folk came for us at dawn. We rode in the Xenobiology lifter. We left the air ducts wide open. The smell of five Folk behind us was rich and strange: not quite an animal smell, but something else, and not entirely pleasant. If the Folk noticed our scent, they didn't seem to mind.

B-beam seemed amazingly relaxed. At one point he told me, casually, "We're in danger of missing a point. We're here to have fun. The Folk don't know we've been sweating and moaning, and they won't. You're being honored, Rick. Have fun."

At midmorning we landed and walked toward a fence.

It was human-built, posted with signs in half a dozen languages. NO ENTRY. DANGER! B-beam took us through the gate. Then the Folk waited. B-beam exchanged yelps with them, then told me. "You're expected to lead."

"Me? Why?"

"Surprise. You're the designated killer."

"Me?" It seemed silly . . . but it was their hunt. I led off. "What are we hunting?"

"You make that decision too."

Well inside the fence, we crossed what seemed a meandering dune, varying from five to eight meters high, curving out of sight to left and right. Outside the dune was desert. Inside, meadow.

A stream poured out of the dune. Further away and much lower, its returning loop flowed back into the dune. The dune hid pumps. It might hide defenses.

The green-black grass wasn't thin like grass; it was a succulent, like three-foot-tall fingers of spineless cactus, nice to the touch. *Fat grass.* Sawgrass would have been a real problem. We wore nothing but swim suits (we'd argued about even that) and the items strung on a line across my shoulders.

Any of the Folk, or B-beam himself, would have made a better killer than one middle-aged bartender.

Of course I had the beamer, and it would kill; but it wouldn't kill fast. Anything large would be hurt and angry long before it fell over.

All five Folk dropped silently to their bellies. I hadn't seen anything, so I stayed upright, but I was walking carefully. Naked humans might not spook the prey anyway. They'd be alert for Folk.

B-beam's eyes tried to be everywhere at once. He whispered, "I got my report on Folk eating habits."

"Well?"

"They drink water and milk. They've never been seen eating. They don't *buy* food—"

"Pets?"

"—Or pets, or livestock. I thought of that—"

"Missing Persons reports?"

"Oh, for Christ's sake, Rick! No, this the *only* way they eat. It's not a hunt so much as a formal dinner party. The rules of etiquette are likely to be rigid."

Rigid, hell. I'd watched them tearing live animals apart.

Water gurgled ahead. The artificial stream ran everywhere. "I never wondered about the canteen," I said. "Why a canteen?"

B-beam yelped softly. A Folk squeaked back. Yelp, and squeak, and B-beam tried to suppress a laugh. "You must have talked about drinking wine with meals."

"I did. Is there supposed to be *wine* in this thing?"

B-beam grinned. Then lost the grin. "The canteen isn't for the hunt, it's for afterward. What about the knife and beamer?"

"Oh, come on, the Folk *gave* me . . . uh." Butterflies began breeding in my stomach. Humans cook their food. Sushi and sashimi and Beef Tartar are exceptions. I'd said so, that night. "The beamer's for cooking. If I use it to kill the prey . . . we'll be disgraced?"

"I'm not sure I want to come right out and ask. Let's see. . . ."

The high-pitched squeaking went on for some time. B-beam was trying to skirt the edges of the subject. The butterflies in my belly were turning carnivorous. Presently he whispered, "Yup. Knife too. Your teeth and nails are visibly inadequate for carving."

"Oh, Lord."

"The later you back out, the worse it'll be. Do it *now* if—"

Two melks were grazing beyond a rise of ground. I touched B-beam's shoulder and we sank to our bellies.

The melks were really too big. They'd weigh about what I did: a hundred and eighty pounds. I'd be better off chasing a bird. Better yet, a boar-pig.

Then again, these *were* meat animals, born to lose. And we'd need four or five birds for this crowd. I'd be totally winded long before we finished. B-beam's exercise program had given me a good grasp of my limits . . . not to mention a raging hunger.

The purpose of this game was to make humans—me—look good. Wasn't it? Anyway, there wasn't a bird or a pig in sight.

We crept through the fat grass until we had a clear view. That top-heavy array of horns would make a handle. If I could get hold of the horns, I could break the melk's long, slender neck.

The thought made me queasy.

"The smaller one," I whispered. B-beam nodded. He yelped softly, and got answers. The Folk flowed away through the fat grass. I crept toward the melks on hands and toes.

Three Folk stood up and shrieked.

The melks shrieked too, and tried to escape. Two more Folk stood up in front of the smaller one. I stayed down, scrambling through the grass stalks, trying to get ahead of it.

It came straight at me. *And now I must murder you.* I lunged to the attack. It spun about. A hoof caught my thigh and I grunted in pain. The melk leapt away, then froze as B-beam dashed in front of it waving his arms. I threw myself at its neck. It wheeled and the cage of horns slammed into me and knocked me on my ass. It ran over me and away.

I was curled around my belly, trying to remember how to breathe. B-beam helped me to my feet. It was the last place I wanted to be. "Are you all right?"

I wheezed, "Hoof. Stomach."

"Can you move?"

"Nooo! Minute. Try again."

My breath came back. I walked around in a circle. The Folk were watching me. I straightened up. I jogged. Not good, but I could move. I took off the loop of line that held canteen and beamer and knife, and handed them to B-beam. "Hold these."

"I'm afraid they may be the mark of the leader."

"Bullshit. Folk don't carry anything. Hold 'em so I can fight." I wanted to be rid of the beamer. It was too tempting.

We'd alerted the prey in this area. I took us along the edge of the forest, where the fat grass thinned out and it was easier to move. We saw nothing for almost an hour.

I saw no birds, no stilts, no boar-pigs. What I finally did see was four more melks drinking from the stream. It was a situation very like the first I'd seen on film.

I'd already proved that a melk was more than my equal. My last-second qualms had slowed me not at all. I'd been beaten because my teeth and claws were inadequate; because I was not a wolf, not a lion, not a Folk.

I crouched below the level of the fat grass, studying them. The Folk studied me. B-beam was at my side, whispering, "We're in no hurry. We've got hours yet. Do you think you can handle a boar pig?"

"If I could find one I might catch it. But how do I kill it? With my teeth?"

The Folk watched. What did they expect of me? Suddenly I knew.

"Tell them I'll be in the woods." I pointed. "Just in there. Pick a melk and run it toward me." I turned and moved into the woods, low to the ground. When I looked back everyone was gone.

These trees had to be from the Folk world. They bent to an invisible hurricane. They bent in various directions, because the Mojave wasn't giving them the right signals. The trunks had a teardrop-shaped cross section for low wind resistance. Maybe the Folk world was tidally locked, with a wind that came always from one direction . . .

I dared not go too far for what I needed. The leafy tops of the trees were just in reach, and I plunged my hands in and felt around. The trunk was straight and solid; the branches were no thicker than my big toe, and all leaves. I tried to rip a branch loose anyway. It was too strong, and I didn't have the leverage.

Through the bent trunks I watched melks scattering in panic. But one dashed back and forth, and found black death popping up wherever it looked.

There was fallen stuff on the ground, but no fallen branches. To my right, a glimpse of white—

The melk was running toward the wood.

I ran deeper among the trees. White: bones in a neat pile. Melk bones. I swept a hand through to scatter them. Damn! The leg bones had all been split. What now?

The skull was split too, hanging together by the intertwined horns. I stamped on the horns. They shattered. I picked up a massive half-skull with half a meter of broken horn for a handle.

The melk veered just short of the woods. I sprinted in pursuit. Beyond, B-beam half-stood, his eyes horrified. He shouted, "Rick! No!"

I didn't have time for him. The melk raced away, and nothing popping up in its face was going to stop it now. I was gaining . . . it was fast . . . too damn fast . . . I swung the skull at a flashing hoof, and connected. Again. Throwing it off, slowing it just enough. The half-skull and part-horn made a good bludgeon. I smacked a knee, and it wheeled in rage and caught me across the face and chest with its horns.

I dropped on my back. I got in one grazing blow across the neck as it was turning away, and then it was running and I rolled to my feet and chased it again. There was a feathery feel to my run. My lungs and legs thought I was dying. But the melk shook its head as it ran, and I caught up far enough to swing at its hooves.

This time it didn't turn to attack. Running with something whacking at its feet, it just gradually lost ground. I delivered a two-handed blow to the base of its neck. Swung again and lost my balance and tumbled, caught the roll on my shoulder, had to go back for the skull. Then I ran, floating, recovering lost ground, and suddenly realised that the grass was stirring all around me. I was surrounded by the black shadows of the Folk.

I caught up.

A swing at the head only got the horns. I hammered at the neck, just behind the head. It tumbled, and tried to get to its feet, and I beat it until it fell over. I used the skull like an ax ... murdering it ... and suddenly black bodies flowed out of the fat grass and tore at the melk. B-beam got a good grip on the horns and snapped the neck.

I sat down.

He handed me the line: knife, beamer, canteen. He was almost as winded as I was. He whispered, "Damn fool, you weren't—"

"Wrong." I didn't have breath for more. I drank from my canteen, paused to gasp, drank again. Then I turned the beamer on a meaty thigh. The Folk must have been waiting for me to make my choice. They now attacked the forequarters.

I crouched, panting, holding the beamer on the meat until it sizzled, until it smoked, until the smell of it told my belly it was ready.

The heaving of my chest had eased off. I handed the knife to B-beam. "Carve us some of that. Eat as much as you can. Courtesy to our hosts."

He did. He gave me a chunk that I needed both hands to hold. It was too hot; I had to juggle it. B-beam said, "You used a weapon."

"I used a club," I said. I bit into the meat. Ecstacy! The famine was over. I hadn't cooked it enough, and so what? I choked down enough to clear my mouth and said, "Humans don't use teeth and claws. The Folk know that. They wanted to see us in action. *My* evolution includes a club."

THE
LEADING EDGE
BOOK REVIEWS
Richard E. Geis

EDITOR'S INTRODUCTION TO:

Richard E. Geis

Book Reviews

Richard Geis has often won the Hugo—otherwise known as the Science Fiction Achievement Award— as best fan writer. His *Science Fiction Review* (PO Box 11408, Portland, Oregon 97211) is understandably one of the most popular of the science fiction fan magazines.

THE FORLORN HOPE
By David Drake

Tor, $2.95, 1984

A future war novel as gripping as this raises questions beyond the writer's skill. There is a fascination in men for equipment, for guns, for valor, and above all for competence. Why?

And there is in humanity a kind of greed for gore, for the physical, vivid, graphic details of death, wounding . . . killing. Why?

These attractions exist—mostly in the human male—on a gut level and are undeniable. If there were no desire (need) for knowing death people would not run to accidents to see the raw, naked face of pain, blood, dying. They would not provide a market for war novels, murder novels, private-eye novels. . . . Novels such as *The Forlorn Hope* would not be written or published or read.

But there is an instinctual willingness in mankind to use force to impose one's will on others, and a willingness to resort to force to oppose the imposition of others' orders on oneself. Because, contrary to the veneer of lies and "morality" and wishful thinking which is necessarily imposed by society (which will use force to impose *its* orders) to prevent maverick, "antisocial" behavior by all its members, death *is* final solution and every man and woman and child on Earth knows it. We make war because we know it does solve some problems. It always has, and always will. We kill and maim because it is natural for us.

This novel, *The Forlorn Hope*, is about a band of highly-trained future mercenaries on a far planet in the not too far future who have been hired by a federal planetary government to help defend itself against a powerful rebel movement of religious zealots.

They are betrayed by a cowardly federal commander and must first fight their way out of the federal installation they had been partly occupying, and then must fight their way through the rebel lines to the safety of the capital of the federal government.

David Drake is a fine writer on many levels: he creates characters who come alive in a myriad of public and private ways—and he is not afraid to kill them.

Drake illustrates constantly the grim terror of a firefight, of being bombed, of putting your life on the line. He creates a real world of trapped, desperate, men and women (yes, some of the mercenaries are women) who must depend on their inner character, their training, physical condition

and intelligence for survival ... and who m
depend on each other's honor, loyalty and love.

Above all, I think he shows the real meaning of
trust.

The meat and potatoes of this fine war novel is
the weaponry of the mercenaries which is superior
in most ways to the federal and rebel arsenal, but
limited to carryable weapons and one self-propelled
cannon.

These guns:

'Fasolini's troopers carried cone-bore weapons. They squeezed down their projectiles at
pressures which only barrels of synthetic diamond, grown as a single molecular unit, could
withstand. At the muzzle, an osmium needle
was expelled at over three thousand meters
per second. The fluorocarbon sabot which had
acted as a gas check in the bore was gaseous
itself by the time it spurted out behind the
needle. The weapons were specialized; but it
benefitted mercenary soldiers, like whores, to
be able to provide specialized services for their
customers. The gun was meant to bust armor
and brick walls.'

But the rebels have imported a limited number
of awesome Terran-made tanks which are armed
with incredibly powerful laser beams. Their armor
is resistant to even the osmium cannon. And the
betrayed mercenaries must face and destroy these
monsters.

The realistic technical detail describing the various aspects of this future, this planet, this war,
this superior band of soldiers and their tactics,
and all of the intriguing weaponry they and their
enemies possess makes this novel come alive and

makes this story of heroism and skill a riveting reading experience.

The final, terrifying touch of realism to be mentioned here is that anyone in this novel can die! Your favorite character can die. Several of mine did. The reader is drawn into a chilling identification with these mercenaries and develops a desperate self-need for them to win. You're never even sure the hero will survive in this book. Hell, the mercenary leader, Colonel Fasolini, is killed in the third chapter.

If hard science fiction of this type is your dish, here is a feast. You'll come away from this novel with a great admiration for David Drake's skill and knowledge and talent, and you'll want to read more of his books.

DR. ADDER
By K.W. Jeter
Bluejay Books, $7.95, 1984

I would describe reading this novel as a depressing and mesmerizing trip through a distorted, warped social hell. Slime and feces and malevolent characters inhabit this ugly, funny, merciless look at a future America in which there is no good, no morality except manipulative self-interest and guilt-ridden masochism/sadism. It stretches from a hypocritical, sexually and commercially intense picture of middle-class life intent on savage conformity and consumerism, to the dregs of the Interface, a street where, in Los Angeles, law is missing and Dr. Adder is king.

He is a plastic surgeon with great skill and advanced technology which allows him to carve young people—mostly girls, prostitutes—to meet the demands of sick middle-class customers who want their evil fantasies to become real flesh.

Enter outsider E. Allen Limmit, a despicable non-hero who has a strange lineage and a vast ignorance of the underground culture of the 'shit strewn' alleys of the Interface.

Add an alien creature, vast and almost dead, being experimented upon for lo these many years in a decrepit, ruined Berkeley. Add John Max's Moral Force movement, various and sundry leftover revolutionaries, terrorists, assassins, drug dealers. . . . Add a high-tech electronic/laser glove which gives its wearer enormous killing power—and madness.

This novel is not a "dirty book" in spite of its constant use of all the four-letter words, all the evil in the human soul, all the descriptions of sexual matters, decay and obscene destruction. It isn't erotic. If it turns you on, you're in trouble!

Dr. Adder is a first novel, a knee-jerk anti-establishment, nihilistic near-future tour-de-force, occasionally brilliant, always brutally graphic, sprung from the soured idealism of a young, very talented writer. How many first novels has the Literary Mainstream seen of this type? Thousands. And now we are seeing it in science fiction.

This trade-paperback edition is handsome—a fine cover by Barclay Shaw—but the interior illustrations by John R. Howarth are totally malaprop in style; they seem grotesquely comic-bookish and subtly amateurish—a joke? They don't match or enhance the nightmarish quality and setting of the novel at all.

IN THE OCEAN OF NIGHT
By Gregory Benford
Pocket Books, $3.95, 1984.

ACROSS THE SEA OF SUNS
By Gregory Benford
Timescape Books, $15.95, 1984.

In The Ocean Of Night is the first book of a trilogy. *Across The Sea Of Suns* is the second book of the trilogy.

These novels revolve primarily around Nigel Whalmsley, born and raised in England, transplanted to America, and an astronaut of extraordinary skill, courage and intuition.

The saga follows his contacts with, first, in 1999, the alien spaceship buried in the ice and rock of the head of the comet known as Icarus which is hurtling on a collision course toward Earth. Nigel is on a hurryup space mission to examine Icarus and plant a nuclear bomb on it to deflect it from its impact trajectory.

But Nigel finds an entrance into the alien ship in a deep crevasse and explores, to find the ship is a derelict, but crammed with invaluable artifacts. And—surprise!—the ship is not quite dead: it sends a short, powerful, automatic message back, into deep space.

Twenty years later, in 2018, a young woman scientist accidentally discovers a crashed, eons-old, almost-dead alien spaceship in a rarely visited section of the Moon. The craft still has an automatic force field and defenses, though its crew had abandoned it hundreds of thousands of years before.

Nigel Whalmsley has managed to be assigned to a team of scientists who explore and analyze its still-accessible computer after the ship's defenses are breached.

There are other, baffling happenings: a mysterious nuclear explosion in the forest near Wasco, Washington, is unexplainable; no Earthly power was responsible.

And there is suspicion in Nigel's mind that half a million years ago aliens interfered with the natural evolution of mankind, and the creatures known as Big Foot, the Yeti, Sasquatch, etc., are somehow involved.

A follow-up alien intelligent-computer reconnaisance spaceship—a "snark"—is detected swinging through the Solar system, and again Nigel Whalmsley is chosen to go out to meet it and if necessary destroy it.

Again, he disobeys orders and has a revealing, extended communication with the alien computer, which he allows to "escape."

In *Across The Sea Of Suns*, 50 years later, when Nigel is an old man, but still active, still keen, benefitting from advanced life-extension medical technology, he is aboard the Earth starship *Lancer*, a converted asteroid, investigating the planet Isis in the system of Ra, because garbled English language radio transmissions had been received years before from the Ra system.

They discover a Guardian, an alien, apparently dead guard satellite near Isis. . . . They discover a strange, warped, hopeless, desperate alien race on Isis who have deliberately changed their forms and metabolism to survive after a devastating attack in their distant past. . . .

Back on Earth the oceans have been seeded with an alien aquatic life form which is maniacally sinking all ships on the surface.

The *Lancer* leaves Ra after a tragic encounter with the suddenly revived million-year-old Guardian.

Another system, another discovery. . . .

The focus is primarily on Nigel Whalmsley and his growing belief that a life-fearing, life-hating machine civilization is systematically seeking out and destroying intelligent organic high-tech civilizations across the galaxy. And that, occasionally, high-tech organic races fight back and have desperately attempted to accelerate primitive peoples' development to create more allies in the battle against the implacable machines.

You'd think this would be enough, wouldn't you, for two novels, with more to come—a final (or maybe not final) encounter with the electronic-life machine civilization.

But Greg Benford is as interested in creating and presenting the whole picture as he is in an absorbing action-adventure epic: both of these books branch out to include Nigel Whalmsley's social life, his preference for a three-person marriage, the killing disease and death of Alexandria, his first prime wife, the phenomenon of the New Sons religion, his life-long struggle with the bureaucratic mind-set of NASA and subsequent agencies, with administrators, with the "democracy" aboard the *Lancer* which presumes to dictate his job, his future, and with the sex-change fad which sweeps the crew of the *Lancer*. . . . All these elements provide a depth and feeling of true-to-life grittiness to Benford's work which are interesting in themselves.

What we have here is success in communication: a fine writer working at the top of his abilities. We may have SF Literature on the hoof, and we may have to wait twenty years for the professors to admit it.

THE MAN IN THE TREE
By Damon Knight
Berkley, $2.75, 1984.

Damon Knight, in this his first novel in seventeen years, gives as much enjoyment and reward as you can take. This because if you know enough about early Christianity your pleasure in reading this story about a runaway boy evading a vengeful man, growing to over eight feet in height and joining a carnival side show, becoming rich and early-on discovering he has a mysterious wild talent which allows him to cure diseased people with a laying on of hands (and mind), will allow you to see the parallels with the life of Christ, and will provide insights into what Damon is doing.

On one level this is a strange suspense story. Eventually Gene Anderson is finally identified and located by the now old, sick man who has been fanatically pursuing him for decades; to avenge his son's accidental death for which he blames Gene.

But on another level this novel is rich with tributaries of meaning and symbolism. And if you are perceptive enough, and remember enough of the detail in this well-written novel, you'll suspect that the world Gene Anderson lives in—apparently our own—may not really be ours after all. And that maybe the alternate Earth Gene Anderson dips into and sends items into, on occasion, is. . . . The clues are there.

Dissatisfaction with this story may come from observing that after building Gene Anderson and a superior man of high intelligence and great learning, Damon made Gene decide to save humanity by creating a new religion with himself as the Christ figure. Gene would have surely anticipated the rabid opposition of the existing established religions and taken measures to neutralize these predictable reactions.

Unless . . . unless Gene knew he had to be killed (or disappear under mysterious circumstances) in order to create the necessary martyr which gives a cult the opportunity to become a full-blown religious movement which can overthrow governments and change the face of civilization.

And, of course, Gene Anderson knew he had a place to go after leaving his world.

WORLDS BEYOND: THE ART OF CHESLEY BONESTELL
By Ron Miller & Frederick C. Durant III
Donning/Starblaze, $14.95, 1983.

This large, quality softcover volume printed on heavy gloss paper, featuring well over 150 paintings, almost all in full color, is a fine tribute to the man who contributed so much to bringing space to the attention of the American public in the years before the moon landings.

But here is a whole-life look at Bonestell's output, ranging from his early work to his latest, from his architectural paintings, his landscapes and seascapes, to his religious and mythological paintings.

His paintings for *Colliers* in 1950 showing the atom-bombing of New York are awesome and terrifying. And his other apocalyptic paintings are marvelous: the spewing volcanoes and raging storms illustrating Poul Anderson's *Satan's World*, and the destruction of ancient Egypt by meteors to illustrate one aspect of catastrophe theorist Immanuel Velikovsky for *This Week* magazine in 1950.

But it is his science fictional and astronomical paintings which dominate this volume and make it special for science fiction aficionados. His breathtaking, painstaking detail and realism are what stunned viewers of his works then and now. He was a stickler for authenticity. Light, shadow, colors, angles, perspectives—all had to be and were precise and true.

Bonestell was born in 1888 and is still alive at 96 years of age. He is still painting. As you read Frederick C. Durant's recounting of the highlights and influences of his life you can understand why he is still going: Chesley Bonestell loves life and loves painting, and he's damned if he'll give them up.

RETURNING CREATION

JANET MORRIS

L5 SOCIETY

FOR SPACE DEVELOPMENT

"I am proud to be an L-5 member."
— **Robert A. Heinlein**

"Membership in the L-5 Society is an excellent way to help get the space program going again."
— **Dr. Thomas Paine**
former NASA Administrator

The L-5 Society leads the effort to promote space development. Since 1975, we have informed the public and Congress about the potential of space, influencing national and international space policy. We are a growing force.

The L-5 Society aims to open space as a *practical* frontier, for industry and eventual settlement. We invite you to join us in this, the great adventure of our time.

Membership benefits include:
- **L-5 News** — brings news of space progress and prospects
- **L-5 Telephone Tree** — to help you influence Washington
- **Local Chapters** — to bring members together for action
- **Space Development Conference** — for sharing ideas
- **Satisfaction** — as you help to open the space frontier

For membership information, write to:
L-5 Society, Dept. L
1060 E. Elm Street
Tucson, AZ 85719